CONNECTION

K.M. GOLLAND

Copyright 2020
Published by Golland Family Pty Ltd

Cover Design: Lilliana Anderson
Editor: Kayla Robichaux
Formatting: K.M. Golland

PREFACE

This book has been written using Australian English and contains spelling, euphemisms and slang that form part of the Australian spoken word, which is the basis of this book's writing style.

Every girl is a princess,
with or without a prince.

CHAPTER ONE

"*V*aginas rule the world!" my flamboyant best friend hollers.

"Really, Carly?" I facepalm then peek through my spread fingers, unable to stop myself from smiling at her idiocy.

"Yes, really." She points a spatula covered in meringue at me. "And it's about time you realised it."

Sliding my hand to my temple, I massage it to release the Carly-tension Carly so easily puts there. "How? How do vaginas rule the world? Please enlighten me."

This should be good.

She licks the spatula and waggles her eyebrows. "Because men are powerless when it comes to the pink taco."

"Oh, my God! Are you for real?"

"I'm for *very* real. The realest real I can be." Carly places her hands on the benchtop and pierces me with her *very real* stare. "That carrot-topped taco between your legs is the most powerful thing you'll ever own, so I suggest you wield it like a weapon."

"*Carly!*"

"What?" She furrows her brow for the slightest of seconds before brushing her inappropriate comment off with the swish of her hand.

Inappropriate. That's the best way to describe my roommate and best friend of several years. She's offensive, fierce, and filterless, but she also has a heart of gold and bears an uncanny resemblance to Barbie.

Snatching the spatula from her manicured hand before she further desecrates our kitchen, I safely place it in the dishwasher, close the door, and rest my backside against it, arms crossed over my chest. "You can't just talk about my vagina like that."

"Yes, I can. You're a redhead, Lib. It's scientifically proven that your taco is redheaded as well."

This is why Carly isn't a teacher and I am.

"Scientifically proven?" I prompt, almost choking.

"Yep." She pokes at the cake she's just covered in meringue and then sucks her finger clean.

"It's *not* scientifically proven." Dismissing her lunacy like I normally do, I walk to the stools at our breakfast bar and slump into one. "You're right about one thing though; vaginas should rule the world—"

"*Do*," she interrupts, "not should. Do."

"Right. Do." I sigh, unconvinced, and then pick at my *un*manicured nails.

"You should see to those abominations." Carly gestures to my fingers while performing a *"blergh"* face.

I fold them into my hands and make fists. "Why?"

"Because they're hideous."

"Why does it even matter? I've no one to impress."

"Yes, you do."

"Who?"

She points to her voluptuous chest. "Me... and your Prince Charming." Carly smiles and bats her eyelids, and I know she's patronising me. "Oh, and you, of course. You should do it for you too."

I scoff. "We both know my Prince Charming doesn't exist."

She pouts. "Yes, he does."

"No, he doesn't. I've been waiting all my life for him to ride in on his horse at sunset and whisk me away to live happily ever after,

2

and he hasn't. Not once." I throw my hands in the air. "So why should I bother 'decorating' myself while waiting for him? I shouldn't. I shouldn't bother at all."

"Oh, Libby Mermaid..." Carly's lips flatten, just like my mum's did before she told me Santa Claus wasn't real.

I bite back my half-smile at one of her nicknames for me—*The Little Mermaid* is my favourite Disney Princess—and snap out a, "What?"

"It saddens me to tell you this, but yes, you're right, Prince freakin' Charming doesn't exist." She leans over the benchtop, her chin propped in her hands. "What's wrong? Something's really bothering you. I can tell."

I divert my gaze to our pastel-pink Smeg kettle. "There's nothing bothering me."

"I call bullshit."

"You can call whatever you like."

"Libby, what aren't you telling me?"

"Nothing!" My face flushes with heat.

"Lies!" she yells, pointing at me and nearly taking out my eye. "Your cheeks are as red as your taco."

Gritting my teeth, I snatch up my handbag and head to my room.

"Where are you going?"

I don't answer her; there's no point.

"Wait! Lib, come back. I'm just kidding. Tell me what's wrong."

Again, I don't answer. I'm just not in the mood.

"Fairy tales, princes, and princesses are all real," she calls out. "I promise. Now come back."

"Have a good time tonight, Carly," I say as I close my bedroom door behind me.

Tears sting my eyes, but I wipe them away with the back of my hand. I'm not going to cry over *him*. Not again. Not a second longer. He's stolen enough tears from me already, and I refuse to let him steal any more. Tears aren't like rain; you shouldn't just let them fall.

Blowing out a long, slow breath, I blink my eyes dry just as

Sasha—Carly's eight-month-old golden retriever pup—scratches at my door. I turn the handle and let her in, and she bounds into the room like a sun-kissed whirlwind.

"Hello, baby girl."

Bending down, I knead my fingers into the base of her ears. She smiles, which makes me smile.

"Did your rude, inappropriate mummy take you for a walk today?"

Sasha barks and whips her tongue across my face.

"My guess is that's a no."

She goes for a second tongue-whip, and I scrunch my nose but laugh. "Who needs men when we have dogs like you, huh?"

She barks again.

"Exactly! Men are jerks."

Sasha rolls onto her back and kicks her legs in the air, so I sit on the ground next to her and scratch her belly, her leg twitching like crazy.

"Oooh yeah." I scratch harder. "That's the spot."

My phone sounds an incoming message, so I abandon Sasha's belly and reach into my handbag, pulling it out to find a text message from Oliver.

Oliver: I'm sorry, Lib. Got caught up. Raincheck?

I roll my eyes at his lame excuse. *Pfft. Caught up? More like forgot.*

Today isn't the first time Oliver—a teacher and colleague at my school—has stood me up, but it will be the last.

I decide not to respond, and a few minutes later, another message sounds.

Debating whether or not to look, curiosity ends up getting the better of me.

Oliver: I swear, Lib. My grandma needed me to fix a leaky tap.

His grandma? Pa-lease. I'm not falling for that. I toss my phone onto the bed and stand up, ready to take a shower and get dressed for my mother's birthday dinner when doubt creeps up my spine like a spindly spider and stops me.

What if he's telling the truth? I mean helping his grandma is quite lovely and chivalrous, and I shouldn't punish him for being a wonderful grandson, should I?

Biting my lip, I clasp my phone and hover my finger over the Reply button until I eventually press it and type him a response.

Libby: It's okay. I hope you fixed the leak.

Oliver: I did. Thanks for understanding, sweet cheeks.

Sweet cheeks? Warmth spreads over my body, and I feel a little fuzzy but also a little weird; he's never called me sweet cheeks before. In fact, he's never called me anything other than Lib or Ms Hanson.

Oliver: So, raincheck?

Libby: Sure

Oliver: Great! Dinner Wednesday?

I smile; dinner sounds perfect.

Libby: Looking forward to it.

Oliver: See you Monday.

Placing my phone back down, I silently curse myself for being too quick to vilify him. Sure, he's stood me up a couple of times before, but he *always* apologises and tries to make amends, and remorse has got to count for something.

Sasha barks her impatience and tries to paw my hand, so I clasp her fluffy face and kiss the space between her big brown eyes. "Your mummy is wrong, Sashy. Prince Charming does exist, and he thinks I have sweet cheeks." I hug her to my chest, and she licks my chin. "I just have to wait for him a little while longer. And shit!" I cringe at my hands. "I need to paint my fingernails."

CHAPTER TWO

"*H*appy birthday!" I hand Mum a bunch of flowers and some bath bombs from Lush and then wrap my arms around her tiny frame. Like me, she could pass as one of Snow White's dwarfs.

Mum buries her nose in a rose and breathes in. "Thank you, dear. They're lovely."

I mouth, *"Hi"* to Dad, who's carving a roast beef at the bench behind her. He slips a small sliver of meat into my mouth, presses his *"shh"* finger to his lips, and winks.

"Mm," I mumble, quickly swallowing the evidence. "Smells delicious, Dad."

Mum pulls back and holds me at arm's length, her eyes suspicious slits. She then assesses my appearance, frowns, and pulls the hair ties out of my braids before flicking my hair with her hands so it fans over my shoulders.

"Hey!" I touch a tendril and frown back at her. "What did you do that for?"

"Piggytails, Elizabeth? Really? You're too old for piggytails."

"I am not. My students love them."

"It's the weekend. You're not seeing your students until Monday."

6

Mum ducks into the dining room, so I give Dad a kiss on the cheek then make my way to where my sister, Fiona, is jiggling her daughter, Isabella, on her hip.

"Hey," I say to Fi and hold my arms out.

Izzy launches into them, so I kiss the crook of her chubby neck, making her giggle.

"Thank God," my sister says. She cracks her neck from side to side then stretches her back. "She's getting too heavy to hold all the time."

"So don't hold her all the time."

Fi deadpans, "It's not that easy, Lib."

I laugh. "Yeah, it is."

She purses her lips. "I was going to tell you not to listen to Mum because I liked your piggytails, but now you can kiss my arse."

Covering Izzy's ears, I turn her away from her potty-mouthed mother and say, "Naughty Mummy said a bad word."

Fi rolls her eyes at me just as Mum returns with a large crystal vase for her flowers.

"Did you girls plan this?" she asks, smiling at us.

"Plan wha—"

"Yes," Fi interrupts, her grin smug.

"How sweet." Mum happily arranges her lilies and roses. "New flowers and a new vase. Aren't I spoilt?"

Leaning closer to my gloating sister, I murmur, "Did you get her that ginormous vase for her birthday?"

She nods. "Yep."

It looks expensive, much more expensive than my flowers and bath bombs.

"You're such a suck," I add.

"That's why I'm the favourite and you're not."

I glare at her, but she's right; she *is* the favourite. Always has been. Mum's golden child—married, successful, the bearer of a grandchild.

I only tick one of those boxes.

Fi pokes out her tongue and then helps Mum get plates out to set the table while I stand helpless with Izzy in my arms.

"Thank you, Fiona." Mum pats her hand.

"Anything for my mother on her birthday."

I almost spew in my mouth. Fi is so blatantly obvious. And as per usual, she has also successfully set me up. I can't help, not with a toddler on my hip.

"How's work, Elizabeth?" Dad asks as he dishes up some roasted carrots.

"Fine. Teaching Grade 3 is a joy." I sneak a carrot off a plate and blow it, cooling it down before handing it to Izzy.

"Libby!" Fi scolds. "She's already had her dinner."

My eyes bulge at my younger sister. "So?"

Izzy smashes the carrot into her gob and hums her appreciation. Dad and I laugh.

"So… she won't drink her bedtime bottle if she eats too many solids."

"If she's hungry, she's hungry. If she isn't, she isn't. Look at her." Izzy sucks on her mucky fingers. "Clearly, she's hungry."

"It doesn't work that way." Fi huffs and hands me a wet wipe.

I take it and clean Izzy's fingers and face, baffled by my sister's logic. "You worry too much about what those stupid parenting books say."

"Those 'stupid parenting books' are helpful."

"Yeah, helpful in stressing first-time parents like you out."

"Don't judge me, Lib."

"I'm not."

"Yes, you are. When you have kids, you can do what you wan—"

I shove Izzy back into Fi's arms, grab a bunch of cutlery, and head into the dining room to set the table. I'm not in the mood for her holier-than-thou attitude. And anyway, I'm older; that attitude should come from me.

As I enter the room, Fi's husband, Ian, is already sitting at the table, his head down, mobile phone in hand. He looks up and smiles then slides the phone into his back pocket.

"Hey, Lib."

"Hey, why are you hiding in here?"

His back straightens. "I'm not hiding."

Smirking, I lay down a knife and fork. "I never said I blamed you for doing so. Why do you think I'm in here too?"

Ian relaxes. "What happened this time, huh?"

I shrug. "Just the usual… my hair wasn't right, and your wife is better than me."

"She's not better than you." He stands and takes a bunch of cutlery from me. "And there's nothing wrong with your hair."

I scoff just as Mum, Dad, Fi and Izzy enter the room.

"Ian, can you help carry some plates?" Fi snaps. "Or better yet, take Iz and put her in her highchair."

He gives me an I-feel-your-pain look, hands back the cutlery, and pries Iz from Fi's arms.

My ten-month-old niece squirms like a worm and says, "Mum, Mum, Mum."

"How about Dad, Dad, Dad?" Ian blows a raspberry into her chest, and she cackles—it's the loveliest sound I've heard all day, maybe ever.

Taking a seat, I ask Mum about her day. "Did you do anything special for your birthday?"

"I'm doing it now, dear."

"No, I mean today. Did you go to the movies, or out for lunch, or something like that?"

"No. But your father did set up a table in your old bedroom for me so I can do my scrapbooking."

"Cool!" I fork a roasted potato, pop it into my mouth, and mumble, "Nice job, Dad."

"What about you, Elizabeth? Did you do anything special today?" Mum asks, her expression hopeful.

I almost groan. "If you mean did I go on a date with a strapping young man, then no."

"I didn't say—"

"You didn't have to. It's written all over your face."

She turns to Dad with a questioning expression.

He nods at her. "She's right, Maria, it's all over your face." Dad dabs her nose with his fork and leaves a smear of gravy.

"Fred!" She wipes it clean then directs her attention back to me.

"I didn't say that. But now that you've mentioned the word date, how's that teacher at your school? Oliver? Is that his name?"

"Yes." I tip my glass of wine to my lips and all but skol it. "We're just friends, Mum, and colleagues."

"Just because you're colleagues doesn't mean you can't—"

"Muuum," I whine.

"What? I'm just saying it's not a crime to date someone you work with." She winks at Dad. "Your father and I worked together for years."

"I know that, but Oliver and I are just friends."

She puts down her knife and fork, and I know what's coming. It's one of the reasons why I moved out with Carly in the first place.

"Elizabeth, you're not getting any young—"

"I'm not even thirty, Mum!"

"You're twenty-nine."

"So?"

"So"—she taps her wrist—"time is ticking. You need to put yourself out there before it's too late."

"Can we please not have this conversation now?"

"I got a promotion," Ian blurts, changing the subject.

Mum smiles. "How wonderful."

I mouth to him, *"Thank you."*

He winks.

"Yes," Fi says while stabbing an innocent piece of broccoli, "but it means longer hours." She sucks on her tooth, and I get the impression she's not happy.

"Oh." Mum gives Dad a sideways glance.

"It's only a couple of hours extra a day," Ian adds.

"A couple of hours that you should be spending with Izzy and me."

The room goes quiet, so I decide to change the subject yet again.

"Scrapbooking? You haven't done that in years, Mum."

"Well, I have a grandchild now, which means lots of photos."

I shake off yet another of her stabs at my single status before enduring more of them throughout dinner until I'm standing in my old bedroom, my fluffy lilac pillow clutched to my chest while I stare at the Disney Princess decals still stuck to the pale pink walls. They were my favourite decorations growing up, and I'd almost taken them with me when I moved out, much to Carly's disgust.

Reaching forward, I trace my finger over Ariel and Prince Eric, both of them about to kiss in a boat—so innocent, so in love. My heart swells; I want to be kissed in a boat under a weeping willow while animals sing in the background.

Never gonna happen, Libby.

Shoulders slumping, I move to where Belle and the Beast are dancing in his ballroom, followed by Prince Phillip leaning over Aurora while she sleeps, and then to Prince Charming on bended knee, securing Cinderella's glass slipper to her foot.

I cock my head and let out a giggle. Prince Charming kinda looks like Oliver—tall with dark, neatly swept hair, clothes pristine, a smouldering smirk.

Pointing my toe like a ballerina, I assess my shoe. *Hmm... maybe I could "accidentally" lose it at school next week like Cinderella did? And maybe, just maybe, he'll find it for me.*

I laugh then leave the room.

Again, never gonna happen.

* * *

MONDAY COMES AROUND RATHER QUICKLY, and during second session—right before recess—I can't seem to get Carly's mantra of *"Vagina's rule the world"* together with *Operation: Oops, where's my shoe?* out of my head. It could work. I mean nowhere in the laws of romance does it say you can't help your own fairy tale along. And sure, Cinderella's missing shoe wasn't intentional, but so what? That's a minor detail.

Lifting my head, I blink a couple of times and focus on Oliver who is at the helm of the double classroom we share. He's filling in an analogue clock on the whiteboard while I grade spelling tests in the corner behind my desk. Beige chinos fit snuggly to his butt, a white shirt to his chest underneath a cute woollen vest with a duck-blue diamond pattern. He looks dashing. Very clean-cut, very... Oxford.

Kicking off my shoe, I nudge it with my big toe until it's under the bookstand next to my desk, instantly regretting my decision to do so as the smell of sweaty feet hits me like a grotty slap to the face. *Abort, Libby. Abort Operation: Oops, where's my shoe? now. Goddamn it, what are you doing? You know your feet pong when you wear these shoes.*

I quickly suck in a breath and inconspicuously slide down my seat to try to fish my fluorescent-yellow Tiek safely back onto my foot, where it should stay... forever.

"Mr Bunt, why is there twelve numbers on the clock?" Jet Bradley asks.

Oliver swivels to look at Jet, his eyes growing wide before they meet mine. I sit back up, unsuccessful with my foot-fishing. *Shit!*

"Uh... because...." Oliver's brow crumples, his expression saying, *"Good fucking question"*, and I can't help but bite my lip to refrain from laughing. "Maybe Ms Hanson can answer that, Jet," Oliver says, looking rather pleased with himself before turning back to the whiteboard.

I smile—not an entirely happy smile because the stench of my foot is near killing me. "Sure," I say. "Time is measured by the movement of our planet Earth in relation to the sun."

My Grade 3 and Oliver's Grade 2 students all turn their heads to where I'm sitting, so I continue. "Earth rotates, or spins—"

"The earth spins?" Jet asks.

"Yes, it—"

"Then why aren't we dizzy?"

"I know!" Hannah Morris's hand shoots into the air. "My dad told me. It's gravity."

I nod. "Yes, you're right, Hannah. But that's a whole other lesson, so let's stick with time today, okay?" Another waft of sweaty feet swims around my face, and I cough, blinking because I'm not

CONNECTION

sure if it's burning my eyeballs or not. "So, Earth spins around an imaginary line—" *Cough.* "—that runs between the North Pole and the South Pole—"

Jet's hand shoots up into the air again, but as per usual, he doesn't wait to be addressed before he speaks. "Can Santa see it?"

"No, Jet, it's imaginary."

His shoulders slump. "Oh."

"As I was saying—" *Cough.* "—Earth turns around the imaginary line you can't see, and when all the places above the line face toward the sun's light, that's when it's daytime. And when all the places below the line face away from the sun's light and it's dark, that's when it's night-time." Cough. "We get daytime and night-time in one whole day, don't we? So that's how long it takes for Earth to do a complete turn, one whole day."

Most of the kids nod their understanding while some shove each other, and one picks his nose.

"How many hours are there in one whole day, Dylan?" I ask, hoping he'll remove his finger from his nostril to answer.

He quickly does but also shrugs.

"Want to take a guess?"

He shrugs again. "Twenty?"

"Close. There are twenty-four. Twenty-four hours for Earth to do a complete spin. "Now—" I cough again, wishing I could fan some fresh air in front of my face. "—can someone tell me how many minutes there are in each hour?"

Emma Johnson bounces on her bum, her arm stretched so high I'm almost afraid it'll tear off.

"Yes, Emma."

"Sixty."

"Very good. And how many seconds in each minute?"

She bounces again.

"Yes, Emma."

"Sixty."

"Uh-huh. Sixty seconds equals one minute, and sixty minutes equals one hour, and how many hours in one whole day?"

Most of the students yell, "Sixty!" and I can't help but giggle.

"No, it's twenty-four. The ancient Egyptians divided the day into two lots of twelve because two times twelve equals?"

The kids shout various answers, some saying, "Twenty-four," some saying, "Ten," and one shouting, "One hundred!"

"Twenty-four," I reaffirm. "They divided the day into twelve hours for daytime and twelve hours for night-time." Standing up behind my desk, I finally breathe in fresher air. "On an analogue clock like the one Mr Bunt has drawn on the board for you, the twelve daytime and night-time hours are marked out around the edge in a circle. The number twelve is always at the top, the number six always at the bottom, and the rest are equally spread out in order between the two. The two pointers, called hands, show the hour and the minutes."

"They don't look like hands." Jet flaps his, and the students copy him, flapping their hands and laughing.

Evan Hunter stands up and spins around, pretending to get dizzy. "I'm Earth, wheee."

"Sit down, Evan," Oliver snaps.

Evan drops to the floor and lands on Emma. She cries out and bursts into tears. Without thinking, I walk around my desk and rush toward her when Jet points to my foot.

"Where's your shoe, Ms Hanson?"

Shit!

"Uh, I lost it."

My cheeks flush with warmth just as the bell rings, and I sigh with relief. As much as I love being a teacher, I love the recess, lunchtime, and hometime school bells even more so.

"You may head outside for recess," Oliver says to the kids before stepping up to where I'm now squatting next to Emma.

"Where does it hurt?" I ask her.

"My hand."

She clutches it to her chest but rotates it so I can have a look.

"Ouch! It looks a bit red," I say, pouting. "I think we should get some ice from Miss Henkley at the sick bay."

As Oliver and I help Emma to stand, his eyes narrow and he

scrunches his nose, almost gagging. My stomach seizes as another waft of foul feet floats around the space between us, my *"lost"* Tiek now dangling from Jet's finger as he steps up to my side.

"Found your shoe!" he announces, pinching his nostrils with his other hand. "And it stinks!"

Oh, my God! Somebody please kill me now.

CHAPTER THREE

*O*liver had pretended he couldn't smell my feet, but there's good reason why he's not the drama teacher, and that's because he can't act for shit.

I appreciated the sentiment, though I'd been so mortified I could barely make eye contact with him for the remainder of that day. Thank God Oliver's timetable included a double session of Sport, which meant he'd been out of the classroom. And thank God Jet never brought it up again, especially when the students practised their "ch" spelling words, one of which had been "stench."

Needless to say, I'd been pleasantly surprised when, at the end of that day, as I'd climbed into my car and Oliver climbed into his, that he asked if we were still on for dinner that coming Wednesday night. I'd been certain he'd ask for another raincheck, or no rainchecks at all.

Now Wednesday afternoon, I slide my feet into a pair of perfectly aerated sandals. I'm preparing to leave for my dinner date with Oliver when Carly leans against my bedroom door.

"You look... nice." She nods toward my ensemble—a pink, floral maxi skirt, white t-shirt, and a denim jacket.

"Thanks." I tilt my head to the side and assess myself in the mirror. "Is it too much?"

"Too much?" Carly steps into my room and unties the silk scarf around my neck. "If you mean too much clothing, then yes."

I roll my eyes and step around her. "What would you have me wear, a swimsuit?"

"Depends, are you and Mr Bunt"—she wobbles her head like an idiot as she says his name—"going swimming?"

I glare at her. "No."

"Where is the dork taking you, his grandma's?" Carly picks up my bottle of Chanel N°5 and sniffs it, pulling a face similar to Oliver's when he pretended my feet didn't smell bad.

I snatch it from her. "No. His grandma lives in a granny flat in his backyard."

"Ew."

"It's not *ew*. It's lovely."

She picks up a pair of my earrings and holds them to her to ears. "It's weird."

"It's not."

"Yeah, it is, and so is he. Why are you even going out to dinner with him?"

"The same reason you go out with Derek."

Carly puts down the earrings and licks her lips, and I know what her X-rated mind is thinking.

I sigh. "Because he asked me to, that's why. You know, courtship? And just because you and Oliver don't get along, that doesn't mean he's a weird person."

"Courtship? What century are you in?" She flops onto my bed and picks up my seashell-shaped cushion. "He dresses like a grandpa, Lib. Enough said."

"He does not! I happen to think he dresses with sophistication."

"Yeah, if you call golf pants and turtlenecks sophisticated."

"When did you become Queen Judge of Character?"

"When I was born."

I take hold of her hands, help her to her feet, spin her to face the door, and give her a gentle nudge to leave. "Goodbye, Carly. Don't wait up."

"I won't have to. His bedtime is probably seven o'clock."

My gentle nudge turns to a playful shove.

"Hey!" She bounces off the hallway wall and stumbles.

Grabbing my handbag from my nightstand, I sling it over my shoulder and pull out my keys.

Her eyes meet mine. "Is he not picking you up?"

"No. I'm meeting him at his place."

"See? Weird. A *real* guy picks you up."

She has a point, but I push it aside.

"He had a lot of class prep to do so thought it would save time if I just met him at his place. No big deal."

"Like I said, weird." She turns her back to me and waves her fingers above her head. "Bye. Have fun, I guess."

Closing the front door behind me, my stomach clenches as I walk to my car and climb inside. *Is it weird that I'm picking him up?* I don't go on many dates, but even I know the guy picks up the girl, at least on the first date.

What am I saying? It's the twenty-first century. And if vaginas are going to rule the world, they should drive every now and again.

* * *

AFTER WALKING BETWEEN TWO CEMENT, white, lion statues sitting atop a redbrick fence that surrounds Oliver's front garden, I make my way up his porch steps, dodging pots of succulents before knocking on his door. Déjà vu sweeps over me, and I realise his home reminds me of my Nonna and Nonno's house. It's weird, considering he's my age and not in his eighties.

I shake my head, silently berating myself for thinking the very word my annoying roommate planted in my head.

"Damn you, Carly," I mutter as the door swings open, revealing Oliver in all his Prince Charming glory—navy chino shorts, latte-coloured shirt, reading glasses perched on the tip of his nose. It's exactly what he'd worn at school today, except now he's barefoot.

I tell myself to repay the favour and pretend his feet don't smell, even if they do.

"Hey, Lib. Come in." He holds the door open and gestures I enter.

"Thanks." I stop on the threshold for the slightest of seconds, expecting a kiss on the cheek or a hug but get neither.

"Just through here, into the living room." Oliver closes the door behind us and then leads the way.

I bend to remove my sandals.

"You can leave them on," he says.

My face burns with embarrassment; of course I should leave them on. I've already near killed him with them off.

"I mean if you want to," he adds. "The carpet is old, so it doesn't matter."

Without intentionally doing so, I laugh the type of laugh you hear in the audience of a TV sitcom then choose to leave my sandals on. Seems stupid to take them off when we're leaving for dinner at any moment.

Following Oliver into the living room through open, amber-coloured, glass doors, I take in his minimalist living style—brown leather recliner sofas, stereo system, gaming console, and a couple of picture frames with photos of him and who could very well be his parents and grandparents.

Because I'm not rude, I say, "This is nice," when it's not nice at all. It's old-fashioned and austere.

He swishes his hand. "It's not my place. It's my gran's."

"Oh! I thought she lived in a flat out the back?"

"She does."

I'm a little taken aback by his answer, and he must notice because he continues. "The house is too big for her, so Dad built her a flat and moved me in here."

"But isn't it too big for you too?"

He narrows his eyes, so I cover my mouth with my hand.

"Sorry. I didn't mean for that to sound rude. I just meant she's one person, and so are you, so it's the same thing."

"Of course it's too big for me, too, but I don't mind. I can keep an eye on Gran."

I nod. "She must love having you look out for her."

"She's the one who looks out for me, really."

I nod again. I have a Nonna, so I know what that's like.

Oliver sits on the leather sofa, a coffee table before it with an open laptop and worksheets fanned out on top.

"Take a seat." He pats the spot beside him. "I'm just catching up on schoolwork."

I do as he suggests and pick up a worksheet, noticing it's from over a month ago. "Have you not corrected these yet?"

He laughs as if it's nothing. "Told you I was behind."

"Oliver! You're *very* behind. These should have been done already. The kids need their results if they're going to progress."

Picking up a red pen, I start marking the children's narratives for their portfolios they'll present in the coming weeks at the end of term.

"I know." He leans back and places his hands on his head. "I've just been so busy."

"With what?"

Not that it's any of my business, but I'm curious as to what he's prioritising over his students.

"Er... Gran. She's been sick."

"Oh!" I put down the worksheet and pick up another. "Is she okay?"

"Yeah. Well, some days. She has angina."

"That's no good."

"She's on meds, but I have to keep an eye on her and make sure she doesn't do too much, you know?"

I nod and giggle at Evan Hunter's narrative.

"What's so funny?"

"Evan's story," I say. "I don't think he likes his mum's boyfriend."

"Oh yeah? Why's that?"

I point to the part where Evan locks his mum's *"friend"* in a lion cage.

Oliver leans forward and reads what Evan wrote. "I reckon you're right." He leans back again, happy for me to continue correcting his work. "Poor kid. With a mum like his, he doesn't stand a chance."

I frown. "You don't know that."

"Have you seen Mrs Hunter?"

"Of course I've seen her."

"Well, then you'll agree she looks like she belongs on a street corner."

My jaw drops. "Oliver!"

"What?"

"That's uncalled for."

"She dresses like a prostitute, Libby."

I shuffle in my seat, uncomfortable with his comments.

"Take you for instance," he continues.

"*Me?*" I turn and glare at him.

"Let me finish." He raises his hands in the air and chuckles. "Take what you're wearing for instance. It's classy, appropriate, and doesn't scream prostitute."

"I should hope not, but..." I pause then decide to bite my tongue. I don't want to get into an argument on our first date.

"But what?" he probes. "Go on... what were you going to say?"

Ah, fuck it!

"Clothing shouldn't 'scream prostitute,' Oliver. A person has the right to wear what they want without being judged or labelled. What's on the outside doesn't define what's on the inside."

"All I'm saying is you look respectable. You're covered up and decent."

"Just because I'm 'covered up' doesn't mean I deserve more respect than if I weren't."

He claps his hands together, reaches for his laptop, and drags it onto his lap. "Let's agree to disagree."

"Yes, let's."

I welcome that notion and focus on the worksheets, and before I know it, they're all corrected, my stomach is grumbling, and sunlight no longer fills the room.

Stretching my arms above my head, I'm about to ask when we're leaving for dinner when the backdoor opens and slams shut, followed by a ruffling sound in the adjacent room.

"Halloo. Olivaaa."

"Be right back." He shoots to his feet and disappears into the next room, Italian conversation soon filling my ears. My mother's mother was born in Bologna, so I'm somewhat familiar with the native tongue.

Making out words and sentences such as *"Not now, Nonna,"* and *"I do it, I do it"*, I stand up and make my way into the same room as them to find Oliver wrestling a washing basket full of neatly folded clothes from the arms of a short, silver-haired woman, a gold crucifix dangling from a chain around her neck. She stumbles backward, and I instantly reach out to steady her.

"Gran, be careful!" He pries the basket from her hands, his laugh uneasy. "She's very stubborn."

"I am no stubborn. I wash and bring to you."

"Yes, Gran. You washed and brought me my clothes. You shouldn't have." He kisses the top of her head and sets the basket down on the table.

I smile, waiting for my introduction, but Oliver doesn't deliver it, instead wrapping his arm around his Gran's shoulders and guiding her back out the door. "Come on, let's get you back to your flat, Nonna."

"But I bring washing and say hallo."

Standing there, a little dumbfounded as they leave the room, I murmur, "Well, that was weird."

And there's that word again. Weird!

Oliver returns moments later, eyes rolling as he sweeps his hand through his hair. "Sorry. She just takes it upon herself to do my washing even though I've told her not to."

Something tells me that's not entirely true, but it's none of my business, so I smile and fiddle with the collar of my jacket. "Are you hungry yet? Perhaps we should go."

"Go?" Oliver rests his knuckle on his chiselled jaw, smiles, and opens a drawer in the kitchen, rifling through it before frisbeeing me a takeaway menu from Pizza Palace. "You pick. I'm not fussy. Just no pineapple, okay?"

Pizza Palace? I almost drop it as I fumble with the catch. *And no pineapple? You weird son of a bitch.*

Sucking on my tooth, I exhale then grit my teeth, forcing a smile as I frisbee the menu back to him. "I'm not fussy either."

"Excellent!" He pulls out his mobile phone from his pocket and dials the number.

"Where's the bathroom?" I ask, my throat tight.

"Down the hall. Last door on the left."

Turning my back to him, I ferociously blink back tears, utterly disappointed, and escape the room. Escape him.

Clearly, Oliver Bunt is no Prince Charming.

Seriously, why do I even bother?

THE REST of our evening turned out as boring as the pineapple-less margarita pizza Oliver ordered us, and I'd realised rather quickly that the purpose of our 'dinner date' had been for him to manipulate me into doing his catch-up work, which I was stupid enough to do. Needless to say, I avoided him on Thursday and Friday as best I could. I was so mad… and an idiot. A naïve, wannabe-princess idiot who thinks fairy tales are real. Well, not anymore. Enough is enough. That shit is for books and movie screens. So-called Prince Charmings don't exist, and men in general are a waste of time.

Okay, so they help grow the human race. I'll give them that. But if I want a baby, there are ways of having one on my own. Not that I want a baby. I'm content with the twenty-plus kids I call "mine" every day.

They fill my child-well.

And speaking of those twenty-plus kids now on their way home to spend the weekend with their parents, I can't help but smile, recalling their responses to a recent task I'd set them while I make myself a cup of tea in the staffroom.

"So, to sum up Emergency Education Month," I say while jiggling the teabag in my mug. "I asked the kids a partial question, and they had to fill in the blank." I giggle, nearly choking on my words. "Some of the answers were hilarious. Want to hear?"

Sally—Ms Taylor—leans over the staffroom table and grabs a handful of M&M's from an open packet. "Yeah, shoot."

"Okay, so I said, 'Where there's smoke, there's...', and I asked them to raise their hands with answers I could write on the brainstorm board." I squeeze the teabag and dump it into the bin before taking a seat next to Carly. As well as being my roommate, we also work together. That's how we met. Carls is the 'office lady' at school.

She shuffles her seat over a little to make room for me. The only other spare seat is next to Oliver, who's sitting next to George—Mr Tims—at the opposite end of the table. Oliver and I haven't really spoken since his fake date, and he'd have to be a few eggs short of a chicken orgy to not know I'm dirty on him.

He smiles, but I ignore it and continue my story.

"Some of their responses were pollution, a smoker, a teepee, a cold morning, burnt toast, a bushfire, and, of course, a fire."

"Burnt toast?" Brooke—Ms Lewis—laughs. "Oh, my God, I love it."

"I know, right? I tell ya, trying to explain to Jet Bradley that our breath on a cold morning isn't smoke is like pulling teeth."

Carly's phone rings from within her handbag, so she pulls it out, stands up, and walks away for privacy.

"That wouldn't be the sexy-arse firefighter, would it?" Brooke asks.

Carly's new squeeze, Derek, was one of the firefighters at our school's Emergency Education demonstration last month. And not only was he very informative with his demonstration, but let's just say he also set a few fires in many a teacher's underwear.

Carly doesn't answer Brooke, instead leaving the room with her phone pressed to her ear. I go to continue my discussion of Emergency Education week when Oliver takes the now empty seat beside me.

"Hey! You got any plans tonight?" he asks.

"Um..." I cup my mug in my hands and bring it to my lips. "Yes. Yes, I do."

He waits for me to explain what plans I have, but I have fuck all plans so don't know what to say.

"Because I was thinking—"

"I'm getting my hair cut," I blurt, setting my mug back down.

His brows pinch just as Carly bursts into the room and says, "Right! Opals... tonight, who's in?"

We all look up.

"I'm in," George offers, eagerly.

"You're too old. You're not invited." Carly pokes her tongue out at him. "And anyway, something tells me Mrs T would have your balls for breakfast were you to accompany us tonight."

George stands and not so subtly covers his package with his hands in a show of protection. "Nobody's havin' my balls for breakfast, especially Mrs T. She can have porridge."

I giggle. I love George.

"Brooke, Sally, you in?" Carly plonks her butt on the table and nearly spills my tea.

I pick it up, finish it off, and stand to take the empty mug to the sink. "I can't, Carls. Sorry."

She laughs, and it reminds me of Maleficent. "Ha! You don't have a choice."

I spin in her direction. "Says who?"

"Me."

"Yeah, I'm in." Sally grabs yet another handful of M&M's and shovels them into her mouth.

"Sal!" Carly points at the candy-covered chocolate.

Sally has appointed Carly as her don't-let-me-put-anymore-weight-on marshal, which Carly has taken rather seriously.

Her eyes flame at Sal.

"I'll work it off tonight on the dance floor," Sal mumbles as she chews. "I promise."

"Oh, I know you will."

"It's all right for you. You can eat whatever you like and—"

Carls cuts her off like the insensitive, no-bullshit marshal she is and says, "Okay, we'll taxi it from my joint then."

Sal glares and sneaks another handful.

25

"Brooke?" Carly asks.

"I'll let you know. I have to see what Lance is doin'. If he's busy, then, yeah, I'm in."

"No probs. Text me later." Pushing off the table, she picks up her handbag. "Okay, you ready, Lib?"

"Wouldn't matter if I wasn't," I grumble. "You'd leave without me."

She shrugs. "You snooze, you lose."

Oliver gives Carly a disgusted look as we walk out the door; he's not her biggest fan.

Well, at least I have *real* plans now.

CHAPTER FOUR

"Why the urgency to go out?" I ask Carly as we climb into her car to make our way home from work.

It's her turn to drive. We take turns and carpool to save money on fuel.

"No urgency. I just want a night out with my friends."

I scoff; she's only ever keen to go to Opals when she wants to pick up a one-night stand.

"You seem to forget, even though I tell you all the time, that you are the world's worst liar."

Rolling her eyes, she leans forward and turns up the radio to avoid telling me the truth. It's typically Carly.

I lean forward and switch it off. "That was Derek on the phone in the staffroom, wasn't it? What happened?"

"Nothing. He just said he's going away for a while, that's all." She shrugs as if she's not hurt by him leaving.

I turn to face her. "That's *not* all."

"Just let it go, Lib."

"No. Not until you tell me the truth."

"Oh, my God! What are you, a mentalist?"

"Maybe." My smile is smug.

Carly glares then returns her attention to the road and murmurs, "More like mental."

I ignore her childish stab and continue, my tone mildly sarcastic. "So Derek said he had to leave for a while and that the two of you are over, is that it?"

"No."

I narrow my eyes as if I'm confused—I'm not—and continue to bait with ridiculous theories. "Hmm... so he said he was leaving indefinitely and wanted to try a long-distance relationship but wasn't sure if it would work?"

She keeps staring straight ahead but taps the steering wheel and sneers. "No."

I groan. "Then what's the problem? I'm not seeing one. He's going away for a little while. So what? That doesn't mean the two of you are over."

"He said he had to go to Sydney for 'family' issues," she snaps, emphasising the family bit with one-handed quotation fingers. "He didn't tell me any more."

"Again, what's the problem?"

"The part where he wouldn't tell me any more."

"Maybe it's personal, or he's not even sure what that 'any more' part is just yet. And maybe when he does, he'll let you know."

"Or maybe he has a wife and kids up there and I'm his dirty little secret," she adds, sulking.

Oh for God's sake.

"Don't be so fucking stupid, Carly."

Her head snaps in my direction, her eyes wide. "Whoa! Geez, I didn't know my love life meant so much to you."

"Yeah, well, it shouldn't, because it obviously doesn't mean that much to you. You're forever sabotaging your own chance at happiness. Finally, a guy comes along who appears to mesh with you, a guy you're clearly smitten with and he with you, and yet you refuse to stop playing this what-we-have-is-nothing game."

"I'm not playing games."

"Then why are you building that wall of yours? For once, don't. Don't build it. Enter a relationship without the fucking wall."

She glances sideways at me again, and I know she knows I'm upset. I rarely swear out loud. It's not a good habit to have when you teach children.

"Now"—Carly drops her hand from the steering wheel and pats my leg—"how 'bout *you* tell *me* what's going on?"

I huff and say, "Nothing," but then decide to tell her what I really think. "Actually, I will tell you. Here you are with a drop-dead gorgeous guy, and you choose to push him away. You do this *all the time.* It's not fair. Where's my drop-dead gorgeous guy, the one who, if he showed even the slightest bit of interest in me as Derek shows you, I would certainly not push away?"

Carly dips her head, and I know she feels bad.

Good.

But now I feel worse.

Because I just inadvertently realised I'm jealous she has her Prince Charming and I don't.

* * *

A FEW HOURS LATER, Carly, Sal, Brooke, and I are at Opals, one of the nightclubs at City Towers.

Contemporary, sleek décor fits out the building, and with three levels dedicated to various musical genres, the nightclub caters to everybody. Carly knows the owner, so when we arrive, we're escorted to a VIP roped-off section near the stage with our very own private bar.

"This is so awesome!" Sal beams. "How do you know the owner again? What's his name... Bryce?" She happily sips her Cosmopolitan, her brown wavy hair pinned into a sexy mess of curls on top of her head. She's wearing a black and gold-speckled off-the-shoulder top and a pair of black dress pants.

"He and my bestie, Alexis, are seeing each other. They live in the penthouse," Carly explains. She smooths down her black-sequinned shift dress, which rests mid-thigh. As always, she looks like a million bucks.

Sal's eyes widen. "No shit! Really? They live in the penthouse?"

"Yeah, really!" Carly sweeps her long, blonde hair off her shoulder and throws back her Slippery Nipple shot.

I give her a sceptical glare. "Are you going to pace yourself tonight?"

She licks her lips. "Probably not."

Just as she's about to scoop up her second shot, a masculine hand darts out of nowhere and swipes it from her, the contents of the small glass disappearing into the hand-owner's mouth.

"Mm." The guy gives her a boyish grin. "I love a good Slippery Nipple."

My jaw drops, and I'm about to shove the jerk for stealing her drink and being an inappropriate pig when Carly smiles at him, recognition in her eyes.

"It just so happens that I like Slippery Nipples as well, and now you"—she presses her finger into his chest—"owe me one."

"Carly—" He licks the rim of the glass, his voice low, playful, and sexy as hell. "—if it weren't for Derek beating me to a pulp, I'd totally give you one."

I swallow and nearly choke, all of sudden craving a Slippery Nipple too—they must be good.

She rolls her eyes at him. "Derek beat you to a pulp? Surrre. I'm almost certain he wouldn't give a flying fuck what you gave me."

"Are you shittin' me?" He steps back and lets out a deep belly laugh, and I'm guessing he knows Derek well.

"No, I'm not shittin' you. Derek has never once hinted he and I are anything more than just 'extra-special' friends, Will." She motions the bartender over. "I'll have four Slippery Nipples. What do you girls want?" Carly turns in our direction, finally acknowledging we're standing next to her.

Sal giggles and waves her fingers, but I just purse my lips at the rude bitch.

"Shit! Sorry! Will, these are my friends and work colleagues, Sally, Brooke, and Labia. Girls, this is Will, Derek's mate."

Heat burns my cheeks. *Did she just introduce me as a vagina?*

"Labia?" The arrogant jerk rests his knuckle on his lips, his amused eyes raking me from top to toe and back again. "Doesn't get any sweeter than that."

I. Beg. Your. Pardon.

"My name is Lib, or Elizabeth," I say, teeth gritted.

He turns his body to face me then leans on his elbow against the bar, and I'm able to get a better look at him—short dark-brown hair, tousled and peppered with a sexy hint of grey, a well-groomed beard and moustache, and pouty lips to rival Brad Pitt's. He's wearing a white shirt—possibly a size or two too small—sleeves rolled up to his biceps that could be easily mistaken as basketballs.

I stare at them and they flex, so I blink and focus back on his face.

"I think I like Labia better," he says and winks.

My eyes narrow into slits, nostrils flared, but I'm too furious to say anything.

"Gee." He raises his hands. "Lib or Elizabeth it is then."

"Thank you," I say, my smile sarcastically sweet.

"So what would your royal highness Elizabeth like to drink?"

"Royal highness? Oh, please." I scoff. "As if I haven't heard that before. And anyway, I'm quite capable of getting my own drink—"

"Actually," the bartender interrupts, "they're on the house."

"Make that five Slippery Nipples and five Cum Shots," Carly announces. "And they're all for me."

"Carly!" I scold.

"Labia!" she scolds back.

Will chuckles then slaps the bartender on the back in a familiar manner. "I'll have a Red-Headed Leg Spreader."

My jaw pretty much hits the floor, but the way he's looking at me—eyes heavy, tongue darting over his bottom lip as if he wants to spread my thighs—I can't help but press them together.

"Is that a real drink?" Carly asks.

"Yep." Will keeps his eyes on me, and my body tingles in response.

Stupid body. It doesn't know what it's doing. He's rude and pigheaded, and rude, and…Jesus, I like his arms.

"Can I get either of you ladies a drink as well?" the bartender asks, looking between Sal, Brooke, and me.

Sal slurps the last of her Cosmo in the most unladylike manner. "Yes, please, another one of these."

Brooke holds up two fingers. "Make that two."

Staring Will square in the eye, I say, "I'll have a Maneater."

He smiles, and it makes me even more annoyed; my drink order was better than his.

The bartender busies himself with the drinks and then lines up Carly's shots and Will's stupid Leg Spreader on the bar.

She starts knocking them back.

"Got something to prove tonight?" Will asks.

She shrugs. "Maybe."

"You may want to pace yourself."

"Yes, Dad."

I'm about to take one of her drinks, just to slow her down, when a woman calls out to Will. We all turn toward her voice—a stunning brunette with hazel eyes and the softest but sleekest cheekbones I've ever seen. *Wow! She could pass as the real-life Belle from Beauty and the Beast.*

"Oh, hi, Carly. This is a nice surprise," she says as she lets herself into our private area.

Carly beams. "Hey, Lucy, how are you?"

"Good." The woman gives Carly a gentle hug.

"Got the night off?" Carly asks.

"You mean from Alexander? Yeah, the crazy kid is upstairs with Bryce and Alexis. I think his presence helps them both, strangely enough."

Carly nods her agreement then gathers up her shots and heads toward our private booth, which is only a few metres away. "Come sit with us," she says to Lucy and Will, and they follow her.

"Who's that?" Sal whispers.

I shrug. "I don't know, but she knows Alexis, Bryce, and that rude jerk."

"You mean sexy jerk." Sal fans her face. "Talk about delicious caveman."

I raise an eyebrow. "Delicious?"

"Uh-huh. Yum!" Her eyes gleam as if he's a big bowl of naughty pasta.

"He looks like a security guard... or a bear." Inconspicuously glancing over my shoulder, I snap my head back toward the bar when I find him staring at my legs. "Damn it! Why did I wear this t-shirt Carly calls a dress?" I wrench it down and grumble when it barely covers my arse.

"T-shirt or not, you look great!" Brooke says. "I've never seen you in something like that." She swirls her finger in my direction.

I glance down at the body-hugging, emerald-green dress. "I look partially naked."

"You look hot!"

"Here you go, ladies." The bartender places three drinks on the bar top. "Two Cosmos and a Maneater."

Brooke snatches hers up and sips on the tiny straw. "I think Caveman agrees with me because he can't keep his eyes off you, Lib."

"That's because he sees me as a piece of meat he wants to rip into."

Sal almost drools. "I wouldn't mind being his meat."

"Really?" I glance over my shoulder again, and he tips his chin up before taking a swig of his drink. "You should go for it, Sal. But I'm sure he'll chew you up and then spit you out. He seems the type."

Picking up my drink, I sniff it hesitantly.

"What's in that?" Brooke asks.

"No idea." I scrunch my nose. "I've never had a Maneater before."

We both laugh, and all three of us make our way back to our private booth, the taste of rum, Coke, and perhaps lime, coating my tongue as I deliberately avoid eye contact with Will. The drink is gross. Fuck Maneaters.

"Lucy, these are my friends, Brooke, Sal, and Lib," Carly says to the woman.

"Oh, thank you for using my proper name this time," I deadpan.

The cheeky bitch pokes her tongue out at me.

Lucy laughs but looks from me to Carly and back to me again, a little perplexed. "Hi." She extends her hand. "Nice to meet you."

I shake it when Carly adds, "Lucy is Bryce's sister."

"Oh!"

That explains her fairy tale beauty. Apparently, the extremely good-looking gene is strong in Lucy and Bryce's family.

Carly offers one of her shots to her. "Would you like a Slippery Nipple?"

Lucy blushes but then smiles and bites her tongue. Will bursts into laughter, and I'm at a loss as to what's so funny. Maybe he's just one of those immature guys who laughs at the stupidest things, like the word nipple. It wouldn't surprise me.

Giving him a playful glare, Carly continues talking to Lucy. "I'd offer you the Cum Shot, but apparently, you're not into that."

"No, I'm not. I'll take a Slippery Nipple over a Cum Shot any day."

I'm so confused.

"Fuck, this conversation is hot." Will leans against the concrete pylon next to our booth then takes another swig of his cocktail. He swallows then pulls a face similar to a cat's bum. I almost laugh— serves him right if his Red-Headed Leg Spreader is as revolting as my Maneater.

"William," Lucy drawls, "when are you going to grow up?" She pats his shoulder condescendingly. "So I'm a lesbian. Big deal."

Ohhh! Okay. I feel a little less out of the loop now.

He smirks and blows her a kiss.

I roll my eyes at his lack of decorum and decide to remove myself from his presence. I don't know why he bothers me so much, but he does. "I'm going to dance. Brooke, Sal, you comin'?"

Sal looks at her drink with an expression of sorrow then puts it down. I do the same—sans the sorrow—and we snake our way through the crowd to an open spot on the dance floor, soon finding ourselves in instant hell.

Sweaty bodies. *Unfamiliar* sweaty bodies. Everywhere. All encroaching on my personal space. There's nothing worse. One guy even has the audacity to place his sweaty hands on my hips.

"Hey!" I swipe them away and move back, ready for fight or flight, when he's suddenly yanked away.

Relief floods me for a second when Will stands in his place, and I'm about to thank him when *he* has the audacity to place *his* hands on my hips too.

I look at them—huge bear-like paws on my silk dress—then look back up at him. "Do you mind?"

He chuckles. "So you'd rather dance with that guy?"

Placing my hands over his, I pry them from my body. "I'd rather dance with my friends."

Turning my back to him, I present my cold shoulder, which heats when his beard tickles the skin of my neck, his breath warm against my ear as he murmurs, "Can I be your friend, Labia? I'd *really* like to be your friend."

His hands once again snake onto my hips, and for a split second, I want them to stay there... until sense slaps me across the cheek and I spin to face him, our eyes locked, our faces mere centimetres apart. He's leaning down, his gigantic frame dwarfing me and creating a shield from anyone else standing close.

Strangely enough, I feel safe but... claustrophobic.

"No, you cannot be my friend!" I shove him again. "And my name is not *Labia!*"

Not knowing what else to do, I growl and storm away.

THE NEXT COUPLE of hours are spent hiding from and avoiding Will. He's like a sniffer dog, and I'm the cocaine. Every time the girls and I change levels, he's not far behind. I even have to slip into the ladies' toilet just to throw him off his scent. I don't know why, but he doesn't seem to understand I'm not interested in his company. I'm sure he's nice, somewhere underneath his offensive tongue, and I mean no offence—or maybe I do—but I'm just over stupid men and their stupid games.

Rounding the corner after leaving the toilet, I stop in my tracks when he pushes off from the wall and takes a step toward me.

"Don't come any closer," I say, holding my hand out like a stop sign.

My palm slams into his rock-hard chest, and I stumble backward, my shoulders hitting the passage wall behind me, his arms caging me in.

"What are you doing?" I ask, barely able to breathe.

His eyes narrow. "Firstly, I'm not playing chasey with you any longer—"

"Chasey? I don't know what you're talking—"

"Secondly, I'm sorry for calling you Labia. I didn't mean to upset you."

"Oh." This second one catches me by surprise. "I... I—"

"And, thirdly, you may want to help me stop Carly from doing something she'll regret."

I stare at his lips, the bridge of his nose, and finally his eyes, grey-blue like an overcast sky. Soft and kind, they contradict the rest of his burly exterior. They're not as dark as I first thought; they're rather lovely, actually.

"Elizabeth?"

I blink. "What?"

"Carly... she's dancing with a dick, a dick who's not Derek."

"Damn her." Closing my eyes momentarily, I sigh then quickly duck under his arm to free myself from his prison. "Where?"

He nods toward the dance floor.

"Right." I gesture to his pocket, where I assume he keeps his phone. "Ring Derek and tell him."

"You shittin' me?" He steps back, runs his hands through his hair, and laughs.

My eyes magnetise to his biceps once again, shirt cuffs straining against the expansion of his muscles. He must lift *very* heavy weights or pull *very* large cars, or—

He flexes them again.

"Am I what?" I shake my head, diverting my gaze back to his eyes, which really aren't less distracting. "No! I'm... I'm not shittin'

36

you. Call him. Tell him exactly what she's doing. He needs to know."

"He's gonna lose his shit."

"Good. He should. That's what she needs right now."

His eyebrows hitch, but he takes out his phone and dials Derek. "Hey, mate. How's things in Sydney?"

I look out at the dance floor, trying to pinpoint Carly, but my eyes keep making their way back to Will, following his every step as he paces the hallway beside me, phone to his ear. His arse looks great in jeans—hard, solid... strong. In fact, every part of him looks hard, solid, and strong. Intimidatingly so.

For the first time since meeting him, I notice tattoo ink creeping out from the collar of his shirt, and I'm curious to know what it looks like in its entirety. I'm not normally partial to men with tattoos, but for some reason, his intrigue me.

"I'm at Opals," Will says then chuckles at Derek's response. "Nah, not playin' a gig without you."

Gig? Oh, Will must also be in the same band as Bryce and Derek. Makes sense considering he seems to know everyone in the building. Carly mentioned Bryce's band often plays here and that he's a *"sexy version of Slash"* and that Derek can *"sing her panties off."*

I wonder what Will's role is. Drummer, guitarist... backup singer?

Unable to help myself, I snort-laugh. He definitely doesn't look like a backup singer. A drummer, yes—he has the arms for it—but a backup singer, no.

Will furrows his brow at me then says to Derek, "I'm with your girl and her hot as fuck friend." He looks me up and down again, much like he did at the bar, then adds, "Fuck yeah. I'm gonna have more than a crack at her."

Jerk! The only crack he'll be having is in his balls when my foot kicks them into his abdomen.

Crossing my arms over my chest, I snarl and walk away, hell-bent on finding Carly and dragging her home. Coming out tonight when she's fragile and hurting wasn't a great idea.

Pushing my way past person after person, I finally spot her ash-blonde hair twirling around like a tornado.

"What are you doing?" I yell, pulling her away from a sleazeball who has his grimy hands all over her.

"I'm dancing with…" She leans into him. "What's your name, sausage?"

"Marco."

"Marco. I'm dancing with Marco." Carly shrugs off my grip. "Want to join in?"

"No, you stupid cow, I don't. And I don't think Derek would want *you* joining in either."

Sleazeball stops dancing. "You're not single?"

"No, she's not. Now bugger off."

He walks away.

"Lib, you just scared him off." She pouts. "I wanted to see the sausage's sausage."

Making claws with my hands, they tremble as I refrain from placing them around her neck and strangling her. "What's wrong with you? What about Derek?"

"What about Derek?" she barks. "He's in Sydney, and whatever it is he's doing there, he obviously doesn't want me to know."

Before I can tell her she's an infuriating fucko—something I've never told her before—Will steps between us and hands Carly his phone.

"You may want to take this."

She squints at it. "It's not my phone. My phone is here." Carly reaches into her bra and pulls it out. Her eyes shoot to Will's phone. *"Is that him?"* she mouths, swaying just slightly.

Sporting a shit-eating grin, he nods slowly.

She groans, grabs his phone, and turns her back to us before nonchalantly answering, "What's up?"

"I could kill her," I say, dancing a little because everyone else around me is and I don't want to look out of place.

Will dances, too, and I'm not stupid enough to deny he has rhythm.

He leans forward. "Derek is pissed."

I nod. "I don't blame him."

"I'd be pissed too."

I smile, not knowing what to say to that. I guess it's fair enough.

He steps closer. "Carly says you don't have a man."

I stop dancing. "That's none of your or Carly's business."

Smiling like I really am a tasty piece of meat he wants to devour, he bends down, wraps his arms around my arse, and lifts me up. "Well, *Elizabeth*, as of this moment, I'm makin' it my business."

CHAPTER FIVE

"*P*ut me down, you prehistoric Neanderthal." I try to
wriggle free, but his arms are like pythons.

"A Neanderthal? Is that code word for Sex Master?"

"What? No! It's code word for *put me down now!*"

"Okay, your highness. I'm sorry." He places me on my feet again
and crosses his giant python arms over his chest. "You're short, and
I can't hear you down there. Conversation is easier when you're
level with my face."

"The only thing that's gonna be level with your face is my
fist."

Will throws his head back and laughs. "Word of advice... if
you're going to make threats, you need to be able to follow them
through."

I punch his arm; it's the only spot I can reach.

He looks at the spot then back at me as if an unexplained
phenomenon just occurred. "What was that?"

"What was what?"

He points to the spot I punched.

"That was me following throu—"

"Everything all right here?" a man asks, his finger tapping my
shoulder.

I flinch, turn to face him, and strangely enough move closer to Will. "Yes, everything is fine. Thank you."

"You sure?" He eyes Will, his chest puffed, which looks ridiculous because if Will were a lion, this dude would be a gazelle.

"Yes, I'm sure." I turn back to Will, his face still crumpled in that unexplained phenomenon kinda way, but now it's directed at the gazelle and not at me.

I can't help but giggle.

"Because if he's hassling you—"

"Oh, my God!" I look over my shoulder at the guy. "No, he's not hassling me. You are! Now go away or I'll punch you too."

The guy raises his hands and says, "Just tryin' to fuckin' help a bitch," then walks off.

Will's body stiffens, and his funny expression turns sinister as his eyes follow the guy. He takes a step in his direction, and I panic, clasping his arm and pulling him to me.

"Don't bother," I say, scoffing.

His hands find my hips again, and this time, I leave them there. I don't want him going after the guy.

"Don't bother what?" he prompts, still focused on the jerk.

"Defending my honour."

His eyes lock on mine. "Why not?"

"Because I don't need nor want you to. I can defend myself."

He lets me go and rubs his chin with his thumb and knuckle. "I'm not convinced."

"You don't need to be."

"Yes, I do."

"No, you don't." I go to leave when he says my name, and for some stupid reason, I like the sound of it on his tongue.

"Elizabeth."

"What?"

"I'm going to teach you how to box."

"Box? What?"

He nods as if that's all there is to it.

"Um… no, you're not."

This time, I do turn on my heel in search of Carly, Will following, his Gigantor arm reaching out to make a clear path through the sea of people before me.

"You need to learn how to defend yourself. You're too small and delicate."

"The only person I need to defend myself against is you."

"Fine! I'll teach you how to defend yourself against me then."

The offer is almost too good to refuse.

"I'll pass, thanks."

"Sorry, no can do."

Stopping at the edge of the dance floor, I spin to face him when he bumps into me, his arms reaching around my back to stop me from falling.

I gasp and grip the lapels of his shirt, my heartbeat escalating as our eyes bounce like tennis balls from each other's lips to each other's eyes. Will's gaze drops to my neck, and my skin instantly heats.

"See?" I wiggle out of his embrace so I'm able to step back for much-needed space. "The only person I need to defend myself against is you."

"Then I'll teach you how. It's settled."

I growl. "No, it's not."

"You don't have a choice."

"No, *you* don't have a choice." Huffing, I wonder why I'm still standing here talking to him. "Now, if you'll excuse me, I need to find Carly and then pretend this night never happened."

Will smiles, greedy-like, then licks his luscious Brad Pitt lips. "It happened, sweetheart, and it *will* happen again."

Swallowing hard, I take another step back and shake my head. "No, it won't."

* * *

"I MEAN who does he think he is?" I move onto the pavement and hold the door of the taxi while Carly ungracefully climbs out.

"He is Will." She giggles.

"He is an arrogant, pig-headed jerk."

Carly sways as she stands, so I loop my arm around hers, bearing most of her weight as I lead her toward the front door of our house.

"Derek and I *are*," she says, her eyes all dreamy.

I have no idea what she's talking about. She's been cooing and mumbling ever since she got off the phone with him. "Are what?"

"We just *are*."

"Jesus, how much did you drink?"

"Enough."

"You can say that again."

We somehow stumble to the top of the porch steps unscathed, so I prop her against the door while I search my clutch for the keys.

"His dad is sick."

"Huh?"

She twirls a piece of hair around her finger, eyes still dreamy. "That's why he's in Sydney. Sick dad."

"Oh. That's terrible."

"It's great!"

"What? Why?" My finger snags the key ring, so I pull it out and unlock the door, twisting the handle and opening it before remembering Carly's still leaning against it.

She slips down the wooden panel and falls to her knees in our doorway. *Oopsies.*

"Ouch!" Carly rolls onto her side and then onto her back, her limbs splayed like a snow angel, her dress pretty much around her waist.

"Shit! Sorry." I reach for her hands to help her up, but she just laughs.

"It's so great!"

I can't help but giggle at her weird happiness. She's never *this* happy. "Why is his dad being sick great?"

"It's not." She frowns at me. "That's horrible."

"But you said—"

"He doesn't have a stupid wife and shitty kids in Sydney."

"Oh." I pull her to her feet again. "I never thought he did."

"I did."

43

"I know."

"They would've wrecked everything."

"Yes, they would've."

"Stupid kids. Stupid wife."

Guiding her into her room, I let go of her arm when she slumps onto the bed. I'm tempted to leave her that way, but I know if I do, she'll be in the same position by morning. So I wrench her dress over her head, then lift one foot at a time and yank off her heels, nearly taking out my eye when one doesn't budge until I'm not ready. The black stiletto flies out of my hand, swiping my head, and nearly landing in Rico's tank.

"Jesus! Sorry, Rico," I whisper to Carly's startled axolotl.

He waves—well, technically, he swims, but tomayto, tomahto—so I wave back.

Rico is adorable. He reminds me of Rapunzel's pet chameleon, Pascal, in the Disney movie *Tangled*. I've thought of getting my own Rico, but I'm happy to play Aunty Lib to Carly's animal children, so I sneak him a few extra salmon pellets while winking at him.

"I know what you just did," Carly murmurs.

Turning my back on Rico's tank, I step up to the bed, shush her, and pull her blanket up and over her body. "Go to sleep. You're gonna have one hell of a hangover tomorrow."

As I go to leave her room, my finger hovering over the light switch, she snuggles her pillow and slurs, "He's the one."

"Who's the one?"

"D—" She inhales deeply then slowly exhales, and I think she's finally passed out when she slurs, "Derrrek."

Tightness pinches my chest, swift and hard, but I breathe through it as an unbearable sadness overwhelms me like a lingering dark cloud. I want what she's found: the perfect guy, a yin to her yang, her happy place. But no matter how hard I search, all I find are jerks.

Blinking through my tears, I drag the back of my hand across my eyes and force a smile. I'm happy for her. Really, I am. She deserves this. And if I can't have the fairy tale I've always dreamed of, then maybe Carly can.

"I hope that's true," I whisper before shutting the door behind me.

* * *

THE FIRST SCHOOL bell of the week rings, reminding me just how quickly the weekend flies by.

"I still have a headache." Carly cups her ears, squints, and then hands me my roll-call folder before sitting at her desk.

I take it from her with zero sympathy. "It's your own fault. You drank too much."

Her phone beeps, and she diverts her attention from me to the screen, so I leave her to it, pushing open the heavy glass door that leads out of the main office building.

"Will keeps sending me annoying texts," she calls out. "He wants your number."

I pause and glance back. "Why?"

"I think he likes you."

I point at her. "Don't you dare give it to him."

She waggles her eyebrows.

"I mean it."

Carly scoffs then says, "Our usual for lunch?"

"Sure."

We always go to the café down the road for lunch on Mondays, and I pretty much gag every time she orders a roasted lamb sandwich soaked in mint sauce. To be honest, I kinda dread it; it really is gross. But I go anyway because Carly loves it. Plus, it's much quieter at the café. No screaming kids and bouncing balls.

"Lib, wait up."

The sound of Oliver's voice followed by his hurried footsteps almost makes me want to power walk, but there's no use avoiding him. It's impossible; we practically teach at the hip.

"Have a good weekend?" he asks, stepping up beside me.

I smile in his direction, instantly noticing his woollen vest—not that it's unusual he's wearing one. For some reason though, the mustard-coloured number he has on today, paired with the red tie around his neck, makes him look like a walking, talking hot dog with ketchup.

I blink. "Yes, thanks, I did. And you?"

He shrugs. "It was nothing special. A bit boring, actually."

"Oh. I'm sorry about that."

He chuckles. "It's not your fault."

"I never said it was."

"Right. Yes." Oliver chuckles again, but this time it's less humorous. "So how was Friday night? Did you and the others go to Opals in the end?"

Surprised by his sudden interest in my social life, I almost clip my shoulder on the brick wall as we round the corner. Oliver has never really shown much interest in anything other than himself and his love of tennis. At the beginning of the year, I thought he was going to invite me to join him at the Australian Open when he showed me two tickets he managed to secure to the semi-finals. But the very next day, I saw a picture of him with his friend on his Facebook page, drinking wine from plastic cups in the stands at Rod Laver Arena.

Remembering how hurt and disappointed I felt, I can't help but exhale harshly through my nostrils. "Yes, we did go to Opals. Carly knows the owner, so we spent most of the night in a private section with our own bar. It was great!"

Oliver's eyes grow wide. "Office-Carly? She knows the owner of Opals?"

My jaw tightens. "Yes, *Teacher-Oliver*, she does."

We stop outside the classroom where our kids are lined up in pairs and chatting about the fun things they got up to on the weekend.

He gives me a sideways glance and murmurs, "I didn't mean it like that—"

"Good morning, everybody," I say, deliberately brushing him off.

"Good morning, Ms Hanson. Good morning, Mr Bunt," the kids chant.

Smiling at their innocent little faces, I gesture they go inside.

"Quickly put your bags on your hooks and sit on the mat, and I'll announce this week's bell monitor, roll monitor, and classroom helpers."

"Can I be a helper?" Jet Bradley asks.

I lovingly cup the back of his head and usher him along—he asks every Monday morning. "Just go and hang your bag up, Jet, and we'll see what happens."

Quickly entering the classroom before I'm bailed up by the few loitering parents, I leave Oliver at their mercy. That's another thing that happens every Monday, and usually I'm the one who's stuck answering queries while Oliver slithers inside like a snake. *Not today, buddy.*

I take a seat at the front of the room and clasp my hands together. "Okay, Grade 2s and 3s, who's ready for Funday Monday?"

Most of the kids say, "Me!" except for Evan, whose head is down, his shoulders slumped. He's not normally the spriteliest of kids, but even so, he looks particularly miserable, so I make a quick change in my notebook and appoint him one of this week's class-room helpers.

"Is Gregory Adams here?" I ask, starting the roll call.

He sticks his hand up enthusiastically, and so I make my way down the list, the kids who are present answering *"Here"*, and I soon discover only one student is absent.

"Excellent!" I close the roll-call folder and hand it to Jet with a knowing smile. "Here you go. You're this week's roll monitor."

He jumps up and says, "Yes!" while the other students clap.

"And the bell monitor is—" I pause while the kids perform a drumbeat on the carpet with their hands. "—Emma Johnson."

Most of them clap while some moan their disappointment.

"And this week's classroom helpers are—" Another carpet drumbeat. "—Zoey Michaels and Evan Hunter."

I wait for Evan to smile, but he doesn't, and it has me a little concerned.

Oliver enters the room, frowning, and I'm childish enough to enjoy his annoyance. He normally announces the monitors and helpers, but again, *not today, buddy*. Instead, he heads to the back of the room, to where our sink and Let's-Make-It table is, and then readies things for the first lesson—Science, and the wonderfully messy shit known as Ublex.

"Hannah and Dylan from Red House, it's your turn for Show and Tell," I announce.

Dylan springs up, goes to his bag, and brings back a pair of boxing gloves, and I'm instantly thrown back to Friday night when Will said he was going to teach me how to box. Large, sculpted biceps dance across my mind, and I delight in them before blinking them away. *What the hell was that?*

"What do you have there, Dylan?" I ask.

"Boxing gloves." He shows the class, and they stare wide-eyed.

"My dad has those," Gregory says.

"My mum has pink ones," Hannah adds.

"Hands up if you have questions," I remind them.

"These are my new gloves." Dylan straps them on and punches the air in front of him.

"Whoa, Muhammad Ali!" I raise my hands. "Be careful. We don't want anybody getting hurt."

"I won't punch anyone." He punches the air again, his demeanour overly confident. "I'm not allowed to unless it's self-defence or I'm in the ring."

"In the ring?" I nearly choke, a little surprised. Surely not. I can't for the life of me imagine one of *my* kids in a boxing ring.

"Yeah, but I'm too young for the ring. I gotta be ten."

Jesus! Is that all?

Jet sticks his hand up.

"Yes, Jet, you have a question?"

He nods. "Can you do an uppercut, Dylan?"

Just as Dylan punches toward the ceiling, Oliver curses under his breath, except it's loud enough for me to hear, which means the students hear it too.

I stand and make my way to the back of the room where he's clearing out the sink. "What's wrong? I'm fairly sure the entire class heard that S-bomb."

"Everything is wet." He holds up a set of containers.

"That's because you left them here on Friday." I point to the faucet, which is dripping much more than usual. "And because that's still leaking."

He huffs, moves the containers aside, and angrily flicks on the tap. Water bursts from the faucet like a fountain and hits me in the face. I scream and hold my hands up to block the spray, but there's too much.

"Shit!" he says.

I step aside, but the water spurts out toward the carpet, so I take one for the team, and once again use my hands and body as a shield. I'm already drenched so why the hell not.

"*Quick! Turn it off!*" I yell.

"I can't. The tap broke off."

"What?"

From his dry position a few feet away, he holds up the rusted brass lever that used to be attached to the sink.

"So? Don't just stand there. Do what you did at your Nonna's house."

"Huh?"

"You fixed her leaking tap, didn't you?"

Oliver appears to search his mind for what I'm referring to, but I'm fairly sure—given his Dumbo expression—that he has no idea, because it never happened.

"Uh… er…." He steps back and scratches his head just as George —Mr Tims—and Carly rush around the corner.

"Wow!" George gives the kids an excited but reassuring smile. "It's raining in your classroom. Cool!"

I laugh a not-so-funny laugh at the oldest teacher at our school while unsuccessfully trying to stem the flow of water with my hands and chest. "A little help, please."

"I'll call a plumber," Carly says and rushes out of the room.

George bends down, reaches under the sink, and the fountain turns to a trickle.

"Oh, thank goodness." I sigh, prop myself against the sink, and wipe my eyes with the backs of my hands, droplets of water falling from my nose, ears, chin, and arms. *Monday Funday, my arse.*

Oliver sheepishly hands me a roll of paper towel, and I have the overwhelming urge to crack him over the head with it, especially when he moves to the front of the room and says, "Okay, kids. It's stopped raining inside, so you can take a seat back on the mat, please." He then picks up the multiplication chart and starts next session's lesson as if nothing happened, as if I'm not standing here soaking wet with a mess to clean and a tap to fix. *Is he kidding me?*

George stands up again. "What happened?"

"I don't know." I offer him some paper towels. "But the tap has been leaking for a couple of weeks now—"

A thunder rumbles from the sinkhole.

George steps back and then looks at my tummy as if it's about to explode. "I hope that was your stomach."

I step back too. "Normally, it would be."

"It might be worth turning the water mains off to this building." He wipes his face with the paper towel and then scrunches it up and tosses it into the bin. "I'll go do that now."

"Thanks, George. You're a lifesaver."

He looks at Oliver then at me. "You gonna be okay?"

I scoff then peel my blouse from my chest and flap it. "Yeah, but I might need to go stand in the sun for a bit."

He chuckles, squeezes my shoulder, and then leaves.

Not one to stand around and do nothing, I head to the storeroom and return with a bucket, mop, and some cloths and begin mopping the floor, towelling the edge of the carpet and wiping down the sink, tables, and windows. It takes me a while because water reached farther than I realised, and when everything is mostly dry—sans me—and safe from hazards, I make my way outside to dry off a bit, still flapping my shirt when I turn the corner and slam into a wall.

A man wall.

A big, hard, familiar man wall.

"Will?" I question, stepping back, perplexed.

He smiles devilishly. "Damn! If it isn't a wet Labia."

CHAPTER SIX

*H*is misty eyes hover over my chest, so I cross my arms, shielding his view.

"What are *you* doing here?" I hiss.

"I've come to clean out your pipes."

"What?"

"Apparently your pipes are blocked."

I pinch my brow, a headache forming.

"You look confused, sweetheart."

"I am."

"Sorry, Will. I had to answer that call," Carly says as she steps out from behind him, a sneaky smile creeping across her face when her eyes meet mine. "Oh, good. You're here, Lib. Can you show Will the tap that burst, please?"

"Why?"

She looks at me like I'm an idiot. "Because he's the plumber."

My eyes bug. "*He's* the plumber?"

Will jiggles a metal toolbox dangling from his hand, his smile full of white dazzling teeth, which look contradictory against his bushy beard.

"Of course you are." Throwing my hands in the air, I turn on my heel and walk away, biting out, "Follow me," not waiting for him to do so.

"You look good wet," he says, voice low but humorous as he falls into step beside me.

"Oh, shut up."

He chuckles. "So tell me what happened."

"I'm not entirely sure. One minute, I'm standing there, and the next I'm soaking wet."

I regret the words as soon as they leave my mouth.

"You wouldn't be the first woman to say that to me."

I pause before opening the door to the classroom, close my eyes briefly, then push it open—my day couldn't have started any worse.

Will follows me inside, and the students grow silent, which is eerie considering they're normally bustling with sound. I look at their faces, all of them staring at Will, wide-eyed, their mouths parted but quiet.

"Whoa!" Jet croons. "You're the biggest man in the world."

I go to correct him when Will nods and says, "Yes, I am."

The rest of the class croon, too, and I have to bite back my laugh.

"You're bigger than my house," Emma Johnson says.

He nods again, nose scrunched. "I'm bigger than *my* house."

This time, I do laugh.

"Hey! That's my boxing teacher."

My eyes dart to Dylan, who has shot out of his seat and is waving at Will like a lunatic.

"Dylan, my man." Will winks at him.

"I brought my boxing gloves for Show and Tell today."

"Nice!" They bump fists as we walk by.

"Class!" Oliver snaps. "Pay attention."

"This way." I motion Will to the back of the room, a little shocked he actually "teaches" boxing.

Will fires Oliver a weird look and murmurs, "What crawled up Colonel Mustard's arse?"

I burst out laughing then quickly cover my mouth, remembering I'm a professional educator and that his comment is inappropriate.

"We're interrupting his lesson. It's hard enough getting the kids' full attention without a new face in the room."

"Maybe the kids should learn some basic plumbing."

"They're not here to learn basic plumbing."

His toolbox lands on the ground by his feet with a thud, and I'm surprised by the sound—it didn't look that heavy when he was carrying it.

"So"—he inspects the broken tap—"run by me what happened, step by step."

"Well, the faucet has been leaking for a few weeks now—"

"Weeks?"

"Yeah."

He huffs. "How bad?"

"Not bad, but it was worse this morning."

"Gushing or dripping?"

My cheeks heat at his words, and I'm almost unable to answer. "Uh... dripping. A lot. Almost a steady stream."

His eyes lower to my damp chest, so I cross my arms again.

"Then what happened?" he prompts, clearing his throat.

"Oliver. I mean, Mr Bunt—"

"Mr who?"

I bite my lip to stop from smiling.

I fail.

"Bunt... with a B."

"Right." Will's eyes bulge before he blinks. "Mr B-unt did what?"

"He turned on the tap, and it broke off in his hand, and then water flew out like a fire hydrant."

Will looks over at Oliver then back at me. "Did he get changed already?"

"No. He avoided the spray. I didn't."

Will scoffs.

"What?"

"Nothing." He bends down, and his shorts pull tight against his thighs, which are like tree trunks—stout, solid, defined.

My nipples tingle as they peak under my blouse, and I shiver then press my arms to my chest, my thumbnail finding its way between my chattering teeth. I'm desperate to change clothes, but that involves a trip home, which I can't do right now.

"Find anything yet?" I ask.

"Did Mr B-unt turn off the shutoff valve?"

"No, Mr Tims did. He also turned off the mains for the building."

"Mr Tims is a smart man."

I smile. "I know."

"Should I be worried?"

"About what?"

"About you and Mr Tims?"

Drawing in a deep breath, I huff it out, letting him know I've no patience for his silly game.

"I'm kidding, Elizabeth. You need to lighten up."

"As you can see, I've had a..." I whisper, "shit of a morning. I'm far from feeling *light*."

"Fair enough," he says, scrubbing his hands together. "I'll need to turn the mains back on for pressure testing."

"Yes, of course. Whatever you need to do."

"Anything else happen?"

"No."

He stands up, unfurling like a giraffe, and I'm almost transfixed.

"Oh, yes, there was also a loud growling noise before the avalanche of water. And after Mr Tims turned the mains off."

"Growling noise?"

I nod.

"What kind of growling noise?" He leans closer, all serious-like. "What did it sound like?"

"Um... it was like..." I do my best growling grumble noise. "Kinda like that."

Will throws his head back, his rumble of laughter nearly louder than the pipes. "Good impersonation! I was almost scared."

I somehow smile and frown at the same time before cottoning on to his childishness, my eyes narrowing, my patience paper-thin.

Forgetting where I am for a second, I punch his arm. "Very funny."

"Hey!" Dylan shouts. "You can't punch Master Will."

Both our heads snap in Dylan's direction, and it's then I notice Oliver glaring at us.

"*Sorry*," I mouth, raising my hand in apology before facing Will again. "*Master* Will?"

He flicks his eyebrows. "Has a nice ring to it, doesn't it?"

"You're unbelievable."

"You wouldn't be the first woman to say that to me," he says for the second time since being here.

I groan. "So can you fix it or not?"

"I can fix the tap, no probs, but I need to look into what made it burst in the first place, and for that, I need more tools from my truck."

"Good."

"So what's the damage?" Oliver says as he steps up next to us and offers his hand to Will. "I'm Oliver."

"Will."

They shake hands, and Oliver stretches his fingers upon release then cups his hand with his other. "Do you two know each other?"

Will hugs me to his side. "We go way back."

I inconspicuously pry myself from his grip. "No, we don't."

Oliver's eyes drop to my blouse, and once again, I'm crossing my arms over my chest. *I really need to change clothes.*

Another grumbling noise sounds, this one much quieter than the last, and I soon realise it's not the sink, instead coming from Will.

"I'll be right back," he says, eyes narrowed at Oliver.

We watch him leave before Oliver breaks the silence. "So how do you know the plumber?"

"I don't. Not really."

"He sure knows you."

"He's a friend of Carly's."

Oliver scoffs. "Now that I believe."

Turning to face him, I'm curious to know why their friendship is amusing to him, as it's somehow less civilised than his friend-ships. "What's that supposed to mean?"

"Nothing."

He walks toward his desk, so I follow him. "No, tell me what you mean by that. I wanna know."

"They just seem like they're cut from the same cloth."

I shake my head, bemused. "And what cloth would that be?"

Oliver goes to answer when, speaking of cloth, a t-shirt is draped over my shoulder.

"You might want to put that on," Will says.

He moves to the faucet, bends down, and fiddles with some-thing under the sink. I hold the black material out in front of me, a picture of a tap and the slogan *Tap That Plumbing* printed in green on the front.

"It's clean," he says, glancing over his shoulder at me, "if that's what you're worried about."

"Oh, no, I wasn't worried about that at all." I smile, a little shocked at his kindness. "Thank you. This is very thoughtful of you."

Will glares at Oliver and says, voice low, "You don't want boys looking at your tits."

And just like that, his kindness dissipates.

Sucking on my tooth, I turn around and address the class. "Grade 3s, start writing your four times tables in your workbooks. Grade 2s, you can write your fives. I'm just going to change my wet top. I'll be back in a minute."

I scurry to the office and stop by Carly's desk, tapping my fingertips on the reception countertop. I don't know how, but Will being here is definitely her doing.

"Yes, Mrs Hunter," she says, pointing to the telephone receiver she's holding to her ear. Carly gives me a *"Suck shit, I'm busy"* grin, so I cock an eyebrow and smile. She can't avoid me forever; I know where she lives.

Ducking into the staff toilets, I remove my blouse and throw on Will's t-shirt. It dwarfs me, but it's dry, warm, and surprisingly soft. Nuzzling the collar, I inhale, a little disappointed to find it smells like brand-new cotton and not him. No matter his caveman appearance and immature persona, nor how many buttons of mine he delights in pushing, I remember him smelling quite pleasant on Friday night when his arms were wrapped around me on the dance floor.

After tucking the hem of the t-shirt into the waistband of my capris so it doesn't look like I'm wearing some god-awful tunic, I stand under the hand dryer and turn it on, lifting my knees one at a time in an attempt to dry the damp sections on my legs.

"What are you doing?" Carly asks.

I swivel to where she's standing at the door. "The can-can, what does it look like?"

Her gaze lands on the t-shirt. "Tap That?" She laughs. "Ha! That's so Will."

I don't get what's so funny at first until Carly performs a hip-thrusting movement.

"Oh, my God! I can't wear a t-shirt in front of my kids that says Tap That."

She clutches her midriff. "You don't have a choice."

"Do you have any spare clothes I can borrow? Surely you've got a blouse or a dress stashed in your desk."

"Nope."

I let my head fall back against the wall and look at the ceiling. "How is he even here, Carls?"

"Who? Will?"

"Yes. Who else?"

"Because I called him." She moves in front of the mirror and adjusts her bra, cupping and rearranging her breasts as if they've somehow moved out of position. "While I was giving Derek head, he mentioned Will is a plumber."

I blink all the blinks. "What?"

"While I was sucking Derek's cock, he said—"

"Jesus! I heard that part loud and clear."

She pulls a lipstick out of her pocket and pops the top. "Then why are you confused?"

"Never mind." I really don't need to understand how that particular conversation materialised while that particular action was being performed, so I let it go. "So Will's a local plumber?"

"Yep." She presses her newly pigmented lips together then places the bullet applicator back into her pocket. "His company holds the contract for the schools in the area."

"Whyyy?" I softly headbutt the wall.

"Because he must be good at what he does?" she says as if my question is a legitimate one.

My eyes meet hers, and she smirks.

"You're enjoying this, aren't you?" I ask.

"Of course I am."

"It's as if you somehow arranged it."

"Maybe I did." Carly holds her hand out and inspects her nails. "Maybe I came here first thing this morning and broke the tap on purpose."

I laugh. "You? Get up first thing in the morning? Ha! If I don't wake you, you'd probably never wake up."

"True." She shrugs. "Okay, so I didn't arrange this. We both know that, which means the universe did."

"The universe?"

"Yes, the universe wants you and Will to get to know each other."

"Why?"

"Because he has a penis and you have a vagina."

I groan. "I don't have time for this. I need to go and... teach."

Stepping around her, I reach for the door when she clasps my arm and yanks me back. "You can't go back looking like that."

"Like what?"

"Like Alice Cooper." Carly spins me to face the mirror.

"*Oh, my God!* My mascara!" I wipe the black smudged pools under my eyes.

"You just made it worse. You need makeup remover."

"No shit!" I wipe some more. "It's not like I have any here at school."

"I do."

"What? Why?"

58

"In case a pipe bursts like a cock and comes all over my face."

I close my eyes for the smallest of seconds. "How are we even friends?"

"Because you need me." She pulls a near-empty wet wipes packet from out of her pocket.

"How—?"

"Don't question my genius. Just do something with that"—Carly lifts her hand toward my face and moves it in a circular motion—"and fix your hair. You look like a Troll Doll."

I smooth down my frizz. "I do not."

She purses her lips, eyes wide, and steps backward out of the room to leave me to my devices.

Sighing at my reflection, I agree; I do look like a Troll Doll. But before I can even decipher what the hell I'm going to do to fix it, the door opens once more and Carly pokes her head in, removes the clip from her perfectly styled hairdo, and tosses it to me before blowing me a kiss and leaving.

I smile and gather my hair into a bun.

She's right; I do need her.

* * *

AFTER OPENING THE CLASSROOM DOOR, I step into the room, and the children all look up and giggle.

"Your t-shirt looks funny," Jet says.

Emma scratches her head. "Tap That? What does that mean?"

I plaster on a smile even though I'm annoyed. It's a crass t-shirt, and I wouldn't be wearing it if Oliver and Will weren't idiots.

Stupid men.

Raising my finger to my lips, I make a shush sound then point to Oliver, indicating they should all pay attention to him before I make my way to the back of the room where Will is packing his tools back into his toolbox.

"All done?" I ask, noticing he's reattached the tap to the sink.

"Not quite." He glances at my attire and smirks.

I smooth the t-shirt down. "It's a little big, but... thank you."

"You're welcome. And, yes, I will."

"Will what?"

He gestures toward me. "Tap that."

A growl emanates in my throat, but I hold it down. "In your dreams."

"Been there, done that."

The growl comes out.

He winks. "I have a few more things to check." Will looks around the room and into the adjoining classroom. "Are there any toilets here?"

"Yes. But they're for the kids. You can use the toilet in the office building if you like."

He lowers his voice. "I don't need to take a piss, Elizabeth. I need to flush out the pipes while the mains are switched off."

My cheeks heat. "Oh, yes, of course."

"Could you let everyone in the building know not to use the toilets or taps until I'm done?"

"Sure."

"Thanks." He gestures to the t-shirt once again. "Looks good on you."

I glance down, my face scrunched as he walks away.

"Ms Hanson?"

I turn to Jacey Preston, who's shuffling on the spot, legs crossed.

I don't need to ask what she wants, so I just say, "You'll have to come with me. Our normal toilets are broken."

Her smile shows more discomfort than relief, so we make our way into the office, and I give her permission to use the toilet adjacent to the sick bay.

"She's not gonna spew, is she?" Carly asks, glancing over my shoulder. "You can deal with her if she does. I've done my quota of kid spew this year."

"She's not going to be sick. She's just using the toilet. Will said not to let anyone use the toilets or taps in our building until he says otherwise. Do you mind making an announcement to that effect, please?"

"Sure. But does that mean I'm gonna be inundated with midgets needing to poop and pee all afternoon?"

"I don't know, probably."

Carly pulls the type of face you pull when you realise you just stepped in dog shit, and I can't help but internally laugh. She's not a fan of kids, which begs the question as to why she works in a primary school... with kids. Lots of kids.

I learned long ago not to try to figure out how her mind works though, because some things cannot be solved. Like chickens and eggs, and which of the two came first. Carly is a chicken *and* an egg.

"Excuse me, students and staff," she says into the school's PA system. "The toilets and taps in Blue Building are currently out of order. Please do not use them. Instead, use Yellow Building, the recreation room, or—" She pauses then pouts."—or the office. Thank you."

"It won't be for long," I say. "I'm sure your friend will have it fixed in no time."

"Afraid not," Will says as his toolbox thuds to the floor at my feet.

I snap my head in his direction. "Why not?"

"Because I've found what appears to be several underground leaks behind the building. I'll need to bring in the excavator and check all the joins."

"So you'll be spending a bit of time here then?" Carly asks, her smile slyer than a Disney villain.

He nods then looks me dead in the eyes. "I'm gonna be here, every day, for the next few weeks."

What?

CHAPTER SEVEN

Carly places my herbal tea on the benchtop as I enter the kitchen. "You're *not* wearing that today."

I look down at my overalls and flannel shirt. "What's wrong with it?"

"Is it Old McDonald had a Farm Week at school? Did I miss the hillbilly memo?"

She has a point—albeit a rude, insensitive point.

"It is a bit 'rural', I'll give you that." I shrug and pick up the mug, cupping it in my hands. "But I like it. It's comfortable."

"And there lies your problem."

"What problem?" I take a sip and scald my tastebuds. "*Ffff*, that's hot."

"No shit! It's just boiling water with a tiny bag of fucking gross steeped in it."

"Green tea isn't everyone's cup of tea, Carly." Supercilious fuzzies wave over me, and I smile, a slight wobble to my head. "Ha! See what I did there?"

She deadpans, "Back to your ridiculous outfit. It's comfortable, which is a bad thing."

"How is being comfortable a bad thing?"

"Because comfortable equals slob."

"Are you calling me a slob?"

"Yes."

I glance at the coffee granules she spilled on the bench and the teaspoon she has no plans to put into the dishwasher, my eyebrow hitching.

"What?" She looks down at her mess.

"And I'm the slob?"

"You're a fashion slob. I'm a domestic slob. There's a difference."

"There's no such thing as a fashion slob."

Carly sighs. "How many times were you dropped as a child?" She tosses the teaspoon in the sink, swipes the coffee onto the floor with her hand, and nudges me toward my room. "Come on. Let me unleash your inner erotic sex slave."

"What?" I stumble and latch onto the doorframe for dear life. "No! Wait! I want to be a hillbilly."

* * *

FIDGETING with the tight-as-fuck leather pencil skirt stuck to my legs, I shuffle in heels toward the school office building. "I can't believe I let you do this to me. I feel ridiculous."

"You look insane! I'm talking librarian fantasy."

"What's a librarian fantasy?"

Carly winks, her smile increasing.

"Ladies!"

The sound of Will's voice behind me sets every nerve ending in my body into a state of panic, and I almost don't turn around.

"Good morning, William," Carly drawls. "Big day ahead?"

His eyes scale my body like Spider-Man would a wall before he chokes out, "Yes. *Very* big."

"Excellent!" She scurries off, and for a second I think she's being chased by a T-Rex.

"Where is she go—"

"You look different," Will says, eyeing my skirt.

"No, I don't."

"Yeah, you do."

My fingers grip my hip, my voice wavering. "I... I always look like this."

He raises his hands. "I don't mean it in a bad way, Elizabeth. I just mean you look different. Still stunning, of course. Just"—he tilts his head—"different." He bends and picks up his toolbox. "After you."

Will gestures toward the office building, his arm outstretched, muscles bulging underneath the sleeve of his fluorescent-orange polo shirt. His collar is up, which I've always found arrogant, but for some reason on Will, it's much more endearing.

"Thank you," I say, dipping my head to his khaki shorts and large tool belt. *Did he just say I'm stunning?*

My cheeks heat a little, so I make my way to the office and am nearly cleaned up by Sally when she wrenches the heavy glass entrance door open.

"Sorry. Oh! Hey, Lib." She gives me a quick once-over. "You look... different."

"That's what I said."

Sally blinks at Will while his giant python arm holds open the door for us. She doesn't speak at first, but then garbled words eventually leave her mouth.

"It's you!" She points at him. "Delicious. Caveman. How? I'm confused."

"You're confused?" he prompts, chuckling.

I put her out of her misery, although she doesn't seem miserable at all, her eyes twinkling like fairy lights.

"He's the plumber contracted to fix the pipes, Sal."

"You fix pipes?"

He smiles. "I do."

"I have pipes," she blurts.

Will nods and smirks at me, then says to Sal, "In or out?"

Her eyes widen and she stutters as if she doesn't know how to answer. "B-Both?"

"Both?"

"Well, yeah." She lets out an awkward laugh. "In and out."

I'm confused, and by the looks of Will's furrowed forehead, he is too.

"How can you be going in *and* out?" he asks.

Sally's face flushes pink. "Ohhh." She shakes her head and blurts, "I thought we were talking about sex." Morphing from a shade of pink to fire-engine red, she also blurts, "Out. I'm going out. Thank you. Goodbye."

She hurries toward her car, and I bite my lip to refrain from laughing.

"School teachers are not like they were when I was young," Will says.

"Yeah?" I giggle as we enter the reception area, unable to hold it in any longer. "How so?"

"They didn't talk about sex." He lowers his voice, his warm breath caressing my ear. "And they certainly weren't as hot as you are."

My heel gives way and I fall sideways, landing in his arms.

"Easy there, sweetheart."

Pythons or not, his arms are warm and strong, safe and lifesaving, because I most certainly would've fallen flat on my face had he not caught me. *Damn heels!*

"Th-Thank you." My eyes meet his stormy grey ones before he helps me upright.

"No probs."

"Right." Smoothing down Carly's ridiculous skirt, I make eye contact again for the shortest of seconds, his eyes now brighter, more amused. "I'll see you around."

"You will."

I nod. "I will."

"No." He pats his chest. "I Will."

"Huh?"

Carly cracks up laughing from behind the reception counter.

I look between the two of them. "I don't get it."

"Me Tarzan, you Jane," she says.

Will gives her the thumbs-up.

Shaking my head at them as I push through the door that leads to my classroom, I cringe as Oliver falls into step beside me.

"See?" he says, gesturing to Carly and Will. "Same cloth."

* * *

DESPITE ADJUSTING my skirt and being incredibly uncomfortable and frustrated for a good part of the morning, every time I catch my reflection in the window, I kinda like what I see. Yeah, I look *"different"*, but it's a good different, an empowering different, and something I might wear again sometime.

Just not at school.

And definitely not on a sports day.

"Rightyo, Grade 2s and 3s," Oliver announces, "please put the dodgeballs back into the bags and line up with your partner. The bell is about to ring for lunch."

I hold out the large net bag as child after child pops a rubber ball inside.

Oliver does the same then tosses both bags over his shoulders. "You'll have to push the trolley," he says, nodding to the metal shelving cart stacked with cones and hula-hoops.

He already set up the equipment prior to our Sport lesson starting, so I hadn't carried a thing.

"Um..." I glance down at my heels, unsure as to how this is going to happen. "Surrre."

Oliver glances at them too. "Why on Earth would you wear those to school?"

"I... I don't know."

"They're hardly practical, Lib."

"Yeah, I get that."

He huffs. "Not your brightest idea."

Oliver walks off, directing the kids back to the classroom, so I clasp the handles of the cart, push forward, and give it a nudge with my hip to begin momentum. It clangs and rolls along the bumpy asphalt, and I stumble behind, trying to keep it straight while also trying to keep up with Oliver, who has conveniently powered ahead.

"Don't wait for me," I mumble.

The wheel of the cart hits a rock, and both the cart and I come to an abrupt halt, nearly toppling over. "Shoot!"

"What's wrong?" Oliver calls out.

He doesn't make a move to double back and help me, so I plaster on a faux smile and shout, "Nothing!" through gritted teeth while trying to right the cart again.

"Just take those ridiculous heels off."

"I would if I could, you idiot," I hiss under my breath.

A flash of orange hits my peripheral vision, and I look up, spotting Will jogging toward me.

"Need a hand?"

"No," I lie. "I'm good. Just a hit a rock."

Ignoring me, he takes possession of the cart and repositions it. "*Now* you're good."

I snatch the cart back, embarrassed. "I said I was fine."

"Actually, you said you were good."

"Whatever."

Kicking off my heels, I pick them up, toss them into the cart, and give it a mighty shove, my barefoot landing on a stone after my first step.

"Ffff—" I limp and close my eyes, willing the godawful sting to subside. "Damn it!"

Before I'm able to inspect the damage, I'm hauled into the air and slung over Will's shoulder, the cart once again clanging and banging as he walks.

"Will! What are you—?"

"Where to?" he asks as if I'm not draped over him like a fur shawl.

"Nowhere! Are you crazy? Put me down!"

"I can't stand to watch you hurt yourself any longer. Just tell me where you need to go, and I'll get you there."

The lunchtime bell blasts through the speakers in the yard, and I panic for fear of someone seeing us. "Please put me down. I can walk." I try to straighten my body, which is when I see Brooke, plastered to her classroom window like a perverted starfish, her Grade 1 students gathered around her and pointing at us as they giggle. "Pleeease," I beg. "This isn't professional."

"You hurting yourself left, right, and fucking centre isn't professional either."

"Okay, okay. I agree. Fine, you can help me with the cart." I slap his back. "Yes. You push the stupid cart, and I'll walk in the stupid heels."

He stops and places me on my feet again. "That I can do."

I quickly wiggle the hem of my skirt down my legs and say, "Thank you." Then, utterly embarrassed, I place my palm to my forehead and sigh. "I'm sorry. I'm just an idiot. I've no idea why I agreed to wear these damn things."

Children spill out of their classrooms and into the yard like bees leaving a hive.

"You don't happen to have a spare pair of shoes, do you, like you did the t-shirt? Size 6? Maybe they're tap shoes that say Tap That?"

Will laughs. "No, but there's an idea."

"This is all Carly's fault, you know." I lift my heels out of the cart and drop them at my feet. "Apparently, I looked like a hillbilly this morning, so she gave me a makeover."

He rubs his chin with his thumb and finger, his eyes sweeping me from head to toe. And for the first time, I don't feel the need to cover myself with my arms.

"While I like Carly's handiwork, if you want to look like a hillbilly, you should look like a hillbilly."

"I don't want to look like a hillbilly," I grouch.

"My point is you should look the way you want to look." He holds out his elbow so I can balance while putting my heels back on.

"Thanks." I steady myself. "In the future, I will. But that'll have to wait until tomorrow. Carly is holding her car keys as ransom, otherwise I'd go home right now and grab a different pair of shoes."

I walk in the direction of the equipment room, Will pushing the cart beside me.

"You don't have a car?"

"No, I do. Carls and I live together, so it makes sense if we ride-share during the week. She drove today."

"So why's she holdin' the keys as ransom?"

"Because she wants me to suffer. She's a villain."

He chuckles. "I'll take you home if you want."

I stop at the equipment room and unlock the door. "Uh…"

"I'm not going to kidnap you," he says, a devious grin creeping onto his face.

I squeak out a laugh. "I know that. It's just I don't want to put you out."

He winks. "I like putting out."

I keep my face stoic.

"Do you want to change your shoes or not?" Will pushes the cart into the corner of the room.

"I do. It would make my life much easier."

"Then I'll take you. End of story. Does now suit?"

"Actually, now is perfect. The students are at lunch for an hour."

"Then it's a date."

"It is *not* a date."

He smiles, all teeth, then holds the door open for me as we exit. "Your chariot awaits."

I roll my eyes but stifle a giggle; I've always wanted to ride in a chariot.

* * *

WILL's truck is indeed no chariot. Instead, it's a white Toyota Hilux utility that smokes more than a dragon and rattles louder than a charity tin.

"Just on your left," I say, pointing at our house through the windscreen. "Number 12."

He pulls to a stop outside, and I open the car door, planning to rush in and out when he opens his door too.

"I'll only be a second," I tell him.

He adjusts himself. "I need to take a piss."

Staring a bit too long at his hand cupped over his groin, I blink and scrunch my nose at him. "Right. Sure. Follow me."

He does, his body a looming shadow as I unlock the front door and push it open.

Distracted by his close proximity, I forget Sasha's tendency to try to escape the house, and she bounds out, nearly knocking me over.

"Oh no! Quick! Catch her!"

Will darts to the side and catches her mid-leap.

"Who do we have here?" he asks, appearing to delight in her enthusiastic, laving tongue.

"This is the naughtiest Golden Retriever to ever live." I grab her head and massage her cheeks with the pads of my thumbs. "Her name is Sasha, and she's an adorable menace."

"My kind of menace." He hoists her higher.

"Please, come in."

Will steps into our entryway hall, and I close the door behind him.

"You can put her down now."

"Nah, I'm good."

I laugh, thinking he's kidding, but the way he has her comfortably reclined in his arms soon tells me he's not.

"I like animals," he says as if it's the only justification he needs.

"You're not taking our dog into the toilet with you."

"Don't need to piss anymore."

My eyes narrow. "You didn't need to piss in the first place, did you?"

He goes to step around me and into our lounge room when I fling my arm out and block him.

"Oh no, you don't." I point to his muddy boots. "Not in those filthy things."

We both look down, and he slides them off with his feet while grinning and jiggling Sasha as if she's a baby.

I sigh. "Fine! Just don't touch anything. I'll be back in a minute."

Letting him pass, I then make my way to my bedroom, hopping as I lever one heel off after the other. The relief is instant, and my toes fan out over the carpet. *Never again will I wear those murderous weapons to school.*

I place them in their allocated space on the floor of my walk-in robe then unzip my skirt and shimmy it down my legs. Grabbing the closest pair of jeans, I step into the legs and wrench them up as I walk back into my room to find Will standing in front of my dresser, inspecting my things, Sasha still comfortably sprawled in his arms while he lightly scratches her belly.

"Jesus!" I shriek. "Do you mind?" I quickly turn away from him until my jeans are secured.

"No, do you?"

"Yes! Get out."

He takes one last look around and leaves the room, but instead of turning toward the front door, he turns in the opposite direction and stops in front of Carly's room.

"Sick! An axolotl." Will disappears from the hallway, and when I find him again, he's bent over, mesmerised by Carly's Mexican walking fish. "I've always wanted one of these."

It's hard to be annoyed; Rico is pretty darn cute.

"That's Rico." I grab his packet of dried salmon flakes and sprinkle some into his tank. "Watch. He waves when you feed him."

And just like clockwork, Rico slowly swipes his foot in an arc.

I smile and wave back. "You're welcome, buddy."

Turning my head to see Will's reaction, because it's an awesome trick, my smile falters when our eyes lock.

We both straighten, and I have a sudden urge to move backward when he lowers Sasha to the floor and takes a step toward me, his pupils dilated, his tongue dampening his lips.

"W-what?" I stutter, my shoulders hitting the doorframe, his body caging me to the spot when his palms press the wall beside my head.

"Go out with me."

CHAPTER EIGHT

"What? No!" I slide out from underneath his arm and back away.

"Why not?"

"Because I don't want to."

"I think you do." He smiles and pushes off from the wall.

"Well, you're wrong." I head back to my room and lower myself onto the edge of my bed, keeping my eyes on him as I feel around my feet for my shoes, snagging one in my hand and smiling back at him. "You're not my type."

Will blinks as if my answer is preposterous. "Of course I am."

"No, you're not." I snag the other shoe and slide it on. "For starters, you're too"—I point to the dried smears of mud on his legs—"dirty."

He glances down then takes a step closer. "There's nothing wrong with dirty, sweetheart."

Shooting to my feet, I back away, *again*, and point, *again*. "And you're rude."

"I am not."

"You are."

"How am I rude?"

"You..." I inch closer to the door. "You touched my things without permission."

"I like touching your *things*."

Heat pools between my legs, and I curse my traitorous body. It's not thinking straight.

Preparing to dive across my immaculately made bed just to put it between us, I realise being anywhere near a bed is a bad idea, given the look of lust in his heavy eyes. Plus, he seems the type of guy who'd destroy my hospital corners and cushion placement in the heat of the moment... which isn't a bad thing, I guess.

Oh, my God! What am I saying? Of course it's a bad thing.

"You're also lewd, and crude," I blurt out, holding my head high as I march past him and into the hallway.

He follows me. "If I'm lewd and crude, then you're a prude."

What? "I am *not* a prude." I spin around, my chest bumping into his, my body fizzling at his closeness.

Will slowly drags his knuckle down my arm, and my treacherous eyelids threaten to flutter.

"I think you are," he murmurs.

The heat from his touch sends chills across my skin, so I blink and swipe his hand away. "You're wrong."

"Am I?"

"Yes."

A smug smile lights his eyes. "Prove it then."

I want to punch him, but that'll only prove, once again, that I can't punch. *Argh!*

Stretching up on my tippy toes, I yank his head close to mine then hover my lips over his ear before whispering, "I like sex, *very* much." I nudge his cheek with the tip of my nose. "But just because I won't let you fuck me here in my hallway"—I shove him, my voice now harsh—"doesn't make me a prude."

Sasha paws my leg, so I lower to my knee to pat her while looking up at him through my lashes. "I respect myself enough not to go out with someone who only wants inside my pants."

He reaches down and tilts my chin up. "You think that's all I want?"

Again, I swipe his hand away. "It's all any guy wants."

* * *

THE DRIVE back to school is quiet until I break the silence when we both climb out of his truck and shut our doors.

"Thanks for driving me home to get changed."

His eyes don't find mine. "No sweat."

"I mean, you didn't have to do that, but you did, so thank you. I appreciate it."

"Like I said, no big deal." He presses his lips together, reaches into the back tray of his truck, lifts out his toolbox, and walks away.

"Okay then," I murmur. I guess I deserved that. *Shit!*

Pivoting to walk in the opposite direction back to my classroom, regret washes over me, and for some stupid reason, I feel bad for turning him down. Well, maybe not for turning him down, but more so for calling him rude, lewd, and crude. It was overkill. And despite him being those things at times, telling him so was perhaps a bit harsh, given he was doing me a favour in the first place.

Damn it!

Turning back around, I'm about to jog over to him and apologise when the bell rings. He raises his hand to acknowledge a guy climbing out of a truck with an excavator loaded on the back. *Tap That Plumbing* is printed along the rusty white panels. They slap each other's back, and I can't deny I'm impressed Will owns and runs his own business. The man might be a player and a bit of a joker, but he's clearly hardworking and successful, and I'm glad that's paid off for him.

Deciding to just let it go because I've no time to linger and wait for him to finish with the other guy, I rush to my classroom just in time for fifth period.

"Nice to see you changed your shoes," Oliver says as I follow the children inside.

I don't respond, instead giving him a half-smile. I already feel like an idiot for wearing them in the first place.

"Why'd you wear them?" Oliver probes.

I shrug. "I don't know."

"Seems odd."

"Why?"

"Because you've never worn anything like that to school before."

"Sure I have."

It's a lie; I haven't.

Oliver shakes his head, a suspicious but playful grin on his face as he claps his hands and announces, "Bums on the mat, eyes on me," to the class.

The kids all sit cross-legged, except for Hannah and Jacey, who stand by my side and continuously inform me Jet went out of bounds not one but three times.

"Take a seat, girls," I say, dismissing their tattling. If I had a dollar for every time one of my kids dobbed another in, I'd be a very wealthy teacher.

"Okay, everyone. Who's ready to make some music?" I ask, eyes wide.

They all cheer, which doesn't surprise me. Behind Sport and Art, Music is their favourite subject.

"Good! Now, Mr Murphy isn't here today, so I'm going to take you to the music room and teach you instead while Mr Bunt marks your math tests."

"You can't teach Music, Ms Hanson," Jet so accurately points out.

"Sure I can."

I can't, but the alternative is cancelling, or Oliver doing it. Oliver doesn't have a musical bone in his body, and I know how much the kids like music, so I don't have the heart to cancel.

"I might not be very good, Jet, but I'm sure we'll be fine and have some fun."

* * *

Music when you're not the music teacher is not fun at all. In fact, I'm fairly sure sand in your undies or a rose thorn in your foot is a whole lot more fun than the hell I'm currently in.

The instrument rotation now has Jet on the drum kit. *Yay!* Five kids are continuously strumming the same chords on the guitars. Another five are bashing the xylophones like a Mole in the Hole game, and the rest are shaking maracas, tambourines, and seeing who can blow the loudest and longest on the recorders. If I wanted to torture my worst enemy, this is how I'd do it. I'd lock them in this very room. Now. Preferably without me. *Why in God's name did I think this was a good idea?*

"Okay, okay!" I shout over the racket. "Hands in the air!" The kids all raise their hands. "Let's try to keep in time. One, two, three, four. One, two, three, four."

The ear-splitting noise resumes, and I'm almost ready to pull out my hair when I notice Will leaning on the doorframe, ankles and arms crossed, an amused grin on his face.

I raise my eyebrows at him in acknowledgement then weave through the kids until I'm at the door. "Hi. Is everything okay?"

"I was just about to ask you the same thing."

"Oh. Is it that bad?"

He nods. "What are they trying to do, kill each other?"

"No." I wrinkle my nose. "Well, I don't think so."

"You don't know what you're doing, do you?"

Offended, because I studied very long and hard to know what I'm doing, I cross my arms and glare at him. "Of course I know what I'm doing."

"Doesn't look like it."

"You think you can do better?"

"At music? Sure."

Waving my hand toward the class, I gesture he enter the room. "Then be my guest."

Will pushes off from the doorframe, makes his way over to the drum kit, whispers something in Jet's ear, and then takes his place, lowering himself onto the stool. Jet steps back, covers his ears with his hands, and nods.

A loud thumping soon fills the room, slow, like a distant roll of thunder, followed by a faster tapping on the snare. Some of the kids stop playing their instruments and snap their heads in Will's direction, but it's not until he unleashes like a madman that everyone in the room freezes like statues, eyes wide, mouths agape.

Including me.

Now, I don't know a lot about music, but I do know Will is an exceptional drummer. The way he moves across each drum, the tempo changing, sticks twirling in his hands. It's impressive, mesmerising even... until he stops, and we all give him a round of applause.

"That was so cool!" Evan says, and it takes me by surprise. He's not normally one to say much, let alone to someone he doesn't know.

"Do you want to try?" Will offers.

Evan nods, so Will stands up and moves out of the way so Evan can sit down.

I grab a seat, and the rest of the kids abandon their instruments, now completely focused on Will. It makes me smile, but at the same time, I'm aggravated he was right.

"Okay, buddy," he says to Evan. "You comfortable?"

"Yes."

"Good. Now place your foot on that pedal and press it down."

Evan does what he's told, and the bass drum thuds, loud. The sound startles him, and he cowers a little but then smiles when Will encourages him to do it again, this time while counting to four.

"Can I try?" Jet blurts.

"You can, little dude. Come, step into my office."

Jet gives him a weird look. "It's not an office."

I laugh.

Will gives Jet the same weird look. "Yes, it is!"

I laugh again.

"No, it's not. It's not an office."

"It is. It's my office."

Jet shakes his head. "No, it's not."

Will places the drumsticks down. "Do you want a go or not?"

"I do."

"Then say it's my office."

"It's my office."

Closing his eyes for a second, a smile creeps onto Will's face. "No, not *your* office, *my* office."

"It's your office."

"Aay!" He holds up his hand for a high-five. "Now we're on the same page."

I shake my head, facepalm, and laugh some more.

"Right. Now we've got that sorted, take this stick, but don't hold it too tight, you want it nice and loose." Will hands Jet the drumstick. "Stand in front of the floor tom, which is this drum here."

Jet takes his position and starts smacking the drum.

"Whoa! Dude! You can't just smack the crap out of it."

I clear my throat, and Will looks in my direction. *"Language,"* I mouth, eyebrow raised.

He pulls an *"oh shit"* face and rephrases. "You can't just bash it."

"But you did," Jet complains.

"No, I didn't. What I did, apart from it being pure class, was time my hits like a champion. If you want to be a good drummer, you gotta know how to count."

"I know how to count."

"Then we're off to a good start. Can you count to four, two times?"

Jet rolls his eyes. "Yes. Derrr. I'm in grade 3."

"Jet," I warn. "Don't be rude."

"Sorry, Ms Hanson. Sorry, Mr Will."

"It's *Master* Will," Dylan says, correcting Jet.

Will winks at Dylan then scruffs Jet's hair. "All good, my man. Now, I want you and…" He looks at me for help with Evan's name.

"Evan," I say.

"I want you and Evan to count to four, two times while playing your drum. The trick is to keep in time. The rest of you," he says, looking out at the kids sitting on the floor before him, "I want you to pat your legs with both hands and do the same. You, too, Ms Hanson."

"Oh!" I point to my chest and smile at the kids, excited that I get to join in, then ready my hands to pat my lap.

"Like this." Will taps the cymbal, counts to four, then repeats himself. "Are you all ready?"

We chant, "Yes," and Will begins to count again.

"One, two, three, four. One, two, three, four."

The kids follow but at different speeds, some counting slow, others racing through it.

Will's eyes grow wide, and he raises his hands to his head, showcasing his enormous biceps. "Let's try that again."

My eyes slide over the rise and fall of his skin, and they flex.

"Ms Hanson," Will says, voice amused.

"Yes?" I snap my attention back to his face, my heart rate accelerating.

"I need you."

"W-what?"

"To be my assistant."

"Oh. Okay." I stand. "What do you want me to do?"

"Come here, next to me."

Walking around the kids, I step up to his side, and he grabs my hand. My first instinct is to wrench it free, unsure of his intentions, especially in front of the kids. But I don't want to cause a scene, so I leave my hand in his, even when he places it on his chest, over his heart.

"A drumbeat is a feeling," he says to the class. "A heartbeat." A smug smile tugs at Will's lips as his eyes zero in on mine, his fingertips tapping my hand. "Go-gong. Go-gong."

I narrow my gaze, a smile tugging on my lips too.

"One, two, three, four. One, two, three, four," he says.

The kids tap the beat perfectly, and I giggle.

"You totally just stole that line from *Dirty Dancing*," I murmur.

He flicks his eyebrows then leans in and whispers, "Patrick Swayze knew his shit."

Throwing my head back, I crack up laughing, which is when Oliver enters the room, a scowl on his face. "What do we have here?"

I slip my hand out from underneath Will's and step back. "Will was just kindly showing us his knowledge of percussion."

"Percussion?"

"Yes." For some stupid reason, I feel as if I owe Oliver an explanation. "How a drumbeat is like a heartbeat."

Oliver hitches one brow at Will.

"I'm a drummer, Mr B-unt."

A rash of red climbs Oliver's neck until it flames his face. "Wow! A plumber *and* a drummer." He plasters on a smile for the kids. "Aren't you lucky to learn from such a professional?"

Will tosses Oliver a drumstick. "Would you like to learn too?"

Oliver tosses it back. "No, thanks."

Will shrugs. "Suit yourself."

"I'll leave you to it." He goes to leave but stops at the door. "Oh, and, Ms Hanson, don't forget about the chocolate fundraiser we have to hand out to the kids before they go home. You might want to finish up 'learning' percussion a bit earlier."

I slap my hand to my head. "Yes! I did forget about that. Right, quickly and quietly, everyone, please put your instruments back where you got them from and form a line at the door."

The kids move about the room, packing up while Will places the drumsticks back on top of the snare.

"Thank you, *again*," I say.

"*Again*, no sweat."

I sigh. "You were right."

"'Bout what?"

"You did do better." Clapping my hands, I address the kids. "Form two lines and head back to class. I'll be right behind you."

They begin filing out through the door, which is when I turn to Will, who begins to leave as well.

"Will?"

He stops. "Yeah."

"Listen, about earlier, I just want to apologise for calling you rude, lewd, and—"

"Crude?"

My cheeks heat. "Yeah. I didn't mean it."

He chuckles. "Yeah, you did."

"Well, fine, I did. But I didn't mean to offend you."

"You didn't."

I sigh, relieved. "Oh, good."

"Because I know I'm not those things."

Placing my hands on my hips, I cock an eyebrow. "Well, you are... a bit."

"Elizabeth"— he touches my cheek—"I'm not who you think I am."

"And who do I think you are?"

"Apparently, someone who just wants inside your pants."

"So you don't want that?"

"Of course I do."

I scoff. "I rest my case."

Pivoting, I go to leave when he grabs my hand and pulls me to him, his eyes searching mine, his voice low and... sincere. "I'm not going to apologise for wanting to bury myself deep between your legs." He glances at my lips, and said legs nearly buckle. "But I want inside your head first, and maybe, just maybe, you'll want inside my head... and pants too."

CHAPTER NINE

*W*ill left me standing in the music room, heart thumping in my chest, an unfamiliar melody dancing all over my body. It didn't make sense—the weak knees and heart palpitations. We're the complete opposite, and we have nothing in common. He's a dirty, burly tradie, and I'm a clean, well-educated teacher. He speaks before thinking, and I speak after carefully considering each and every word to leave my mouth.

And... and he has no manners. Manners are important. They show maturity and decorum, qualities every adult should possess. We're chalk and cheese, summer and winter, Elsa and Anna. So, yeah, feeling this... this giddy just doesn't make any sense.

Now a few days later, I'm staring out of the classroom window at Will and his apprentice, Jeremy, as they set up a safety area with construction tape. He informed all staff this morning that they'll be driving the excavator within the taped-off area and to warn the children to stay well away. Other than that, we haven't spoken since the music room, but I've been very much aware of his presence around the schoolyard. He's hard to miss—fluorescent-yellow and orange high-vis vest flashing on my peripheral vision every time I glance out the window.

Just now, for instance, Sally was heading to—I assume—the

library with a stack of books when two slipped from her grasp. Before she could squat and retrieve them, Will jogged over and picked them up for her. It was rather lovely, until they conversed longer than I thought necessary. And then it didn't seem so lovely anymore, Sally blushing and blinking profusely. At one point, I thought she had something stuck in her eye.

She didn't, beside her eyeballs, which I felt like poking out. Which is just weird, because I'm not jealous. I can't be—one has to form an emotional connection to experience jealousy, and I haven't done that… I don't think.

Will hammers in a star picket then animatedly drums a beat on top of it. I smile; it's something I've noticed he does a lot, tapping fence tops, walls, and nothing but air several times a day. At first, I thought it was childish and stupid, but the silly tapping has kinda grown on me. I've also noticed he lifts his baseball cap and runs his hand through his hair a lot, as if in contemplation, or perhaps because his head is sweaty.

"Lib!"

"What?" I snap my vision to Oliver, and he ducks his head to see what, or rather who, I'm looking at through the window.

His eyes narrow. "The bell just rang."

I take note of the clock and let out a noise that's supposed to be a laugh but isn't. "Oh, really? I must've been in a world of my own."

"What are your plans?"

"For what, lunch?"

"Yeah."

"Um—"

Carly and Sal poke their heads through the doorway. "You ready?" Carly asks.

"Um, yep." I look at Oliver. "We're just heading down the street to the café."

"I might join you if that's okay?"

Carly vehemently shakes her head.

"Sure," I say. *I mean what choice do I have?*

Carly pretends to bang her head against the doorframe, and Sally quickly nudges her when Oliver turns in their direction.

She smiles, all teeth and sarcasm. "I've invited Will and Jeremy too," she adds.

I grab my purse. "Greeeat. The more the merrier."

Ffffk! This will be interesting.

We head out of the classroom, the sun high in the sky, breaking through rainclouds and casting a rainbow over the horizon. Warmth and joy fill me as I admire the pretty spectrum. I've always loved rainbows. There's just something magical about them as if they only belong in fairy tales, and if you do happen to find the bottom of one, it's not a pot of gold you'll find but instead a castle in a faraway land.

"You fantasising about my body on top of yours?" Will asks, snapping me out of my rainbow-daze by nudging my shoulder.

Sal chokes then coughs, and Jeremy chuckles.

I sigh, my eyes playful. "The only way your body will be on top of mine is if we both trip and I cushion your fall."

Oliver scoffs and shakes his head at Will. "Ouch!"

Will ignores him, eyes fixed on mine. "Best you watch your step then."

"I will." I look down at his feet. "Best you watch yours."

He follows. "I won't."

Oliver scoffs again.

The footpath we're walking on is narrow, wide enough for two abreast. So Sal and Jeremy walk ahead, Oliver and I not far behind them, Will mere steps behind us, and Carly at the tail end, her phone pressed to her ear. The café is only a short walk from the school, so it's pointless to drive.

"So how are the repairs coming along?" I ask Will, trying to include him in conversation because my roommate is a rude bitch. "Any closer to fixing the problem?"

"Yeah, you've been at it for a while now," Oliver pipes in before Will can answer.

"Everything's on schedule. Why? You want to get rid of me?"

I glance over my shoulder and smile at him. "Of course not."

Slowing my pace a little, I drop back to walk beside Will. "I'm just curious as to when we'll have water connected to the building again, that's all."

Will arranged for makeshift portable water tanks with taps and drinking fountains to be installed just outside my classroom, and while they're a satisfactory replacement, I miss having a functional sink and student toilets.

"Water should be connected by tomorrow."

"Oh! That's... that's great!"

"Does that mean you'll be finished?" Oliver asks, not masking the hopeful tone of his voice as he, too, drops back and walks beside me but on the grass, both men flanking my sides.

I suddenly feel like a piece of meat in an awkward sandwich.

"Finished? Nah, not even close," Will says. "There are numerous leaks around the school grounds, which will cause the same problem to other buildings if we don't fix them." He slides his hands into his pockets and grins. "It's gonna take *weeks* to replace various sections of piping." Will enunciates the word weeks, and I feel weirdly settled about it.

"Wow! That much damage, huh?" I say.

He nods at me. "Yep."

We round the corner, and Sal and Jeremy enter the modern chic café. Oliver goes next, and just as I'm about to follow him, Will reaches out and holds the door open.

I pause then blink. "Thanks!"

"You say that like no one's ever held a door open for you."

Diverting my gaze from his stormy eyes, I step past him. "That's because no one has."

We all take a seat at a large wooden, rustic, picnic-bench-style table at the back of the café, and once again, I find myself sandwiched between Oliver and Will, somewhat uncomfortably, given the sheer size of Will.

"Perhaps we should request a larger table," I say.

Carly glances around, waiters and waitresses bustling about. "Doesn't look like they have one."

I sigh. "I think you're right."

"You can sit on my lap if you like," Will offers.

I roll my eyes at him. "Thanks, but no thanks."

He chuckles, and once again, Oliver scoffs, which I've realised isn't unusual. He scoffs at everything.

We order drinks and food and soon settle into our own conversations, mostly one, which we all contribute to.

"So how long have you been working for Will, Jeremy?" I ask, sipping my soda water.

"I started my apprenticeship with him when I was eighteen. I'm twenty-two now, so four years."

Will leans forward. "He sits his final exam next month, then he'll be fully qualified."

Jeremy sprinkles a little salt on the table then fingers it into a pile. "I gotta pass first."

"Piece of piss, mate." Will leans back against the wall behind us. "You got nothin' to worry about."

Oliver swigs his Coke and adds, "It can't be that hard, right?"

At least three sets of eyebrows rise, including mine.

He swallows and quickly continues, "I mean, you've been learning it for four years. You already know what you need to know."

Will's brow relaxes, but only slightly, his eyes still locked on Oliver. "He does."

"I'm not very good with reading and writing," Jeremy admits. "I'm not dumb or anythin'. I just get nervous with tests and end up screwin' 'em up."

Sal blows his pile of salt off the table and giggles. "I'm sure you'll be fine, but if you need any help with the reading and writing, you can give me a call sometime."

Jeremy nods, dips his head, and pours himself another pile of salt.

"And anyway, it's natural to be nervous," Sal adds.

"Yeah," Carly pipes in. "Just ask Lib. She failed her driving test twice!"

I kick her under the table. "I did not! It was once, and my testing instructor was a dickhead. He was more interested in my breasts than my three-point turn."

"So why'd he fail you?" Will asks.

"Because my three-point turn was more a six-point turn." I lay my napkin on my lap. "And I might've forgotten to give way once or twice."

Carly shakes her head, eyes wide. "Never get into a car with her. She's scary as fuck." She picks up her drink. "I'm serious. She nearly got into a punch-on with a biker once."

Will turns to face me. "Even more reason for me to teach you boxing."

I laugh. "We've been through this already. You're not giving me boxing lessons."

"Oh! Pick me!" Sal raises her hand like a student would. "I'd love to learn boxing."

"Hold on just a second." Oliver raises his finger. "So you're a plumber, drummer, *and* boxer?"

Will crosses his arms over his chest. "I can also knit."

I nearly spit my drink. "You knit?"

"Yes. Blankets and mittens for babies in Africa."

I wait for him to laugh or nudge me and say he's kidding, but he doesn't. He just sits there, expressionless, as if him knitting for children in need is as natural as breathing.

Carly narrows her eyes and points her taloned finger at him. "You for real?"

"I am."

"Can you knit me a scarf?"

"I can."

"Hot pink?"

"Sure."

"Awesome!"

My jaw is like cement, heavy and weighted open, so I close it just as our waitress approaches the table.

"Two pizzas: one Supreme, one Hawaiian. I also have a burger with the lot, and a roasted lamb sandwich swimming in mint sauce." She places the pizzas on the table, the waiter behind doing the same with the burger and sandwich.

"What the hell is that?" Will asks, nodding to Carly's lamb sandwich.

She slides it in front of her. "The yummiest thing you'll ever taste."

"I can promise you that is *not* the yummiest thing I'll ever taste. Not even close." He lifts the lid of her sandwich with the tip of his fork. "Is all that green shit mint sauce?"

"She loves the stuff," I say, leaning forward to help myself to a slice of pizza. "It's hideous."

"It's not hideous. When I see Derek next, I'm gonna smother it all over him and lick it off."

Will lets out a belly laugh. "Now that I'd like to see."

"You want to see a woman lick shit off another man?" Oliver asks. He gives me a disgusted look as if I'd be disgusted too. I'm not, strangely enough.

"I wanna see my pretty-boy best mate covered in sticky shit and nothing he can do about it."

Oliver presses his lips together. "Charming."

I'm about to ask him what his problem is when Will hands him a slice of pizza and says, "Here, eat a piece of pizza, ya cranky fuck."

Carly bursts into laughter, a chunk of lamb flying out of her mouth and hitting Oliver in the face.

It bounces off his chin and lands on my plate.

I look at it, then look at her, then look at Oliver.

Everyone else does the same until we're all laughing, sans the cranky fuck.

* * *

AFTER EATING LUNCH, Will and Jeremy head back to school to get the excavator ready while the rest of us take care of the bill.

"I think Will is a bit smitten with you, Lib." Sal hands her credit card to the woman at the till then pulls out a packet of gum from her handbag.

I shake my head. "He's not. He's just a massive flirt."

"He's wasting his time," Oliver says as he calculates what he owes for lunch. "Will isn't her type."

I stare at him. "And how would you know what my type is?"

Digging into his pocket, he pulls out some notes and change. "Lib, I work with you every day. I know your standards, and Mr Steroids doesn't even come close."

"And who does come close?" Carly asks before I do.

"Someone more refined, more educated. Less… moronic."

Carly taps her chin. "Let me guess. Someone like you?"

He smirks and hands over his money. "Yes, someone like me."

She turns her back to him and opens her eyes so wide I'm afraid her eyeballs might pop out and I'll have to catch them.

"Thanks for your input, Oliver, but I think I'll decide for myself who my type is."

"Well, we both know it's not him."

Carly doubles back. "It's not you either."

He glares at her.

I give her a little shove. "Come on, you two, we gotta go."

We arrive at school just as the bell rings, kids running in all directions back to their classrooms.

Will is supervising Jeremy manoeuvre the excavator from the car park into the roped-off area, his arms crossed over his chest, his legs shoulder-width apart.

I detour over to him on my way to class. "Hey, sorry about Oliver. I don't know what's gotten into him. He acted like a complete jerk at lunch."

Will doesn't look at me, instead completely focused on his apprentice. "It's not an act, sweetheart. The guy is a jerk."

"Yeah." I bow my head. "I'm just beginning to realise that."

"Better late than never, I guess."

"True. Anyway, I better get to cla—"

"Stop!" Will shouts.

He darts off and dives behind the excavator, his python arms wrapping around one of the kids who somehow snuck into the roped-off area. I scream, horrified, as they tumble to the ground,

Will bearing the brunt of the fall, his head colliding with the back of the machine.

"Will! Toby!" I rush to their side and drop to my knees. "Are you okay?"

"I…" Toby starts crying, his tiny body trembling all over. "I was just getting my b-ball."

I quickly scan his face, running my hands from his head to his arms. "Are you hurt? Can you walk?" I glance at Will, who's not moving. "Will!" I touch his arm, but he's unresponsive. *Oh no! No, no, no.* Dread climbs my spine like a flame, my chest seizing.

Jeremy is by my side in an instant, one hand covering his mouth, the other gripping his hair. "I'm so sorry. I… I didn't see the kid. I—"

"It's not your fault."

"My knee hurts," Toby whines.

"Jeremy, take Toby to the office and get Carly to call an ambulance. Tell her Will hit his head. He's… he's unconscious." I scoot closer and gently touch the side of his face. "Will! Can you hear me?"

He doesn't answer. *God! Please be okay.*

Jeremy carefully scoops Toby into his arms and dashes off.

"What happened?" Sal asks as she kneels on the other side of Will, her eyes wide, her hands tentative as they hover over his still body.

I slip my hand under his head, cushioning it from the concrete. A sticky warmth coats my fingers, and I know beyond a shadow of a doubt they're covered in blood.

"Toby snuck in here to get his ball and nearly got hit by the excavator. Will jumped in the way and hit his head." I cup his face with my other hand. "He's bleeding, Sal. I can feel it."

"Shit! What do we do?"

"We—"

A groan leaves Will's mouth, and his eyelids flutter open. "W-what happened?"

"Oh thank God!" I mutter, finally able to breathe again.

He shoots upright and nearly knocks me out too. "The kid? Where's the kid? Is he okay?"

"Yes! Yes, he's fine." I scoot closer again, this time guiding his head back down to rest on my lap, crimson staining the side of his face. "Just stay still."

He exhales and relaxes into my embrace. "He's okay?"

"Yes, he's okay. You, on the other hand, aren't."

His eyelids grow heavy. "I'm good."

"No, you're not. Just... just stay still. The ambulance is on the way."

"Don't need an ambulance."

"Yes, you do."

"Don't."

"Damn it, Will, stop being stubborn for once."

He reaches up, touches my cheek, and slurs, "You're an angel."

"What?"

"Beeauutiful."

"Shut up, you goose. You don't know what you're saying. You've hit your head."

"Go out with me, Elizabeth."

Staring into his glassy eyes, my heart practically in my throat, I shake my head as I smooth his hair away from his face. "No."

"I might die."

I chuckle. "No, you won't."

"You'll regret it."

Drawing in a deep breath, I let it out slowly. "Fine, I'll go out with you."

He smiles, and his eyes fall shut.

CHAPTER TEN

I rode in the ambulance with Will to the hospital, and after numerous tests and scans, he was released, suffering a mild laceration and concussion. Toby sustained a graze to the knee and was understandably shaken, but it was Jeremy who I think suffered the most. The poor guy was ashen and intermittently slapping his head in frustration as we drove away.

"I nearly died," Will says as the glass doors part and we step outside of the Emergency Department.

I roll my eyes and smile then reach up and touch the bandage covering three stitches on his scalp. "You did not."

"I did. For you."

"For *me*? What do you mean for me?"

"I nearly died so you'd agree to go out with me."

Halting my steps, eyes narrowing, my finger pointing, I laugh. "You. Did. Not. You can't pin this on me."

An incredibly adorable smile creeps onto his face. "Yeah, I can."

"Well, I can take back my agreement to go out with you."

He pouts.

I groan. "Fine, I won't take it back. I said I'd go out with you, and that's what I'm going to do."

His pout magically vanishes.

"But only *once*," I reaffirm, my finger pointing again.

Will slides his hands into his trouser pockets and rocks back on his heels. I shriek and reach out, ready to catch him should he fall—not that I'd be able to catch him, even if I tried.

"Whoa!" I say, scanning his eyes. "Steady there."

He dips his head and lowers his voice. "Afraid I'm gonna fall on you, your body under mine?"

"Yes, are you diz—" I pause, remembering his smartarse remark at lunch about being on top of me. "Hey! Don't even think about it."

"I'm tempted, trust me." He rocks back again, this time teasing me, then chuckles and pulls out his phone. "Want to share an Uber?"

"Don't be silly. Put your phone away. I called Carly. She'll be here any min—"

Just as I mention her name, a car horn blasts through the car park to the tune of "We Will Rock You".

I facepalm and mumble, "Right on cue."

Will chuckles and taps his foot. "She's actually got good rhythm."

"She's got problems, that's what she's got."

Carly's red Suzuki Swift pulls to a stop right in front of us. I take hold of the door handle and pull it, but it's locked. *What the?*

Bowing my head, I knock on the window, and it slowly winds down. "What are you—"

"Hey, sugar," she interrupts with an awful American accent, "you lookin' for a date?"

Recognising the line from *Pretty Woman*, I raise an eyebrow at her. "Carly, open the door."

"I want head and a threesome. How much?"

Heat burns my cheeks, and I tug at the handle. "Oh for God's sake," I say, laughing. "Open the damn door."

"Okay, okay." She giggles. "Spoilsport."

Imbecile Barbie finally unlocks the door.

Will goes to climb into the back but stops. "Jesus! Is this a Matchbox car? It's not even big enough for my balls."

I glance at the backseat. He's right. "Wait! You sit in the front. I'll sit in the back."

He peers over the headrest. "Not sure that's gonna be any better."

"Stop dissing my Suzi and decide where you're gonna sit," Carly says.

We swap positions.

"Watch your head," I blurt out, worried as he squeezes into the front seat, me sliding into the back behind him.

The car grows silent until both Carly and I crack up laughing.

"Yeah, yeah, go ahead." Will shuffles. "Laugh at the big guy all curled up like a turd."

"You're not having a good day, are you?" Carly asks him.

"Besides the fact that my balls are lodged somewhere in my gut and my head's about to explode, the day's been pretty fuckin' good actually."

I can't help but smirk at his response.

"Good? Why's that?" Carly gently accelerates then glances over at me, her brow crumpled. "He hit his head, right?"

"He did."

"How's that a good day?"

"Because your roommate finally agreed to go out with me."

"What?" Drama-llama Barbie slams her foot on the brake, stopping before exiting the car park.

We all jerk forward.

"Jesus, Carly! Be careful. He has a head injury."

"Sorry." She pulls an oopsies face then glances back at me. "You're going on a date with Will?" A huge smile spreads across her face. "Like a *real* date, one that might end in sweaty hot sex?"

Will opens his mouth first. "Yes—"

"There'll be no sweaty hot sex," I say, setting him straight.

"Yes, there will."

I hold up my hand. "I'm not even going to argue with you about this."

"Good," both he and Carly say simultaneously.

Groaning, I deliberately headbutt the window. *What have I gotten myself into?*

* * *

WE DROP Will off at a cosy mud brick home in Diamond Creek, which is only twenty minutes from our place. He invites us in, but I decline, suggesting he get as much rest as possible and to ring—no matter what time—if he feels unwell. As intriguing as his home appears—because it reminds me of a Disney cottage, nestled at the base of several gigantic gum trees—all I want to do is get home, throw on my PJs, and snuggle with Sasha. So much happened today, and even though I never hit my head, it feels ready to explode too.

"So how'd that come about?" Carly asks as she pushes our front door open after unlocking it.

I squat, ready to catch Sasha should she miss. "How'd what come about?"

"You agreeing to go out with Will."

I laugh. "Ha! I can't believe you lasted the entire car ride home before asking me this."

"I was hoping you'd just tell me."

"There's nothing to tell."

The skittering rumble of Sasha's paws on the wood flooring as she rounds the corner into the entry hallway prepares us for her imminent presence. I'm confident Carly will catch her when, instead, she steps aside at the last second and allows Sasha to nearly barrel me over.

"Don't give me that bullshit. There's always something to tell."

"Fine. He's asked me a couple of times."

"And you didn't think to tell me this?"

"It's none of your business."

"It is so my business." She steps into our house and pats her knees. "Come on, Sashy. Who wants a treat?"

Sasha follows Carly, jumping up every other step. I get to my feet, close the door behind me, and follow them into the kitchen.

"What is that?" Carly screeches and points to a part of the room I can't yet see.

I'm almost afraid to move closer, her horrified face is well... horrifying.

"Nooo!" Carly plunges her face into her hands then covers her nose with the sleeve of her top. "You shit *outside*, Sasha. That's why I got you a damn doggy door."

"Did you unlock said doggy door?"

"Of course I di—Wait." She pushes on the door flap, and it doesn't swing. "Shit! I didn't. Damn it!"

Walking into the room, the unmistakeable waft of dog poo assaults my nostrils. "Jesus! It's fresh."

Carly dry retches. "It's foul."

"It's... *on my flip-flops!*"

"Yeeeah." She shrugs. "Sorry. Forgot to mention that part."

"Carly! Why are my flip-flops even in this room?"

"I borrowed them."

"Did you not think to put them back?"

"I was going to, but then... but then you rang and asked me to pick you and Will up from the hospital. And being the kick-arse friend that I am, I dropped everything and came to your aid, so you can't be mad at me."

"I sure as fuck can be mad at you." I point to the shit-piled flip-flop stack. "Look at them! They're covered."

"It'll wash off."

"Wash off?"

"Yeah." She grabs my cardigan, which is lying on the dining room table and not in my wardrobe where I left it.

I step toward her. "Why is *that* in here too? And... and what are you going to do with it?"

She ties it around her head. "I'm using it for protection."

I could kill her, outright murder her arse.

Carly bends down and tentatively reaches for my flip-flops, gagging as she lifts them and balances the shit on top like you would jelly on a plate.

"Don't you dare spew on my cardigan," I warn.

"Shut up! I'll drop it. You're making me nervous."

"*I'm* making *you* nervous?"

She ignores me, slowly pivoting toward the back door. "Open it. Quick! The stench is burning my eyeballs."

I lunge for the sliding glass door and wrench it open, expecting her to walk through it and outside, when she stops and tosses the dog shit *and* my flip-flops onto the back lawn.

"Carly!" I stare at them.

"Phew." She wipes her brow with the back of her hand and smiles with relief. "That was close."

"But... my flip-flops!"

Inconsiderate Psycho Barbie swishes her hand. "I'll buy you a new pair. Those were hideous anyway."

"They were not."

"They were."

"Argh!"

"So back to Will asking you out...." Carly shuts the back door and casually takes a seat at the table, one foot propped on the chair, her knee pressed to her chest as if she didn't just destroy my property.

Sasha lays at her foot, so Carly drops her hand to pat Sashy's head.

"What about it?" I snap, turning my back on her to switch on the kettle. I need a tea, preferably one with chamomile to ease my elevated stress levels.

"What made you say yes to Will this time?"

I shrug. "He nearly died."

She laughs. "So it's a pity date?"

I consider that for a second and decide it's not, or maybe it is. "I... I don't know."

"Well, do you like him or not?"

"I don't *not* like him. I just...." Realisation that I now have to go out with Will hits me, and I rest both hands on the edge of the benchtop and hang my head. "What have I done? And why on Earth did I say yes? I'm such a sucker. Sure, he was a hero today; he risked his safety to ensure Toby's, but ... but is that reason enough to let him take me out?"

"Yes."

I turn to face her. "Of course you'd say that. Just waking up in the morning would be reason enough for you."

"Hey!" She gives me a look that says, *"Be nice"*, so I adhere—sometimes, I step over the line.

Shoulders slumping, I pick at my nails. "We have nothing in common, and I mean *nothing.*"

"How do you know that if you've never been out with the guy?"

"I can just tell."

"Oh, that's right, you're"—she taps her head with her pointer finger—"psychic."

"You just have to look at us to see we're not going to mesh."

"You shallow, narrow-minded, princess wannabe."

I flinch at her words. "I beg your par—"

"You of all people shouldn't judge a book by its cover."

"Me? Of all people? Why?"

"Because you have red hair."

Oh, my fucking God! "So?"

"So… redheads are mutants!"

I deadpan. Dead. Pan.

She points at me. "You know it's true. We saw it on that—" She clicks her fingers. "—that *Human Bodies* show you're always making me watch, remember? You have a fucked-up gene or something. You could be in the X-Men."

I laugh; she's actually right for once.

"I also produce more Vitamin D and am more likely to be stung by a bee, but that doesn't make me shallow or narrow-minded."

"But judging Will before giving him a chance does."

"I'm not judging him," I say, offended.

"Yeah, you are. Just because he doesn't fit your perfect, prissy, Prince Charming expectations, doesn't mean he's unworthy."

"I never said he's unworthy."

"Yeah, you did, without actually saying it." She stands up and calls Sasha. "Come on, baby."

Strangely enough, I don't want her to leave. When she's a bitch like this, she often helps me find clarity.

"Where are you going?"

"I'm going to have phone sex with Derek."

"Oh." I pout. "Really? You guys do that?"

Carly pulls a face that nearly has her going cross-eyed. "Yes, really. It's what us non-royal types do."

I cross my arms over my chest, feeling a little remorseful. "I'm not a royal type, and I never meant to judge Will. I'm not like that. You know I'm not like that. Hell, I live with and love you, don't I?"

She steps up to me and cradles my face in her hands, and I can't help but admire the perfect smoky eyeshadow framing her eyes. "You're just scared of the unknown."

I nod, tears pooling.

"You've placed yourself in a make-believe fairy tale with make-believe heroes." She wipes a stray tear from my cheek. "They don't exist, Lib. But men like Will do. They may not have a castle on a hill, horses, and a crown, but they do have other things to offer."

"Like what?"

"A huge cock." She double-slaps my cheeks. "Wake up. You've got to give someone a chance to know whether they deserve it or not."

"Ow!" I rub my face.

"Now, goodnight. If you hear noises coming from my room… enjoy them."

I turn back to the kettle as Carly skips out of the room, and I'm not entirely sure what just happened. All I know is I'm willing to give Will a chance. But a chance at what, I'm not too sure.

* * *

THE NEXT MORNING, as I'm pegging my hosed-down, freshly cleaned flip-flops to dry on the clothesline, my phone buzzes in my pocket.

I reach in and pull it out to see a text from an unknown number.

Unknown: Tonight's the night

Weird! I ignore it.

Unknown: Don't ignore me

How rude!

Me: Who is this?

Unknown: The man you're going to have hot, sweaty sex with tonight

Will? How'd he get my numb—Damn it, Carly!

The blinds at the window to our kitchen move, and she waves her fingers at me, her phone pressed to her ear.

I type a response.

Me: You've got the wrong number. Sorry, I'm celibate

Will: Are you really?

I'm tempted to say yes.

Me: No!

Will: Wouldn't matter if you were

I laugh. *Yeah right!* But then I remember what Carly said last night and decide not to assume or judge.

Me: Really?

Will: Yes, because once you see my cock, you'll change your mind

And there you have it. I place my hand on my hip and glare at my phone.

Will: Take your hand off your hip. I'm kidding

I do as he says then freeze, dread or perhaps excitement waving over me. Spinning to look around the yard, I stop when I see Carly laughing.

My eyes narrow.

Me: Are you on the phone with Carly?

Will: I am

I slide my finger over my throat in a slicing motion then point at her. I know it's melodramatic, but so is she, so she'll get my drift.

Will: Back to tonight. I'll pick you up at six.

Will: Wear something warm

Me: Sorry. No can do. I'm busy

Will: No, you're not

Me: How would you know?

Will: Carly

Me: How would she know?

**Will: She said you were just gonna watch *Bridget Jones's Diary*
with her**

I flip Carly the bird.

Will: Six o'clock. Be ready. Dress warm

I don't want to answer, but I do because I'm not an adolescent.
Plus, he said he's gonna pick me up.

Oliver didn't.

Me: Fine

* * *

AT SIX O'CLOCK ON the dot, there's a knock at the door. Quickly
trying to secure the back of my earring, I fumble when Will strolls
into my room, Sasha—once again—in his arms.

I can't help but smile.

Will smiles, too, his eyes slowly raking me from head to toe. I
feel violated but in a good way until he shakes his head, places
Sasha on the ground, and enters my wardrobe.

I'm about to object when he comes out with my grey duffel coat.
"You're gonna need this." He hands it to me.

I try not to frown when I take it from him, and say, "Thaaanks."

"What's that look for?"

"I'm just confused. You're trying to cover me up. Don't guys like
you try to undress girls like me?"

His eyebrow hitches. "Guys like me?"

I regret the words and how I said them almost instantly. "Sorry,
I didn't mean it like that. What I meant was don't men in general
want women to wear less, not more?"

Will steps closer and helps drape my coat over my bare shoulders. "You'll wear much less when the time is right, sweetheart. For
now, I don't want you to get hypothermia."

I shiver. "Hypothermia? Where are you taking me? Antarctica?"

"All you need to know is we're gonna get *high*."

"What?"

* * *

Turns out, by high, he didn't mean weed, which I'm very grateful for.

"Sky High, Mt Dandenong?" I read the sign as we turn off the main road. "I've never been here before." I sit straighter. "I've always wanted to though."

"We've made good time, so you'll get to see the sunset."

"How lovely." I cock my head a little, surprised by this thoughtful, sweet side of him.

"It's even better after dark." The skin at the edge of his eyes crinkles as he smiles, and he quickly glances my way before focusing on the road again.

Will's profile is rather handsome, but it's his full lips and mischievous eyes that I find most alluring. I can't help staring at them, which I realise I'm doing when an amber glow swims across his face as we drive through a break in the trees, hues of orange, pink, and purple painting the sky as far as the eye can see.

I gasp. "Oh wow! You can see the city from here. And is that Port Phillip Bay?" I lean forward and exhale. "That's... that's beautiful."

Swinging the truck into a parking spot, he kills the ignition and turns to face me. "Not as beautiful as you."

CHAPTER ELEVEN

"$\mathcal{I}$'m not sleeping with you, Will."

He laughs and props his head on his hand, his elbow resting on the door trim. "You think I said that so you'll sleep with me?"

I press my lips together and nod, my smile deliberately sarcastic.

"Then you're wrong. Again." Will unbuckles his seatbelt. "You're beautiful, Elizabeth. And I am allowed to tell you that with or without your permission."

Swallowing hard, I blink all the blinks, my mouth suddenly dry when he pushes off from the steering wheel, opens his door, climbs out, and walks a couple of metres in front of the truck to the safety barrier, his arms stretching toward the sky before resting atop his head.

I don't know what to say so don't say a thing, instead choosing to take the moment alone to scale his body with my eyes, happily settling on his arse, which is nicely accentuated in denim. My teeth clamp my lip, and I squeeze my thighs together. He has a football player's arse—firm, round, high.

Will doesn't look back nor call out to see if I'm coming to join him. He just basks in the magical sight before us, looking the perfect picture of serenity.

It's very inviting.

Wanting nothing more than to stand out there with him and breathe it all in, I unbuckle my seatbelt, climb out of the truck, and make my way to stand by his side, the silence beautiful but deafening.

"Thank you," I finally bring myself to say after swallowing my often-stupid pride. "No one's ever said that to me."

Will throws his arm around my shoulders and hugs me to his side, his body warm and... comforting. "Just because no one's said it until now, doesn't make it untrue."

I nod but leave it at that. I don't know what else to say, especially because I'm pressed to the side of a man who I think I like but also like to despise.

Sucking in a deep breath, I hold it for a few seconds then exhale, mesmerised as the sun melts into the sky, oranges and pinks soon turning grey, a cooler breeze now chilling the air.

"You warm enough?" he asks, his grip firmer.

The muscles in my neck relax, and I rest my head against his shoulder and sigh. "Yes. Thank you." Realising what I'm doing, I immediately sit straighten. *Damn it, restful head.* "I... I'm so glad you made me bring my coat," I say, trying to direct all focus on that and not me cuddling up to him. "I would've frozen without it."

"You're welcome."

Will slips into quiet territory again, and at first, I'm grateful but then realise I need him to speak more, to clarify and follow through. I mean he can't just say what he said in the car and act like it didn't make my heart flutter and my head spin.

"So—" I pick at my nails then stop and fold them into my hands. "—do you come here often?"

He chuckles. "Is that supposed to be a pick-up line?"

"No." I giggle and give him a gentle nudge. "I'm genuinely curious."

He doesn't answer straight away, and I wonder if he simply wants to stand in silence and enjoy the view, not my stupid questions. Can't say I blame him—the view is much more appealing right now, given I'm an incoherent nervous wreck.

"I do. Molly and I visit quite a bit in summer and autumn. She likes the gardens and walking tracks."

I look up at him. "Molly?"

Will doesn't look down at me, his eyes still fixated on the view. "Yeah, one of my roommates." I wait for him to explain further, but he doesn't, instead taking my hand in his. "Come on, we're gonna be late."

"For what?"

"Dinner." He points to the restaurant atop a small slope behind us, floor-to-ceiling glass windows jutting out around the circular building. "They have the best Parma and chips."

Excitement travels the length of my body as we walk hand in hand—which I don't really mind, strangely enough—until I'm guided to a fancy, candlelit table with nothing but a sea of sparkling lights as far as the eye can see.

"Wow!" I pause and stare for a moment before Will pulls my seat out for me, a boyish grin on his face.

"Pretty cool, huh?" he prompts.

"*Cool* is an understatement. It's spectacular." I sit and clasp my hands in my lap. "Thank you so much for thinking to bring me here."

He winks then sits opposite me, and before we can say a word to one another, a waiter is by our table side, ready to order us drinks.

"Pot of Carlton Draught," Will says.

"Ooh. Make that two."

His eyebrows arch high. "You drink beer?"

"Of course." I remove my coat and drape it over the back of my chair, the night air cooling my bare shoulders. "Why do you sound so surprised?"

"Because I pegged you for one of those rosé types."

"And I pegged you for one of those I-take-my-dates-to-McDonald's types."

Will leans back in his chair, a laugh rumbling from his chest. "Touché."

I lean back too. "And he speaks French!"

"*Oui.*"

My mouth falls open, an impressive smile creeping onto my face. "Do you really?"

He nods once. "*Oui.*"

"*Je suis tellement surpris. Comment connais-tu le français?*" I ask, eagerly, enquiring as to how he knows the language.

His eyes crinkle just slightly, and I'm excited for his answer when he casually says, "*Oui.*"

Thinking he may have misunderstood my question, I ask him when he learned to speak French instead. "*Quand avez-vous appris?*"

He steeples his hands together and rests his elbows on the table. "*Oui.*"

I narrow my eyes, suspecting he has no idea what I'm saying. "*Oui?*" I ask.

He nods again. "*Oui.*"

Biting the inside of my cheek, I decide to have a little fun with him and ask if his penis is small, knowing his answer will, of course, be *oui*.

"*Votre pénis est-il petit?*"

"*Oui.*"

I crack up laughing. "You have no idea what you just said yes to, do you?"

He chokes out another "*Oui.*"

Giggling, I cover my face with my hand and peek through my spread fingers. "Well, for what it's worth, I highly doubt it."

"Doubt what?"

I lift my napkin from underneath my cutlery, flick it loose, lay it over my lap, then lean forward and lower my voice so only Will can hear me. "That your manhood is undesirably small."

He blinks. "My manhood… undesirably small?"

I shrug. "Well, that is what *you* said."

"Well, shit. I can't have you thinking that, sweetheart." He pushes his chair back and stands, his hands on his belt buckle.

"Will!" I whisper-hiss, my eyes as wide as saucers. "What are you doing?"

"Setting the record straight."

Quickly glancing around, my cheeks turn pink when I spot an older couple watching us. "Sit down! I believe you."

"Not sure that's gonna be good enough."

"Will, please!"

He chuckles and lowers himself back down. "You honestly think I'd just flop it out here, in this restaurant?"

I lower my head to my hand, my heartrate decelerating. "I honestly don't know what I think when it comes to you."

He's silent for a moment, so I look up.

"And that bothers you, doesn't it?" he asks.

"Well, yes, you're… you're unpredictable."

Will smiles as if he's figured me out. "You're a bit of a control freak, aren't you, Elizabeth?"

"No! I… I just like to know what I'm getting myself into."

He presses his lips together as if to say *"Hm, interesting."* And then he asks, "So you speak French?"

"Yes, but only the little bit I picked up when I backpacked Europe during my gap year."

He moves his cutlery and napkin to his right in a messy pile so he can rest his elbows on the table. "You backpacked Europe?"

"Sure did"—I pick up my menu—"much to my mother's reluctance."

"She wasn't on board?"

"No."

He pushes his menu aside.

I stare at it then at him. "You're not even going to look?"

"No. I know what I'm having."

"The Parma and chips?"

"The one and only."

I'm tempted to order the same, given he's so convicted, but decide to open the leather-bound folder and see what else they have on offer, scrolling my finger down the choices and stopping when I land on the venison eye fillet with truffle mash and steamed greens. *Oh, my goodness! Yumm.* My stomach grumbles, but the fifty-dollar price tag next to it prompts me to keep scrolling.

"So why wasn't your mum on board with you backpacking?" he probes.

"She didn't want her eldest daughter roaming Europe on her own."

"You backpacked on your own?"

"Uh-huh. I do a lot of things on my own."

A devious glint lights his eyes. "Like what... self-care?"

My mouth falls open like a fish, so I close it and keep scrolling. "I don't know," I say, my tone deliberately disinterested. "Like sleeping and bathing, going to the toilet, that sort of thing."

Thankfully, our waiter returns, places two beers on the table, and says, "Are you ready to order?"

I nod but don't look at Will. "I'll have the crispy-skinned salmon, thanks."

"I'll have the Parma and chips." Will hands the waiter our menus. "And she'll have the venison, not the salmon."

"What?" I shake my head, my laugh uneasy. "No, I'll have the salmon."

He ignores me. "She wants the venison."

"I'm sorry, but how do you know what I want?"

"Because your eyes lit up when your finger stopped on it, sweetheart."

The waiter takes a step backward and smiles. "I'll come back in a min—"

"No. The lady will have the venison, and I'll have the Parma."

"Will!" I shriek.

"Elizabeth!" he shrieks back.

I almost laugh but grit my teeth instead, frustrated with the gall of him when he reaches across the table and places his hand over mine, his squeeze ever so gentle, his eyes ever so sincere.

"Order whatever you want, your choice, my treat. But be honest... you want the venison, don't you?"

I sigh. "I'm more than happy with the salm—"

He looks at the waiter one final time. "A venison and Parma, thanks. End of story."

The waiter gingerly nods then flees toward the kitchen.

"Oh, my God!" I try to retract my hand. "Are you happy now?"

He holds it firm. "Are you?"

"I was happy with the salmon."

"But you're happier with the venison." Will smiles, all teeth and sparkly eyes.

I try to retract my hand again, but *again*, he holds it firm. "Stop it," I say, laughing. "And you can't just say 'end of story' like that. It's rude."

"No, it's not."

"Yes, it is."

His smile grows bigger. "You have the cutest nose."

"What?" Unable to help myself, I wiggle it. "Can I have my hand back now?"

"Depends."

"On what?"

"Are you mad at me?" He grazes my knuckles with the pad of his thumb, the small gesture sending a rush of emotion through my body. "Don't be mad at me. I just want to give you what you want."

My throat thickens at his sweetness, so I pry my hand loose and reach for my beer, eyeing him over the rim of the glass as I take a sip. "Why? Why do you want to give me what I want?"

"Because it'll make you feel good."

"And how do you know that?" I place the glass back down and swallow my mouthful.

Will leans back and crosses his arms over his chest, his grey shirt pulling taut, sleeves down, top button undone. "Because it'll make me feel good too."

"I'm not sleeping with you, Will," I reaffirm, my lips lifting as I tip my glass to him.

The waiter approaches the table once again, hands behind his back, face contorted, almost as if he's about to break the news of a loved one passing. "I'm so sorry to interrupt, but the chef informs me that we've run out of venison. He offers his sincerest apologies."

I burst into laughter. "Salmon it is then."

Will just huffs.

* * *

AFTER A DELICIOUS DINNER AND DESSERT—A chocolate fondant I thought we could've shared but was politely told, *"Who the hell shares dessert?"*—we huddled in his truck, watched the dancing lights below, and listened to music before heading home.

"So how long have you been playing the drums?" I ask.

Will taps out a beat on the steering wheel while waiting for the traffic light to turn green. "Since I was four."

"Four!"

"Yeah. Santa got me a drum kit, and I've never looked back."

"You're very good."

"I know!" He flicks his eyebrows, and the car accelerates.

I scoff. "You've also got a big head."

"Nothin' wrong with a big head, sweetheart."

Probably for the billionth time, I playfully roll my eyes at his inappropriate comment. "So what's this song?"

He glances my way. "You've never heard it?"

"No. But I like it. It's different."

"It's Knights of Cydonia by Muse. Great fucking song. One of my favourites to play at gigs. Derek nails the vocals."

His excitement and passion make me smile. "Carly's mentioned one or two times that he's good."

"Yeah, and he knows it."

"So how often do you guys play?"

"Once a month at Opals, and whenever or wherever we want. Bryce has contacts."

I glance out the window, rain now streaking the glass. "I bet he does."

"Perks of being a billionaire."

"Must be weird being friends with someone like him."

"Yes and no. Sometimes it's no different than being friends with someone like you or Carly. Other times, it's fucking unreal. Like whenever I need to stay in town, I've got a room at City Towers. No questions asked."

I look his way again. "Wow! That's pretty generous of Bryce."

"He's a good bloke." Will's misty eyes meet mine. "Been through a lot though. Shit ain't been easy. Deserves everything he's achieved."

I rest my hands on my lap. "Carly speaks very highly of him too."

Will chuckles and focuses on the road again. "It's the smirk."

"The smirk?"

"Yeah, the man does this thing with his face that makes all the women drop their panties."

I laugh. "Sounds... interesting."

"You'll see soon enough."

"How?"

"We have a gig soon, and you're coming."

"I'm coming?"

He glances my way, a grin tugging at the corner of his mouth. "Not how I wanted to hear you say that for the first time, but I'll take it."

Drawing in a deep breath, I bite back my smile and shake my head as I exhale. "Very funny."

"Sweetheart"—his voice deepens—"when I make you come for the first time, it'll be far from funny."

I legitimately squirm, the muscles between my legs pulling tight. "Okay," I choke out, "let's change the subject." I swallow. "So, your band... none of you play for a living?"

He chuckles. "No. Never have. Bryce is made of money. Derek's got some coin, too, and not to mention is high up in the MFB. Matt's in the army. And I'm expanding my business. Live Trep is just time with the boys."

"Live Trep? Is that the name of your band?"

"Yeah. Pretty much."

"Isn't that woman from Opals in the band too?"

"You mean Lucy?"

"I think so. The one who looks like Belle."

His eyebrows draw together. "Whose Belle?"

"From *Beauty and the Beast*."

When his baffled expression doesn't change, I offer a different explanation. "The one who likes the Slippery Nipple shots."

He chuckles. "Yeah, that's Lucy. She's one of the boys. Likes chicks not dicks."

My jaw drops. "Will!"

"What?" He full-on belly laughs. "Man, you offend easily."

I cross my arms. "I do not."

"Yeah, you do."

The song changes, and I recognise the new one instantly so lean forward and turn it up, ending our discussion.

"You like The Police?"

I nod. "Sure. Every Breath You Take was my parents' wedding song."

Will's eyes stretch, like really stretch, but he doesn't say anything.

"What's wrong?"

"Nothing." He doesn't look my way.

I point at him. "That wonky smile of yours is not nothing."

He finally glances at me, his expression remorseful. "Every Breath You Take is a fucked-up choice for a wedding song."

"What? No, it's not. It's a love song." I press my hand to my heart. "Every breath you take... that's so romantic."

"Yeah, if you're a stalker."

"What?"

"It's a stalker song, Elizabeth."

Covering my mouth with my hand, I mumble, "Nooo. Really?"

"Afraid so. Sting wrote it about his ex-wife at the time."

"Shit! That's not good." I try not to laugh. "Every time my parents hear that song, they sing it to each other so lovingly."

He glances my way again and shrugs. "Songs can be interpreted in different ways. I wouldn't worry about it."

I nod. "Good. But whatever you do, don't tell my parents. It'll crush them."

He winks. "I won't... when I meet them."

Will focuses on the road again, and it takes me a second or so to realise what I just said. *Crap!*

"So when will that be?" he asks.

"When will what be?"

"When do I get to meet your parents?"

I laugh, which comes out more like the noise Sasha's squeaky dog toy makes. "Who said you're going to meet my parents?"

"You just did."

"No, I didn't."

"Yeah, you did."

"I did not."

He gives me the 'end of story' look. "It's just a matter of time."

Sucking on my tooth, a smile creeps onto my face—I kinda like his cockiness. He's confident in an endearing way, and that speaks a lot about a person.

Deciding not to argue, I concede. "Tonight was nice, Will," I say, sincerely. "I haven't been out like this in a long time, so thank you."

"My pleasure. Next time will be even nicer."

Closing my eyes for the smallest of seconds, the screech of windscreen wipers scraping the windscreen even louder than before, I rest my head on the headrest. "Who says there's gonna be a next time?"

"There'll be a next time. I nearly died for you. The least you can do is give me *two* dates."

I pry an eye open. "You *did not* nearly die."

He runs his hand through his hair and flips some of it to the side, revealing a small shaved area with stitches. "I have a battle scar."

I sit up straight and reach out, barely grazing my fingertip over it. "Ouch! That does look sore."

"It's very sore. I'm in agony."

"You are not."

I go to retract my hand, but he catches it and brings it to his mouth, his soft lips pressing my knuckles. Warmth shoots across my body and pools at my chest, the air thick and suddenly hard to breathe.

"Will you give me a second date?" he asks.

Not wanting to but knowing I should, I tug my hand free of his grip, and say, "We'll see."

He grins, turns the car onto my street, and parks by the curb before cutting the engine. As I'm about to pull on the door handle to get out, he dips his head and looks through the windscreen toward the house.

"All the lights are off."

"Yeah, Carly's out with Alexis."

"It's dark. I'll walk you to your door."

He gets out, jogs to my side of the car, and holds his jacket over my head, sheltering me from the rain as we hurry up the steps to my front door.

Laughing, I turn to face him as I step out from underneath the jacket, droplets of water streaking down the sides of his cheeks and nose. Our eyes meet before his gaze falls to my lips.

My breath hitches, and I stare at his, too, before taking a step back. "I'm not sleeping with you, Will."

He steps closer, moonlight illuminating the humour in his eyes as he slides his arm behind my back and pulls me to him. "I know. But I am going to kiss you, Elizabeth. So if you don't want this, stop me now. Because once my lips meet yours, there's no going back."

Tilting my chin up, he dips his head, slow enough for me to stop what he's about to do, but I don't. Because I want this kiss.

I deserve it.

CHAPTER TWELVE

*W*ill lets go of his jacket and threads his hand through my hair, cupping my nape and cradling my head as his soft, wet lips touch mine. My body sparks to life. Receptive. Alert. Except for my eyelids, which collapse when his tongue sweeps into my mouth.

He tastes like chocolate and beer, winter and warmth, and I fall into the kiss, fall into him.

Reaching up, I glide my fingertips over his beard, surprised at the silky soft feel. I've never kissed a man with a beard before, always thought I'd hate it, but I don't. Quite the opposite, actually. Will and his beard are nothing but sweetness and strength, and I've never felt more relaxed in someone's arms before.

He trails his lips across my cheek to just under my ear, then down my neck before gently sucking on my skin. My body tightens in anticipation, and I gasp, gripping him hard. Wanting more. Wanting all of him.

I can't for the life of me remember the last time I craved sex, let alone participated in it. It's safe to say it's been years, on a cruise ship to New Caledonia, I think. I was drunk and very much embracing the leave-your-worries-behind sea life.

"You want to come in?" I ask, breathless.

His voice is rough, like gravel. "Yes."

Fumbling behind for the door handle, I go to open it when Will covers my fingers and holds the door closed. "But I'm not going to. Not tonight." He grinds his body into mine and presses his erection against my belly. "If you want this, you're gonna have to give me that second date."

Holy shit!

He pulls away, his eyes dark, his lips glistening. Unable to help myself, I look down at his jeans, pulled taut over an impressive mound I can't seem to take my eyes off.

"How 'bout it, sweetheart?" He covers my view with his hand as he adjusts himself. "How 'bout that second date?"

Blinking, I look up and focus on his sexy grin and amused eyes, which help me find my words again. "I'll..." I swallow. "I'll think about it."

Fumbling once more, I turn the door handle and step backward until I'm inside and slowly closing the door, our eyes glued to one another's.

"Wait!" Will's hand shoots out and covers the doorframe. "I'll call you tomorrow."

I cock my head and give him a lazy smile. "You do that."

He groans and hangs his head.

Giggling, I close the door and lean against it in a daze of body tingles and hard-ons, when something furry brushes my leg.

"Hi, Sash," I say as if she knows why I'm smiling.

She barks.

"Yes, I had a great time. Thanks for asking."

Joy dances around me, and I want to sing to the tune, to believe in Will and give him a chance. I haven't felt this... this uplifted in a long time, and I like it. But how can I trust a guy who acts and speaks like he does, a guy I don't know? And do I really want to get to know him, only to be disappointed and have my faith in men shattered all over again?

Sighing, I make my way toward my bedroom when I see small bits of white litter the hallway. "What the...?" I move closer, squat, and pick one up, thinking at first that it's a cottonwool ball.

Following the trail, I steer into Carly's bedroom and am hit by what can only be described as a winter wonderland—the stuffing of Carly's pillows strewn across the bed and floor.

"Oh, my God!" My hands fly up to cover my mouth. "Sasha, what have you done?"

She barks, sits, and wags her tail, happy with her artwork.

"Oh, baby girl. You're in deeep shit when Mummy gets home."

A piece of pillow stuffing floats into the air. I blow it away then laugh, because I'm not cleaning this shit up.

I'm in too good of a mood to do anything but go to bed and dream about misty blue eyes and a devilish grin.

* * *

"WHAT THE FUCK!"

I spring up in bed, my heart hammering in my chest.

"Libby!" Carly yells.

Tossing off my blanket, I nearly trip over it when I try to grab my robe. "What? What's wrong?"

"Why has a snowman blown his load all over my bedroom?" she screeches.

Stopping in my tracks, I leave the robe and climb back into bed. *Damn her.* I was happily dreaming of a castle in a faraway place.

Just as I start to doze again, my bedroom door springs open, and Carly appears with pillow stuffing in her hands.

"I was sleeping," I grumble.

"What the hell happened last night?"

"The sun visited the other side of the earth."

The pillow stuffing hits my face. "Very funny."

"Your dog happened, that's what."

"But I shut my door."

"Are you sure about that?"

Crack-smoking Barbie moves farther into my room and picks up my long, black dress I draped over the back of my chair. "Did you wear this last night?"

"I did."

"Nice!"

She also picks up my coat. "Please tell me you didn't wear this too."

"I did."

"God help me. I take it you didn't get laid then."

"No."

"You can blame that on the granny coat."

"Go away, Carly. Go clean your snowman sperm."

"It can wait." My bed moves, and then she's lying top to toe with me when her big toe pokes me in the eye.

"Jesus!" I swipe it away from my head. "What are you doing? Get out."

"I wanna know how your date went."

"It was fine."

"Did Will touch your boobies?"

"No! Oh, my God, Carly, you're such a child."

"Did you touch Will's willy?"

I choke on my laugh. "No! We just went out for dinner. That's all."

"That can't be all."

"It is."

My phone buzzes on the bedside table, so I pick it up to see a message from Will.

Will: Mornin', beautiful. I'm picking you up at midday

I smile.

She nudges me with her toe again. "That's him, isn't it?"

"No."

"Liar."

"It's Sal with a new book rec."

"I don't believe you."

"I don't care."

I quickly send him a reply.

Me: No, you're not. I'm busy.

He replies straight away.

Will: Yeah, busy with me.

Me: No, I'm serious. I have an appointment

Will: What kind of appointment?
Me: None of your business.

He doesn't answer, so I put my phone down and sit up.

"Get out." I throw a pillow at Carly. "I need to shower and head off."

"Where are you going?"

"To see Dr Tao."

"Is it that time again?"

"Yup."

"Want me to come?"

I shrug. "It's up to you."

Carly sits up, too, and tosses the pillow back at me. "I'm sorry you have to go through this so often." She pouts and blinks her black-rimmed, puppy dog eyes.

I smile appreciatively. "I'm used to it."

"Still. It can't be nice to always have it looming over you like a giant turd cloud."

I've never thought of it as a "turd cloud" before. A constant shadow that survives without light, yes. But a turd cloud? I guess that works too.

"It is what it is," I say. "I can't change it. I can only play the cards I've been dealt."

She stands up. "What time's your appointment?"

"Midday."

"Okay. We'll take Suzi and make a girly day out of it."

"Girly day?"

"Yeah. We'll hit the shops, and I can help you buy better clothes."

"There's nothing wrong with my clothes."

She swishes her hand. "That's debatable. You're dating now, therefore you need dating clothes."

"I'm not dating."

"You will be."

"Says who?"

My phone beeps again.

She points to it. "Him."

* * *

CARLY and I drive to Dr Tao's specialist rooms at Bundoora Private Hospital. I see her monthly for check-ups and referrals to manage my condition. She's an exquisite Asian beauty in her forties, and I admire her dedication to her career—not everyone happily works on a Sunday—but I also feel sorry for her tireless work ethic.

"Elizabeth Hanson," she calls out from her office doorway.

Smiling, I place the well-read copy of *Vogue* back in the magazine holder and stand up.

"Want me to come in?" Carly asks.

I shake my head. "No, I'll be fine."

"Good, 'cause this article on vaginal squirting is really interesting." She flips the page of her *Cleo* magazine and gives me the thumbs-up.

My cheeks flame, and I move toward Dr Tao while shooting another woman in the waiting room an apologetic look.

"How have you been?" Dr Tao extends her arm and gestures I enter her office.

"Fine, thank you. And you?"

"Nice and busy. Just the way I like it."

"That must be a catch twenty-two."

She winks. "It is. Busy means many people like you with an illness, which isn't nice at all. But busy also means I'm helping people like you manage your illness. So, yes, it's definitely a catch twenty-two." She nods toward her desk. "Please, take a seat and tell me how you've been since our last appointment."

I do as instructed and sit down. "For the most part, I've been fine, except for a lump on my lower back."

"Let's take a look." Dr Tao washes her hands at the basin and puts on a pair of surgical gloves.

I stand, turn around, and lift my t-shirt. "Just here," I say, pointing to the protruding mass.

She prods and squeezes it. "No pain?"

"No."

"Hmm... my guess is it's a lipoma, like the last one. But let's get an ultrasound just to be sure." She scans the rest of my back then turns me to face her, scanning my abdomen, neck and face, until her eyes meet mine. "Good. Trichilemmomas are minimal. How about any new oral papillomas?"

I shake my head and smile. "None."

"Excellent!" She pats the examination table. "Lie down and I'll examine your breasts. You know the drill, bra and t-shirt off."

Like I've done countless times before, I remove my clothing and rest my arms above my head.

Dr Tao rubs her hands together then places them on my skin, gently kneading my breasts with her fingertips. "Have you been checking weekly?" she asks.

I scrunch my nose. "Mostly."

"No changes?"

"I don't think so."

She pauses and moves her hands back over the same spot. "You're due for a breast scan, so let's get that done, as well as your thyroid." She steps back, removes her gloves, and washes her hands again. "When was the last time we scanned your ovaries?"

"Three months ago."

"Any pain or changes to your menstruation?"

"No."

"Good."

"No ultrasound of the ovaries too?" I ask.

She smiles and shakes her head. "I don't think it's necessary so soon, but if you'd like to do—"

I raise my hands. "No. Just the three scans will do."

She chuckles, taps on her computer, and then prints out my referrals. "Okay. Book these in as soon as possible and make an appointment to see me again next month. If the results show anything we need to address, I'll give you a call, and we can go from there."

I take the sheets of paper from her. "Thank you. See you next month then."

"You will. Goodbye, Elizabeth."

As I exit the room, Carly stands and smiles, her smile faltering when she sees the referrals in my hand.

"Everything okay?" she asks.

I nod. "Yeah. Just the norm."

Hesitation clouds her eyes, so I reassure her with a little more information. "Routine thyroid and breast scan and a scan of a lump on my back, which Dr Tao isn't concerned about."

Carly loops her arm in mine and rests her head on my shoulder. "I hate this."

I scoff. "Then why do you come?"

"Because you need me to."

I don't, not really. This is my life and has been for a long time.

Lying, because sometimes a lie is the kindest gift you can give a person, I rub my hand over hers. "I do need you. Now, let's go and have this girly day thing."

She lifts her head and proceeds to skip, my arm still linked with hers. "I'm gonna start with your lingerie."

I roll my eyes but then lock my feet to the ground and gesture to the magazine rolled up under her other arm. "You have to put that back."

"No, I don't. It's complimentary."

"Carly! It's *not* complimentary. Put it back."

"But, Liiib, it has detailed squirting techniques and a homemade facial recipe."

My eyes widen. "Please tell me they're two separate articles."

"Ha!" She shoves the magazine into my handbag. "Wouldn't you like to know?"

No, no, I wouldn't.

CHAPTER THIRTEEN

*N*umerous times during the week that follows, Will asks me for a second date. But each time he "pencils me in", I have to decline, as I'm busy with ultrasound appointments.

Come Friday, I suspect he's sulking or shitty with me, because after texting him back the night before with a *"Sorry, no can do"* for the third time, he hasn't spoken to me since.

It's not like I'm deliberately evading him, because I'm not. I just can't tell him why I'm not available. Not yet. And, anyway, it's none of his business.

"Okay, kids," I say to the class fifteen minutes before home time. "Let's finish the week with some quiet reading."

A handful of them moan while others happily grab their books and find a place in the room to get comfortable.

"Ms Hanson, Jet won't get out of the beanbag, and it's my turn."

I squint toward the whiteboard, finding Dylan's name on the reading corner list. "Yes, you're right. Jet, please hop out of the beanbag and find somewhere else to sit and read."

The door to the classroom opens, and Will enters, a looming giant over the kids sporadically spread out around the room.

I smile at him. "Everything okay?"

He tips his chin. "Yeah, just checking the taps."

"Sure. Be my guest."

"Jet, stop!" Dylan yells.

Frustrated, because it's three o'clock on a Friday afternoon and my teacher-tolerance is super slim, I step around Will to see Jet punching Dylan, Dylan blocking each punch with his balled fists held on either side of his head.

"*Jet!* That's enough." I quickly place myself between the boys and hold Jet's flailing arms, coping a whack to my ribs in the process. "We *do not* use our fists. We use our words instead." Turning my back to him, I rub my side and give Dylan my attention. "Are you okay?"

He nods. "Yes. Master Will taught me to block." Dylan points to my ribs. "He should teach you too."

I glance up at Will, who's now next to Jet. He winks at Dylan.

"Master Will is a very good teacher," I say.

Dylan nods so fast I'm scared his head will fall off.

"Okay, take a seat in the beanbag and start reading." I turn back to Jet. "As for you, you can spend the last ten minutes writing Dylan, *and me*, a sorry note."

"But I'm not sorry."

"Jet," I warn.

He crosses his arms over his chest. "I'm not."

Will squats down so that he's at eye-level with Jet. "Any dude that deliberately punches someone should be sorry. That's not cool, buddy. We learn to punch to defend ourselves. Like Dylan did."

Jet's head dips.

Will continues. "Cool dudes say sorry. It's the only way."

Tears pool in Jet's eyes, but he blinks them back and murmurs, "Sorry", then trudges to his seat and gets out a piece of paper and a pencil.

I draw in a deep breath then let it out slowly. "Thanks for that."

"No sweat." He lays his palm on my side. "You okay?"

"Yeah."

Oliver enters the room, his eyes narrowing as he looks between Will and me. "Everything all right?"

"Everything is fine." I step back, and Will pushes up from the ground. "Will's just checking the taps one last time."

Oliver lays his clipboard on his desk then perches his reading glasses on the bridge of his nose. "Does that mean you're all done?"

"With this building?" Will clarifies. "Yes." He picks up his toolbox and makes his way toward the sink.

Oliver murmurs, "'Bout time."

I glare at him, and he mouths, *"What?"* so I turn my back and begin to wipe down the whiteboard, ready for Monday's lesson plan.

Warmth climbs my spine when I sense Will's eyes on me, so I glance over my shoulder, an endearing grin on his face. I can't help it and blush. I even giggle, which is just outright stupid.

Oliver clears his throat, steps up beside me, and picks up a whiteboard wiper. "So what's your plans for the weekend?"

I pause, shocked that he's helping me. Oliver *never* helps me, let alone wipes down the board.

"Uh… not much—"

Will drops his toolbox at my feet, and I startle. "She's getting a boxing lesson from me."

Oliver grimaces then laughs. "Lib's getting a boxing lesson… from you?"

Offended, I straighten my shoulders. "Yes, I am."

"Why would you need a boxing lesson?"

I go to answer, but Will does it for me.

"Because there are a lot of *creeps* in the world," he says, insinuation in his tone. "And I'm gonna teach her how to defend herself against them."

Placing down the wiper, Oliver says, "How nice of you," his grin far from friendly as he walks away to assist the children with packing their bags.

"Master Will?"

We glance down at Dylan, who's tugging Will's shorts, Evan standing beside him with hope in his pleading eyes.

"Can you teach Evan to box too? His mum's new boyfriend is a creep."

My hand shoots up to cover my mouth, eyes wide as I look from Will to Dylan, then to Evan, and back to Dylan again. "What do you mean by creep?" I ask the boys.

Evan doesn't speak, so Dylan says, "He's really mean. He yells a lot, doesn't he, Evan?"

Evan curls into himself, looks at the ground, and shrugs.

"Right. I—"

"I'll teach you how to box, mate." Will lightly squeezes Evan's shoulder.

His head springs up, and he smiles, hope returning to his eyes.

"How 'bout you boys go pack your bags then line up at the door."

"Okay. See you tomorrow at boxing class, Ms Hanson," Dylan says and runs off with Evan.

"You can't just offer to teach the kids how to box, Will," I murmur behind my hand.

He ignores me. "You think there's truth to what Dylan just said?"

I look at Will, his eyes fixed on Evan. "I'm..." I rub my forehead. "I'm not sure."

"Because if there is, I'm gonna need to find out who this new boyfriend creep is."

I turn to face him as the bell rings and the kids filter out of the room. "You will do no such thing. There are proper avenues and channels to go through."

"Shit like that takes time." Will's eyes follow Evan like a cat would a mouse. "Time a little kid like Evan might not have."

I watch Evan, too, as he meets his mother, and she quickly ushers him toward the car park.

"Will, as noble as your concern might be, this has nothing to do with you."

"As a human fucking being who doesn't like to stand by while the strong hurt the weak, it has *everything* to do with me."

I touch his arm, and his eyes meet mine, fury blazing within them. I can't deny I feel the same wrath because I do, fear and anger rolling through me like thunder. To think one of my kids is possibly being harmed makes me sick to my stomach. But something like this needs to be dealt with correctly, and I intend on doing that.

"Just let me do my job. I'm mandated to report any suspected abuse. I have no reason to suspect it right now based solely on what Dylan just said, but I'll fill in a report and speak to Evan on Monday. I promise."

He clicks his jaw from side to side but nods.

I relax. "Good. Now tell me about this boxing lesson. What time and where?"

The skin at the corners of his eyes crinkle. "I'll pick you up at nine."

* * *

WILL'S truck engine cuts outside the front of my home, and I smile as I glance at my watch. One minute to nine. *Impressive!* He might not be Prince-Charming-perfect, but my God he's punctual.

I quickly throw on a loose tank top over my sports bra, smooth down my Lorna Jane yoga tights, and pull my ponytail taut.

"Let's get this over with," I say to my reflection in the mirror before grabbing my water bottle and handbag.

Carly and Will's voices travel along the hallway until I find them both in the lounge room, Sasha once again in Will's arms.

I scruff her golden fur, smile, but shake my head. "Such a spoilt girl, aren't you?"

Her jaw opens, and her tongue flops out of her mouth.

"Ready to be jabbed?" Will asks, his smile all teeth.

"Pardon?"

"Are. You. Ready. To. Be. Jabbed?"

My brows draw together. "That doesn't sound pleasant."

"Sweetheart, when I jab, it's as fuckin' pleasant as it gets."

Carly laughs, shoves a mouthful of cereal into her gob, and mumbles, "'Ave a 'ood 'ime." She waves her fingers and dribbles milk onto her chin.

"Charming." I turn to Will and point at Sasha. "You need to put her down. We can't take her with us."

He pouts. "Goodbye, beautiful."

Sasha's wayward tongue smothers his face, and he lets it before placing her on the ground.

"After you," he says, gesturing with his arm that I walk ahead of him.

"Thank you."

Smiling, I take note of his chivalry, bookmarking it right next to his punctuality.

Will groans, low and carnal, so I glance over my shoulder, which is when his eyes rise from staring at my arse.

"Really?" I ask, eyebrow cocked.

He goes to speak, but Carly beats him to it. "Yes, really, your arse looks unreal in those pants. If you weren't my best mate and a know-it-all superior bitch, even I'd want a chunk of that."

My jaw drops. "I'm not a know-it-all superior bitch. Well... maybe superior."

Will looks at Carly and she shrugs.

Growling, I storm out of the house, down the front path, and wait by the passenger side door of Will's truck.

He follows and reaches out to open the door for me. "Don't worry. I'll help you release all that pent-up anger and frustration."

"Ha! Funny you should say that because you're partly the reason I have it in the first place. Between you and Carly, it's a miracle I haven't been admitted to an asylum yet."

He rubs his hands together. "This is gonna be fun."

After climbing into the truck, I secure my seatbelt. "I'm glad you think so."

"Have a little faith, Elizabeth," he says before closing my door. "I'll take *good* care of you."

* * *

FAITH? Faith is the absolute last thing I have when I step into the boxing studio not even thirty minutes later. Mirrored walls skirt three quarters of the large, well-lit room, and people of all ages, genders, and sizes punch each other and boxing bags suspended from metal stands and the ceiling, a constant slapping sound rhythmic in the air.

It looks barbaric.

"Master Will, Ms Hanson!" Dylan calls out.

I search in the direction of his voice until I see a small hand frantically waving in the air.

Will waves at the same time I do, then says, "Drop and give me ten." He puts his bag down at the edge of a cushioned mat and fires me a sadistic grin. "That goes for you too."

I point to my chest. "Me? Do push-ups?"

"You need to warm up to help prevent injury."

"But I am warm. Feel me." I hold out my arm.

He wraps his hand around mine and pulls me flush with his chest before turning me around and whispering into my ear, "I have every intention to *feel* you at some point, but for now, while you're under my supervision in this gym, you will drop and give me ten."

Heat rockets up my spine, and I can't help but squirm in his embrace. "But I... I don't know how."

"I'll make it easy for you." He gently guides my bag off my shoulder and places it next to his. "On your hands and knees."

The sheer sexiness of his command tells me this isn't going to be any easier, but I do as I'm told, and he drops to one knee by my side.

"Your hands should be shoulder-width apart." He leans over me and places his paws on my shoulders then slowly skates his fingertips down my arms to reposition my hands, my skin buzzing everywhere he touches. "Back straight." He gently presses down on my arse. "Ankles crossed."

Will scoots backward to my feet, so I glance over my shoulder and laugh, my arms already like jelly before even attempting my first dip. "I'm definitely not cut out for this."

"From my angle, sweetheart," he says, voice low, "you definitely are."

My cheeks flame. "Behave, Will, or I'll sit and watch."

He chuckles and gets to his feet again then moves to stand at the helm of the cushioned mat. "Good morning, Beginner Boxers."

"Good morning, Master Will," several people reply.

If he thinks for one second that I'm going to refer to him as Master Will, he has another think coming.

Slowly lowering my chest to the mat for the second time, I take note of five kids and two adults—one woman and one frail-looking man—all of them rising and falling at a much quicker pace than me.

Dylan springs up first and proceeds to jog around the outer edge of the mat, and the rest of the group follow. I'm only up to push-up number four.

"You may want to speed it up a little, Elizabeth," Will says, amusement in his voice.

Arms straining, I glare at the son of a bitch.

He raises his hands in defence. "Okay. That'll do. Jog around the mat twice then come back here and we'll get started."

Rising to my feet, I nearly stumble and fall flat on my face when Will unzips his jacket and shakes it off, revealing a loose black singlet that barely covers his hulk-like chest. *Oh my!*

"Come on, Ms Hanson!" Dylan yells as he passes me. "You're too slow."

I quickly focus on him but can't help taking peeks at Will as I start my second lap, this time launching into a coughing and choking fit when he pulls down his tracksuit pants. *Sweet legs of Hercules!*

He steps out of each pant leg, now wearing nothing but light-weight jogging shorts that perfectly accentuate well-defined quads. I whack my chest with my palm, forcing it to wake up and help me breathe again.

"You all right?" he asks as I slow to a stop.

Bending at the waist, I nod then join the rest of the group who are standing before him, spaced roughly two metres apart.

"This is my special friend, Elizabeth," he says, gesturing to me. "She's—"

"She's my schoolteacher," Dylan blurts.

Will continues. "Yes, she is. This is her first time boxing, so I hope you all make her feel welcome."

Everyone smiles, so I give them a sheepish wave.

"Right, let's get started. One hundred air jabs, fifty air jabs and hooks, then a hundred uppercuts."

What the fffk? I'm exhausted just listening to that.

Everyone starts punching the air, kinda like a *Cobra Kai* karate class. I try to copy when Will slides in beside me and rests his hand on my lower back.

"Not you, sweetheart. We gotta work on your technique first."

"My technique?"

He nods, eyes roaming my arms, shoulders, and chest. "You left-handed or right?"

"Right."

"Step forward on your left foot." He squats, and I can almost see up his shorts.

"You won't see much."

I look straight ahead. "See much of what?"

"What I'm packin'."

I snort. "I wasn't trying to see what you're packin'. They're all the same anyway."

"Oh, sweetheart, you are in for a treat." Will palms my thigh and slowly glides his hand down over my knee and calf until he's repositioning my foot. "God *did not* create us all equally."

"Is that right?"

"*Oui.*"

I laugh.

"Now, shift your weight onto your right leg and turn it out on a slight angle." He grips my hips, firm but gentle. "Soft knees," he murmurs.

I'm about to say thanks and that I use a milk bath powder from the Body Shop when he continues.

"Don't lock your knees. Relax. We call this 'soft knees.'"

"Oh."

"Footwork and posture are very important. If you don't have good balance, you can't throw good punches." He stands and moves back, hand on his chin as he assesses my position. "Does that feel comfortable?"

I look down at my feet then back at him. "I think so."

"Good. The power of your punch comes from your hips and your knees as you properly distribute your weight." He moves behind me, his chest pressed to my back, his large, masterful hands on my shoulders. "As you punch forward," he says, cupping my right fist with his right hand, "your body pivots."

Will's lips and beard skim my earlobe, his breath tickling my neck, and I almost topple into his arms.

"Posture, Elizabeth." He places his hands on my hips again. "You gotta hold your body strong. All movement stems from this very spot."

Guiding my hips back and forth, he moves me in unison with him as if we're doing some kind of erotic Hokey Pokey dance—my right arm in, my right arm out. And for a second, I'm tempted to shake it all about.

I don't.

Master Will is very serious.

And the last thing I want is to be forced to do more push-ups.

"When do I get to punch something?" I ask.

"You don't rush what you want to do right," he whispers into my ear. "You gotta take your time and pay attention to every detail."

The tip of his nose nudges my neck, and my eyelids flutter then close.

"Look in the mirror," he says.

I snap my eyes open and focus on our reflection.

"Think of it like fucking." He pulls my hips inward, his cock pressing above the apex of my arse. "Sure, we can go at it hard and messy and get there in the end. And, sure, it'll be fun and wild." His eyes flare, and so does my uterus. "But when you want perfection, you gotta take it slow, be precise, learn, and appreciate every little aspect involved. Once you've done that, you can go as fast or as slow as you like."

I swallow, hard, just as Dylan shouts, "Done!"

All of a sudden acutely aware that one of my students can see us,

I quickly step forward, away from Will, now internally grateful for Dylan's interruption. I make a note to give him extra house points next week. He deserves it. Because little did I know, boxing was like fucking, and little did I know it would turn me on just as much.

I'm not here to be turned on; I'm here to learn how to punch.

"Okay," Will says to the group. "Repeat those punches, but this time grab your gloves and a set of pads, and pair up. Elizabeth, you're with me."

I wrinkle my nose.

"You'll like this. You get to punch me."

A sinister gleam creeps onto my face. "Finally!"

Will bends down and takes out a set of gloves and pads from his bag, and his shorts pull tight across his arse. *Fuck me, he's right. God did not create us all equally.*

I quickly look away but notice his tickled expression in the reflection of the mirror. *Shit! Busted!*

He inconspicuously cups himself as he stands then hands me a pair of gloves. "Chuck them on."

I cock my brow. "They're pink."

"Yes."

"Why do they have to be pink?"

He gives me the same puzzled look he gave the sleazeball the night we met at Opals. "I don't friggin' know. Why is the moon round?"

I'm tempted to tell him it's not, that it's actually oblate, but I don't. There's a time and place for that type of scientific discussion, and it's neither here nor now.

I shove the gloves at his chest. "I find it sexist that I'm expected to wear pink boxing gloves solely because I'm female."

He blinks, then blinks again. "Fuckin' pink sexist shit," he mutters under his breath. Will drops them back into his bag and takes out another pair, this time red, and dangles them in front of me. "These better?"

"Yes. Red is fierce." I snatch them. "They also match my hair." Slipping my hands into the gloves, I tighten the Velcro straps and fire him a devilish smile. "I'm ready to punch you now."

* * *

FOR THE NEXT FORTY-FIVE MINUTES, Will teaches me various techniques in punching and blocking until I'm drenched in sweat and exhausted.

"Head up," he says, tilting my chin to look at him. "Lock your frame."

I slump like a non-compliant puppet, arms and body akin to a piece of flailing string.

"Look, spaghetti arms. This is your boxing space, and this is my boxing space."

Bursting into laughter, I bend at the waist and prop my hands on my knees. "Oh, my God! You just quoted *Dirty Dancing* again. I swear you have a crush on Patrick Swayze."

"Maybe I do." He claps his pads together then holds one up high, prompting me to punch it again.

Still laughing, I stand straight, stretch my back, and barely swipe it. "Are we done? Please tell me we're done. I'm stuffed."

Will glances at the clock on the wall then places his padded hand on my shoulder. "Yeah, we're done."

"Thank Christ for that."

"You did good."

"I did?"

"For a first-timer." He takes the pads off and hands me my water bottle. "Now have a drink and meet me back on the mat."

"What? Why? You just said we're done."

"You need to stretch."

I need a shower and a sofa.

Grumbling, I have a quick drink then sit on the mat where the rest of the class has congregated.

"At the end of every session, we need to stretch the muscles to break the release of lactic acid and assist in muscle recovery. Ain't that right, Dylan?"

"Yep." He jumps up and does a warrior pose, and everyone else moves into various stretching positions.

I go to get up, but Will stops me.

"I want you on your knees, Elizabeth."

Taking in his lecherous stare, I bite the inside of my cheek and shuffle to my knees, ready for further instructions that, at first, aren't forthcoming.

"Now what?" I look up through my lashes.

He runs his hand through his hair and shakes his head. "Sit back on your heels and hunch forward, tucking your head into your knees and stretching your arms out before you, breathing slow and deep. You should feel the stretch in your quads, neck, and shoulders."

I do as I'm told and close my eyes, steadying my heartbeat. "I like this part of boxing," I say, my voice a little drowsy.

He chokes out, "So do I."

Lifting my head, I find him staring at my arse again. "I might report you for sexual harassment."

He squats, and again, I chance a peek down the leg of his shorts.

"I should do the same to you," he says.

I giggle. "Fair enough."

"Okay, now lie on your tummy then push up with your hands and arch your head back. This is called a cobra. It stretches your lower—"

"Jesus! You're not wrong." Fire burns my lower back and abdominals.

"If it's too painful, creep your hands forward a bit to relax the stretch, but not too much or it's pointless."

Once again, I do as I'm told, and the discomfort soon eases.

Will kneels beside me, his hand resting on my arse. "How's that, better?"

I scoff. "Is that a trick question?"

"No." He chuckles. "On your back and open your legs."

I snap my head toward him. "What?"

He points to the rest of the class who are all on their backs with their legs open like frogs.

"Oh. Okay." Shuffling onto my back, I copy my fellow class-mates, my inner thighs now screaming their disgust. "Oh wow! Yep. Feelin' that."

"Breathe," he says. "Relax your hips and let your knees fall as close to the ground as they can."

"I... I am," I struggle to say, my muscles too tight.

He scoots along the mat until he's kneeling in front of me, his knees pressing into my shins. Will leans forward, rests his hands on my legs, and gently kneads the pads of his thumbs into my inner thighs.

I moan, and it almost sounds pleasurable.

"Nice, slow, deep breaths," he says, thumbs biting deeper.

Will scoots forward again and ever so slightly presses down on my legs, his eyes not wavering from mine.

I grimace. "That hurts."

"Just relax."

"I can't."

"You can. Just let go."

"No, I ca—"

He pushes a little harder. "It'll be worth it."

For a second, I'm not sure if he's talking about the stretching or about us. He's but a hair's breadth away, and I'm so defenceless and... vulnerable.

I swallow.

"Trust me, sweetheart."

Sucking in a deep breath, I close my eyes and relax as much as I'm able to, my knees falling to the ground, the stretch severe at first but then pliable. It's almost comfortable, freeing... liberating, until he slaps my leg and jumps to his feet.

"Well done, everyone. Class dismissed. See you next week."

My eyes shoot open, and I prop myself on my elbows. "That's it?"

He offers me his hand. "No. I'm not finished with you yet."

CHAPTER FOURTEEN

"What do you mean you're not finished with me yet?" I take his hand, and he helps me stand but doesn't let go, his fingers sliding between mine.

"I want you to meet someone."

"Who?"

"Molly."

"Molly?" My stomach tightens, and I frown. I don't want to meet Molly. I've had a somewhat lovely day, and meeting Molly will surely ruin that. "Er... I really should just go hom—"

"It won't take long."

I pry my hand loose from his and scratch the back of my neck. "So, who's Molly again?"

"My roommate. She's awesome." He slings his bag over his shoulder and grabs my hand again. "Come on. You'll love her."

I highly doubt that.

* * *

ROUGHLY TWENTY MINUTES LATER, we pull up outside his home, and it's even better in the daylight—moss-covered rocks, flowers, and cobblestone paths weaving around gum trees and various shrubs.

I gleam. "Your house looks like a magical fairy garden."

"Yeah, I know." He takes my hand and leads me up the path to the front of the house, a cement troll-looking creature standing guard by his door.

Its existence is entirely odd, and yet it looks as if it belongs nowhere else.

"Are you sure Molly wants to meet me?" I whisper, leaning in just a little too close.

His eyes meet mine before dropping to my lips, and the sudden urge to lean in even closer is like an invisible, magnetic pull. My mouth parts as I inhale, and I almost do lean in farther, my heart-beat an unsteady thump in my chest.

A low growl emanates from Will's throat, and he unlocks the door and pushes it open. "Yes," he says, clicking his neck from side to side while momentarily closing his eyes. "She does want to meet you." He gestures inside his home. "Come on in."

I gingerly step into his entryway, his hand once again finding mine before guiding me into his lounge.

"Molly, meet Elizabeth. Elizabeth, meet Molly." Will points to a black Labrador curled up in a bed at the base of the sofa, and my heart settles to a pleasant rhythm again. I'm fairly sure it even swells a few sizes.

Molly raises her weary head, white hair peppering her face and ears, and she slowly rises to her feet before waddling over, her tail wagging happily.

"Molly's one of the loves of my life," he declares.

I drop to one knee and pat her head, and she sits. "*One* of the loves of your life?"

He points to the far end of the room. "They're some of the others."

Following his extended arm, my jaw nearly hits the floor when I spot a tropical fish tank filled with an array of brightly coloured fish, a reptile tank with what I think is a bearded dragon, and a white, lop-eared rabbit peeking out from a plastic tunnel on the floor.

"Oh, my God—"A bird screeches behind me, and I almost piss my pants. "Jesus!"

Will smiles, all teeth and pride. "That's Romeo and Juliet, my love birds."

Clutching my chest, I blink all the blinks then burst into laughter. "You weren't kidding when you said you like animals, huh? You're like a male version of Snow White."

He strides over to the rabbit, squats, and picks it up. "Hey, buddy. Come meet Elizabeth." Will hugs the ball of fluff to his chest, and if I had fallopian tubes, I'm sure they'd explode. It's the most adorable thing I've ever seen. Slightly paradoxical but immensely adorable.

"Want to cuddle Casper?" he asks, holding him out like Rafiki the mandrill did Simba in *The Lion King*.

"Sure!"

He places him on my chest, and I cradle his bum and back. "Hi. Are you as friendly as your namesake?" He makes a sniffy sound and snuggles into the crook of my neck, and I decide I love him unconditionally. "I always wanted a rabbit, but Mum is allergic to fur, so I never got one. Nor a cat or dog."

"You didn't have a cat or dog?"

I shake my head.

"I can't imagine that horror."

Casper undulates as I laugh.

"So what's stopping you getting a rabbit now?"

"Probably Sasha. I reckon she'd eat it. And that wouldn't be great pet ownership."

He strokes Casper's back, his fingers gently grazing my jaw. "Golden Retrievers are smart dogs. You could easily train her not to eat other pets."

"I've told Carly to send her to doggy training numerous times. She hasn't... clearly."

After strolling over to the fish tank, I gently bend my knees and dip my head. "You have a Nemo, how cute."

"I do. And Marlin and Dory."

"What?" I eagerly search the tank for the other clownfish and the blue tang, but then shake my head, shocked he even knew the Disney characters in the first place.

"What's wrong?" he asks, brows knitting together.

"I'm... I'm just surprised."

"By what?"

"By you."

"Why?"

"You're not like I thought you were." I divert my gaze back to the tank, ashamed. "You're actually a really sweet, down-to-earth guy."

"So what's your problem then?"

Focussing on Dory, she zigs and zags around the tank. "I don't have a problem."

"Good. So be my woman then."

I snigger. "Your woman?"

"You know what I mean, sweetheart."

Turning my back to him—because it's easier to be a coward than not—I move closer to the reptile tank. "N-No. I don't think it's a good idea."

"Why not?"

"Because I... I don't need a man to fulfill my life. As much as I want the fairy tale, I don't *need* it. Men let you down. They tell you what you want to hear then disappoint you." Desperate to change the subject, I point to his lizard. "What's his name?"

"*Her* name is Princess Fiona."

"Princess Fiona?" I burst out laughing and turn to face him.

"Yes, and the little dude hiding in the corner is Shrek."

Scrutinizing the corners of the tank, I spot a tortoise just as Will takes Casper from my grasp, puts him on the ground, and stands directly in front of me, arms crossed over his puffed chest, eyes stern.

"What?" I ask.

"Not all men do that."

"Do what?"

"Let you down."

I cross my arms too. "Well, I haven't come across one who hasn't."

"Yeah, you have." He steps forward, his wrists bumping mine.

I step back. "That's yet to be seen."

He steps forward again. "So let me show you."

"I..." I hold up my hand like a stop sign. "I don't know. I'm—"

"You're basing that judgement on him, aren't you?"

"Him?" I ask, confused.

His eyes narrow. "Oliver."

I almost choke on the name. "Oliver?"

"Yes."

I shake my head. "Oliver and I have never dated." Pausing for a second, I doubt my own words. "Well, I don't think we have. I'm not really sure."

"That says a lot."

Stepping back once again, I scratch the base of my neck. It's not really itchy, so I don't know why I do it. "I'm not following."

"Oliver is a fucksqueak who wouldn't know pure gold from a pile of shit even if he shit it out himself." He takes my hands in his. "But I do. I know you're gold, sweetheart. A prize. And I know I wanna win you." He closes his eyes. "No, I wanna *earn* you," he says, opening them again. Will lets go of my hands and cradles my face. "I wanna be the man who doesn't let you down, the man who gives you your fairy tale."

Unable to speak or think, I stand there with nothing but my racing pulse, a heavy throat, and a chest so tight I'm not sure if I'm breathing or not. I've never felt this... this alive and useless at the same time.

"Why, Will?" I ask. "Why me?"

His eyes crinkle, and he tilts my chin so that I've nowhere else to look but at him. "Because, from the moment I first saw you, I haven't been able to unsee you. You're there when you're not, in my head and in my bed. You're all I think about, Elizabeth. And that means something." He gently rubs the pad of his thumb across my cheek. "So let me be that man for you. Let me give you your fairy tale."

"You can't." I swallow, blinking back tears I don't want him to see. "No one can."

"Then let me at least try."

Staring at his lips, I bite my own. *Should I let him try?* I want to. *Really* want to. Threading my fingers through his hair, I give in and pull his head down to mine, kissing him like I've never kissed a man before. Deep. Sincere. With purpose.

Will envelops me in his arms and lifts me from the ground, our mouths magnets as I wrap my legs around his waist and squeeze him tight, gently grinding against him for the need of friction I didn't know I craved.

He tastes like Powerade and candy, and I'm finally ready for a sugar rush.

"Fuck, sweetheart. You keep doin' that and I'll blow where I'm standin'."

Giggling around his tongue, my hands are feverish as I grab at his shoulders, face, and hair, desperate to taste, touch, and feel every part of him. I've never wanted anyone as much as I want him, here, now, against the wall or on the floor. It's unlike me, but for the first time in my life, I simply don't care.

"I'll let you try, Will," I say, panting as I pull away from him. "I'll let you try to give me my fairy tale, but... we need to keep it between us, for now."

Hesitation darkens his eyes. "You don't want people to know?"

"Not yet."

He pulls back a little. "Why? You ashamed of me?"

"No! Of course not." I peck his perfect lips twice. "I just... I don't want the pressure of other people knowing and sticking their heads in where they're not needed. I want it to be *us* first. I want to get to know you, and you to know me. No interference. Does that make sense?"

He searches my face, his eyes settling on mine. "Us first, people later?"

"Yes." My lip quivers. "If that's okay with you."

Letting out a surrendering sigh, he kisses the tip of my nose. "If that's what it takes to earn your trust, then it's okay with me."

A wave of heat surges up my spine and bursts at my cheeks. "Good." I grind my hips a little more. Hungry. Frenzied. A little messy. "So can we fuck now?"

He chokes. "Thought you'd never ask."

Mashing my lips to his once again, I practically climb his body like a koala climbs a tree, his hands firm on my arse, his strides determined as he walks us to his room. My back hits his mattress moments later, and I shimmy out of my yoga pants and help him wrench my t-shirt over my head.

Will grunts, animal-like, his eyes wide as they rake my body. "Don't let me break you, sweetheart."

I unclip my bra. "I'm not as delicate as you think."

Something sinister crosses his face, and he lowers his shorts, his cock springing free unapologetically.

This time, I grunt. "Shit! I take that back. Don't break me."

He drags his palm up and down his length, slow, purposeful, his smile lazy, then lowers to the bed and hovers over me. "Your fairy tale include my face between your legs?"

He licks my nipple, and pleasure shoots straight to my core.

"Y-Yes. Yes, it does."

Will moans, licks, nips, and sucks my nipples some more then trails kisses down my stomach and around my bellybutton, his beard a delightful tickle. I squirm, but he holds me still before pressing his nose into the apex of my thighs and sucking in a deep breath.

I gasp and buck into him, desperately wanting more. The last time someone went down on me, I'd had a few drinks of the alcoholic kind. I'd wanted it to happen, consensual and all, but my expectations hadn't been high. They'd just been blah. I'd known it was just going to be sex. Intoxicated, emotionless sex. This time, though, my emotions are high. My expectations are high. I want this to be epic. I want us to work.

He growls, nudges me again and again, then wrenches my underwear aside and swipes his tongue across my skin, deliberately slow and precise.

"Oh God," I moan.

He does it again, this time faster. The muscles in my core pull tight, and my body soars to a height I'm not yet ready to reach.

"Jesus, Will!"

Clenching my thighs around his head, I try to hold him still for fear of coming too soon, my nerve endings dancing the Carnival in Rio de Janeiro.

He looks up at me, eyes glittering before he pries my legs apart like scissors and dips his tongue once more, this time flicking my clit ferociously.

I cry out, grip the doona, and nearly rip it from the bed.

"That's it, sweetheart. Come for me," he murmurs, sucking, licking, and nipping while sliding two fingers inside me.

I climax so powerfully my back bows and leaves the mattress, my pussy clenching, my toes curling. Heat flushes my face, chest, and fingertips, and I'm about ready to incinerate when he places his palm on my tummy and gently holds me down, letting me ride the wave of pleasure until I gain my breath and prop myself up on my elbows.

"Wow! That was…. I mean, I haven't done that in a long t—"

Will crawls up my body, his lips glistening, his eyes gleaming, then he leans over the bed, takes out a condom from his bedside table, and rolls it onto his cock, his movements smooth and confident. He makes me want to touch myself… *in front* of him, which is mind-boggling, considering I don't like to touch myself in front of me, let alone anyone else.

I tug on my lip—it's strangely erotic.

Will's eyes flare before he clasps my ankles and drags me to him, my knees bent, my legs spread wide. Positioning the tip of his cock, he slides it through my wetness before pushing inside me, one glorious inch at a time.

I moan, long, low, languorously.

"You okay?" he asks, his voice tense.

"Uh-hm," I mumble, unable to articulate words.

Will glides his hands over my stomach and cups my breasts, his hips gyrating, his soft but calloused fingers delightful as they knead my skin. I move with him, in rhythm, rocking and breathing as if we're one.

A bead of sweat slides from his temple, down his cheek, and onto the muscles straining in his neck. It's sexy as hell, and I have the strange urge to lick him, so I lift myself up and straddle his knees.

Using his shoulder for balance, I wrap my hand around the back of his head and lean in, swiping my tongue up his neck, over his cheek, until I'm tasting his mouth once again.

"Fuck, Elizabeth." He pistons into me faster and deeper, and I bounce against his lap, the sound of skin slapping skin a rhythmic beat filling the room.

"Yes!" I cry out, kissing him harder, my breasts pressing his chest as I hug him to my body.

He glides his hands up my back and rests them on my shoulders, holding me down as he thrusts deep, long, and full. My core pulls tight, my head near exploding as pleasure once again ripples through me.

Will hardens and grunts, guttural and raw, and I throw my head back and cry out his name before my body falls limp against him.

I can't move.

I can't think.

Everything I just experienced was as if I'd experienced it for the first time. Which is crazy, considering I'm somewhat experienced.

He chuckles. "Did I break you?"

"Yes, I think so."

Trailing his lips down my neck and across my collarbone, he slides out of me, lies down, and pulls me to him, hugging me to his chest until we both fall asleep.

* * *

MY EYES SPRING OPEN, and for the smallest of seconds, I forget where I am and who I'm draped across, naked, until the scent and feel of his skin beneath mine triggers every vivid memory.

Blinking, I take in his room. Wood panelling halfway up fog-grey walls. Charcoal-coloured dresser topped with aftershave. A pair of drumsticks and an expensive-looking watch. And a chair in the corner, covered in worn clothing. I smile then bite the inside of my cheek, my finger tracing the pattern tattooed to his arm. Need once again pools between my legs as flashes of Will's impressive, virile body pistoning into mine surges to the forefront of my memory.

"Mm," he garbles.

I tilt my head to look up at him, and he peeps one eye open.

"You ready to go again, sweetheart?"

Crawling on top of him, I lick from one of his nipples to the other before venturing toward his abdomen until I'm sucking the silky-smooth crown of his cock.

He groans, harsh like gravel.

I consume as much of him as I can and work his shaft with my hand, pumping as I lick, suck, and tease him. Sucking cock has never really interested me. It cramps my jaw and makes me gag, and there's nothing pleasurable about that. Strangely enough, I'm enjoying Will. His cock is rather pleasant in taste and texture, and although it's bigger than any I've sucked before, it's neither daunting nor boring.

I'm a happy Libby. A happy lip-locked Libby.

Will slides his hand into my hair and grips me gently. "Elizabeth."

"'es?"

"You want me to blow in your mouth?"

I pause. *How sweet.* I've never been asked this before, never been given the choice, and for that, I say, "'es," again.

Will jerks once then twice before warmth hits the back of my throat, slick and thick. I swallow, which is when I realise my eyes are watering and I'm in desperate need of oxygen.

Releasing him from my lips, I gulp all the air I can when he reaches down, cups my face, and guides me to his mouth, his tongue slipping between my lips as he kisses me long and hard but oh so tenderly.

"I like you very much," he says as he pulls away, his eyes alive with humour. "And so does Molly by the looks of it." Will gestures to where Molly is sitting by the bed, head resting on the mattress, staring at me like I'm her long-lost love.

"Oh, my God!" I roll off him. "Did she just watch me give you head?"

"Probably."

"Will! That's—" I pull the blanket over my head. "—so embarrassing."

He chuckles. "She's a dog."

"A perverted dog."

"Hey! You just hurt her feelings."

"Are you kidding me?" I wrench the blanket down again.

"Look." He points toward the door. "She's leaving."

"Good!"

Rolling on top of me, he bears his weight on his elbows and nudges my nose with his. "What do you want to do now?"

"Wipe Molly's memory."

He chuckles again. "Besides that."

"Take a shower."

"Done. Then what?"

"Er... watch a movie?"

"Then what?"

I laugh. "I don't know... have something to eat?"

"Then what?"

"Go home?"

"Wrong answer."

I cock an eyebrow. "Are you asking me to have a sleepover, Will?"

The cutest boyish smile illuminates his eyes, and he nods.

Covering my face with my hands, I peek through my spread fingers. "Okay. I'll sleep over."

* * *

AFTER CLEANING OURSELVES UP, making toasted cheese sandwiches, and watching—you guessed it—*Dirty Dancing* while Casper sporad-

147

ically jumped in the air around us, which I now know is called a binky, Will shows me the rest of his house. It belonged to his grandma before she passed away a couple of years ago and bequeathed it to him, her only grandson. His sister ended up with a beach house in Dromana.

"You're very lucky," I say, admiring the cathedral ceilings in the kitchen and living area. "This house is incredible."

"I know. Ma always knew I loved her home." He leans against the woodgrain kitchen cabinetry. "When I was a boy, and my sister and I stayed with Ma and Pa on school holidays, we used to spend every daylight hour outside, pretending the house was enchanted and under threat of an evil sorcerer."

I cock my head and smile, imagining their fun game. It's definitely something I would've played.

"I also spent most weekends here as I grew older, clearing gutters, mowing the lawn, and fixing odd things Ma couldn't after Pa died. It's always felt like home and always will."

Touching my hand to my heart, I say, "That's really lovely, Will. It sounds like you had a special relationship with your grandparents."

"I did. Mum and Dad were often away for work, so we stayed with Ma and Pa a lot."

"What line of work were your parents in?"

"Dad's a pilot for a commercial airline, and Mum's an air hostess."

"Oh. I guess they were away a lot then?"

"Yep."

His quipped answer stirs my curiosity.

"Did it bother you?" I ask tentatively.

Will puts the glass of water he's been holding down on the benchtop. "They were part-time parents, so, yeah, it bothered me sometimes."

He pushes off from the bench, which is when my eyes land on a ball of wool and set of knitting needles jutting out from an empty fruit bowl near his hand.

"Are you kidding me!" I point to them then cover my mouth, laughing behind my hand. "You really do knit."

One of his eyebrows hitches. "Yeah."

"I thought that was a lie."

"Why?"

"Because men like you don't knit."

"Who says?"

"I don't know, the vast majority of society."

He shrugs as if the vast majority of society are wrong, and maybe they are. "Ma taught me and Faith."

"Faith?"

"My sister."

"Will and Faith?"

He shrugs again. "Yeah, part-time parents or not, they were both optimists."

"Seems so," I say as he takes my hand and leads me into the hallway.

"Want a tour?"

I smile, enjoying the feel of his fingers entwined with mine. "Sure! I thought you'd never ask."

"That's my room." He points to his left. "Which you've already seen."

I blush at the crumpled sheets on his bed and keep moving.

He opens the next door. "Main bathroom."

I poke my head in and marvel at the glass bay windows and ceiling, showcasing the surrounding majestic mountain ash gum trees. "Oh wow! That's... magical... and a little nerve-wracking."

He leans on the doorframe. "Why's that?"

"Because one of those trees or a branch might fall and smash all this glass."

"Ah, but this house is enchanted, remember?"

The crooked smile I give him lacks confidence.

"Reinforced, laminated glass," he explains. "Extremely tough. And safe." He winks and moves to the next room. "Toilet."

I perform the same head poke, relieved to see no glass ceiling.

"And this room," he says as he opens the last door at the end of the hall, "is my music room."

In the centre of the room is a drum kit, black and silver in colour, the words *Live Trepidation* printed on the bass. Framed photos of various drummers hang between white carpet-panelled walls, and in the corner is a computer and some kind of sound recording system.

"Who's that?" I say, pointing to the first framed picture.

"God."

I laugh. "No, seriously."

"Dave Grohl. Nirvana."

"Oh, I thought he looked familiar." I point to the next one. "And is this Phil Collins?"

"Sure is."

I glance over my shoulder at him. "I like that song he sings where the gorilla plays the drums in the Cadbury advert."

"In the Air Tonight."

"Yeah, that's it."

I turn back to the picture, and before I can ask about the next one, Will drums that very part of the song, frightening the bejesus out me.

Clutching my chest, I nearly have to pick myself up off the floor, my eyes alight in wonderment. "If only you had the gorilla suit."

He cocks his brow.

I move to the next picture. "Who's this?"

"John Bonham. Led Zeppelin. And that last one is Neil Peart."

"Are they all your idols?"

"Yeah, you could say that."

"I think it's really great that you have them in here, surrounding you when you play. It's inspirational."

Sounds stupid, but it kinda reminds me of the Disney princesses on my childhood bedroom wall that used to surround and inspire me.

"That's the idea, sweetheart." He tips his chin. "Come here."

I move behind the drum kit, and he grabs my hips and pulls me onto his lap.

"I'll be fine," I playfully groan.

* * *

TURNS OUT I AM FINE. Biopsy: negative. Thyroid: clear. Lump on my back: a benign lipoma. Will noticed it in the shower the other day, and I had to explain what it was, which he seemed content with. I didn't offer any further information; I'm not ready for that. But I do know I'll have to confess the extent of my illness sooner or later, especially because, over the past few weeks, we've spent more time together and have grown much closer.

I'm now a permanent member of his boxing class, and he's well-versed in assessing spelling homework. I can complete a killer seed knitting stitch, and he knows just how I like my tea. He has five tattoos—my favourite is on his foot. He's memorised my bra, panty, and shoe sizes, and I now like to listen to Led Zeppelin and Muse.

He likes white chocolate; I like dark.

We both love Mexican food.

The more time we spend together, the more I fall for him. Like how he cares deeply for animals and the underdogs of the world, how he challenges me even when I don't want to be challenged, and how his mischievous smile lights up the darkness that often creeps up from within. I've loved sharing every moment with him, even the times when we've nearly been busted by Carly, like when she unexpectedly came home while he was between my legs.

Needless to say, he had to hide in my wardrobe for roughly thirty minutes while she told me all about some satay sauce sex session she had with Derek. I had to bite my lip the entire time to prevent myself from laughing, which would've worked because her satay sauce story was kinda funny. Messy and entirely unhygienic, but funny all the same. Thankfully, she eventually left me to my devices and had a shower, which was when I could finally sneak him out of the house. How she never noticed his car in the street is beyond me.

Other than a couple of close calls with Carly, and one at school when he snuck a kiss behind the excavator, our secret relationship has successfully remained secret.

We did, however, have our first proper fight on Christmas Eve. He wanted to tell our families about the two of us, and I told him I didn't. I mean, deep down I want what he does, but I'm still not ready. Call it denial, I don't care. I just want our bubble to remain intact for as long as possible, so we can continue to float through a world of pretend and insurmountable bliss. A world where shadows stay in the darkness, and where things are easier done than said—floating through a world with no risk because refusing to acknowledge the stakes is not something I get to do often. And if I tell Will the whole truth and nothing but the truth, there's a good chance our blissful bubble will burst, and I'll stop floating and fall back to earth among the soil and shit. I don't like soil and shit. No one does. And the more people who know we're together, the greater chance my fall will happen.

Anyway, I ended up storming out of his home, and we didn't speak until New Year's Eve when he snuck up to my bedroom window and scared the absolute shit out of me and Sasha.

Great guard dog she is.

Pushing open the door to the school office with my hip, I balance my empty mug, mobile phone, and a stack of paper. It's one week before the new school year commences, and it's all hands on deck for teachers and staff in preparation for the students' arrival. I'm teaching Grade 3 this year, on my own without Oliver, thank God, but I do have some of my Grade 2 students from last year, Dylan and Evan to name a couple.

Carly's behind the reception counter, radio blaring as she claps her hands and dances in her seat.

"Why are you so happy?" I ask, suspicious. She's been giddy ever since Derek dropped her off this morning.

She stops clapping. "I'm not."

"Yes, you are."

"So I'm singing, big deal."

I laugh and steadily place down the things I'm holding. "Carly,

"Want to have a go?"

I giggle. "Sure."

He places the drumsticks in my hands, then as if I'm a puppet, he guides me in hitting the drums.

I laugh, feeling a little silly but also liking the feel of him beneath and behind me. Not to mention it's nice someone else being the teacher for once.

"I'd love to see you play with your band," I say.

Tap.

"We're playin' a gig next weekend when Derek gets back from Sydney. You should come."

Tap. Tap.

"I'd love to. When next weekend?"

Tap. Tap. Bang.

"Saturday afternoon."

I'm about to say *"sure"* when I remember my breast biopsy. Dr Tao rang yesterday to notify me that my ultrasound showed a lesion in my left breast, and of course we need to investigate immediately. It's not the first lesion we've found—and it won't be the last —so I'm not losing sleep over it, but I can't cancel the appointment. I know how important these things are. I've been dealing with them most of my life.

Tap. Tap. Bang.

"Crap!" I say, shoulders slumping. "I can't. I'm busy."

"Then become un-busy."

"I can't."

He doesn't say anything, and I suspect it's because he's waiting for me to tell him why, so I do... kinda.

"I have a doctor's appointment."

Will rotates me a little so that we're face to face. "Everything all right?"

"Yes, of course." I nod. "It's just routine."

He searches my eyes for a second, and I'm as used to this type of response as I am buttering toast.

"Okay," he says, leaving it at that. *Bang. Bang. Bang.* "Maybe next time then."

Yes. *Definitely* next time.

CHAPTER FIFTEEN

"*D*o you want me to come with you?" Carly asks, her shoulder propping her body against the doorframe to our lounge room.

I look up from the sofa and swish my hand. "No. Derek gets back today. You should be with him." Flipping the page of my *Better Homes and Gardens* magazine, I add, "I'll be fine. This isn't my first biopsy, you know."

She huffs.

"Hey!" I point at her. "Don't give me that sad puppy dog look."

"But, Lib—"

"No 'But, Libs'." Flipping the next few pages, I admire the double-page spreads of summer garden ideas. "I'm a big girl, remember?"

"More like a big pain in my arse," she groans.

I shut the magazine with a snap and frisbee it onto the coffee table before tucking my feet under my bum. "Sooo, are you and Derek finally gonna have sex tonight?"

Part of me feels terribly guilty—not to mention a little trampy— that I've slept with Will before she's had a chance to sleep with Derek. I mean, they've been seeing each other for several months now, and I've only been *"seeing"* Will for a week. But, then, am I technically seeing him if we haven't revealed it to anyone? Kinda like the fallen-tree-in-a-forest-when-no-one-is-around scenario. Did it really make a sound if nobody heard it? *Ugh.*

I don't know what I'm doing. I like Will a lot, and every part of me wants to grab a megaphone and blare to a crowd of unsuspecting strangers in the street that Elizabeth Regina Hanson—the quiet, Disney-fairy-tale-loving teacher—finally has a boyfriend and is happy. That she's not some miserable nearly-thirty-year-old spinster cat lady sans the cats. Then there's my mother; she'll be thrilled. Not to mention a genuine relationship is something I've wanted and deserved for so long. I just... I know it can't come without hard truths and unsurmountable sacrifice, and I'm not sure Will is up for that or *should be* up for that. Just telling him the entire truth about my life terrifies me.

"...I'm desperate to fuck his brains out, like really fuck them out of his sexy head and into the next century, but I'm so nervous and scared, and I don't understand why, and—"

I realise I haven't been listening to a word Carly's said for the last minute or two, so I nod, pretending to agree with full comprehension. It's a tactic that always works.

"So what do you think is wrong with me?" she asks, and I also realise my tactic is flawed.

"Uh..." There are so many things I could say here, like, *"You act before you think, Carly, and you're an extremely unkempt housemate, not to mention the worst dog owner and dishwasher."* The list goes on. Instead, I choose to go with, "There's nothing wrong with you, hon. Just go with your gut and have a good time. Like you always do. Don't think about it too much."

God, I hope that's good advice. For all I know, she could've just admitted to being a nymphomaniac without morals.

It's not entirely farfetched.

She pushes off from the doorframe. "Okay. Yes. I will."

"Good?"

She nods. "Good." Carly approaches and kisses my forehead. "Good luck with the biopsy. Ring me if you need me, for anything at all."

"I'll be fine," I playfully groan.

* * *

TURNS OUT I AM FINE. Biopsy: negative. Thyroid: clear. Lump on my back: a benign lipoma. Will noticed it in the shower the other day, and I had to explain what it was, which he seemed content with. I didn't offer any further information; I'm not ready for that. But I do know I'll have to confess the extent of my illness sooner or later, especially because, over the past few weeks, we've spent more time together and have grown much closer.

I'm now a permanent member of his boxing class, and he's well-versed in assessing spelling homework. I can complete a killer seed knitting stitch, and he knows just how I like my tea. He has five tattoos—my favourite is on his foot. He's memorised my bra, panty, and shoe sizes, and I now like to listen to Led Zeppelin and Muse.

He likes white chocolate; I like dark.

We both love Mexican food.

The more time we spend together, the more I fall for him. Like how he cares deeply for animals and the underdogs of the world, how he challenges me even when I don't want to be challenged, and how his mischievous smile lights up the darkness that often creeps up from within. I've loved sharing every moment with him, even the times when we've nearly been busted by Carly, like when she unexpectedly came home while he was between my legs.

Needless to say, he had to hide in my wardrobe for roughly thirty minutes while she told me all about some satay sauce sex session she had with Derek. I had to bite my lip the entire time to prevent myself from laughing, which would've worked because her satay sauce story was kinda funny. Messy and entirely unhygienic, but funny all the same. Thankfully, she eventually left me to my devices and had a shower, which was when I could finally sneak him out of the house. How she never noticed his car in the street is beyond me.

Other than a couple of close calls with Carly, and one at school when he snuck a kiss behind the excavator, our secret relationship has successfully remained secret.

We did, however, have our first proper fight on Christmas Eve. He wanted to tell our families about the two of us, and I told him I didn't. I mean, deep down I want what he does, but I'm still not ready. Call it denial, I don't care. I just want our bubble to remain intact for as long as possible, so we can continue to float through a world of pretend and insurmountable bliss. A world where shadows stay in the darkness, and where things are easier done than said—floating through a world with no risk because refusing to acknowledge the stakes is not something I get to do often. And if I tell Will the whole truth and nothing but the truth, there's a good chance our blissful bubble will burst, and I'll stop floating and fall back to earth among the soil and shit. I don't like soil and shit. No one does. And the more people who know we're together, the greater chance my fall will happen.

Anyway, I ended up storming out of his home, and we didn't speak until New Year's Eve when he snuck up to my bedroom window and scared the absolute shit out of me and Sasha.

Great guard dog she is.

Pushing open the door to the school office with my hip, I balance my empty mug, mobile phone, and a stack of paper. It's one week before the new school year commences, and it's all hands on deck for teachers and staff in preparation for the students' arrival. I'm teaching Grade 3 this year, on my own without Oliver, thank God, but I do have some of my Grade 2 students from last year, Dylan and Evan to name a couple.

Carly's behind the reception counter, radio blaring as she claps her hands and dances in her seat.

"Why are you so happy?" I ask, suspicious. She's been giddy ever since Derek dropped her off this morning.

She stops clapping. "I'm not."

"Yes, you are."

"So I'm singing, big deal."

I laugh and steadily place down the things I'm holding. "Carly, you're beaming so bright you practically blinded me when I walked in."

"Am not."

She's lying. She's elated, and she doesn't want me to know why.

Realisation hits and I squeal. "Oh, my God! Either Derek said the L-word, or you have. Or both."

Plonking my arse on her desk, I deliberately mess her paper-work piles, karma for the pile of laundry she kicked off the sofa during the week.

"You're an idiot," she grumbles, and yanks the documents poking out from underneath my butt.

"It was you!" I point at her. "You said it!"

She tries to remain aloof by bunching the paperwork in her hand and tapping it on the desktop. "Was there something you wanted? I'm super busy."

Carly saying the L-word, let alone acknowledging it exists, is a *big* thing. My love-is-bullshit best friend is, indeed, in love—it's written all over her lovestruck face—so I'll be damned if I'm going to let her off easy by pretending it isn't so.

Pressing my fingertip to my chin, I try a different tactic. "He said it, didn't he? God knows you wouldn't."

"Yes! All right," she concedes. "We both said it. So what?"

I hug her then childishly pat her on the head. "Carly has finally become a grown-up. Congratulations. I'm happy for you."

"Seriously, Lib," she says, unsuccessfully trying not to smile, "is there anything I can help you with? I'm swamped."

Picking up my phone, I quickly scroll through my newsfeed. "Nope, I'm—" My words cut short when I notice a breaking news post about the penthouse at City Towers, where Alexis and Bryce live.

"Nope, you're what?"

I don't answer, instead reading that there's been an explosion and one person is reported dead.

"Lib!"

I look up, eyes wide. "Y-You might want to see this. It's breaking news. I don't know how true it is, but—"

She snatches the phone, the colour of her skin draining as she reads. "Oh, my God!" Her other hand shoots up to cover her mouth. "Oh no! No, no, no."

Tears pool in her eyes, so I place my hand on her shoulder to keep her composed. "Calm down, honey. Let's ring Alexis."

She nods, hands back my phone, then fumbles for her own, her finger trembling as she taps Alexis's profile in her contacts list.

Pressing the phone to her ear, she impatiently bounces her foot. "She's not answering. I've got to go. I've got to go there now." She shoots up from her seat, grabs her keys, and heads for the door.

"Carly!" I call out. "I'm coming with you."

* * *

AFTER DRIVING to the City Towers precinct and being informed by one of Bryce's employees that he and Alexis are fine and that Alexis has been taken to the Alfred hospital for treatment of smoke inhalation and shock, we head there instead.

"If Bryce and Alexis are okay, and the kids are staying with Rick this week, then who died?" Carly says as we take the front steps, two at a time, and enter the hospital through sliding glass doors.

I scurry behind her, trying to keep up. "Maybe no one died. Maybe the media got it wrong."

"I hope s—" She turns a corner and slams into a guy. "Sorry, I— Oh, hi." Carly smiles with relief when she realises it's Will she slammed into. I almost smile, too, but remember I'm supposed to despise him, so I groan, feigning anger instead.

Carly glares at me then mumbles like a seasoned ventriloquist, "What's your problem?"

I match her skill and utter, "Nothing."

"Hey, Jaws," he says to Carly before his eyes land on mine and light up like a Christmas tree.

Jaws is a weird nickname, and not one I've heard her called before, so my *what the fuck?* expression is genuine.

"And nice to see you again, Labia." His lip curls seductively, eyebrows waggling.

Oh no he didn't.

My glare is genuine too.

"You don't happen to know what room Lex is in, do you?" Carly asks. "It'll save me the trouble of asking."

"I know what rooms they're both in." Will licks his lips, eyes glued to my chest.

My nipples tingle, and I can't help but fiddle with my hair.

He winks, so I inconspicuously grit my teeth and shake my head at him.

Carly looks between us as if we're hiding something, which clearly we are, so I panic a little to try to throw her off her scent.

"Yes, these are breasts, Will," I hiss, shoving my hands on my hips. "They are two protruding glands and their purpose is to secrete milk after childbirth."

He licks his damn lips *again*. "They have more purpose than that, sweetheart."

Oh my God, I want to kill him, but I also want to take off my bra and let him prove what he's saying.

My thighs tremble and my tummy tightens, so I cross my arms over my chest and heighten my glare. "You're a pig!"

"Wait a minute." Carly holds up her hand. "You just said both, as in plural."

He diverts his gaze to her. "Yeah, Alexis and Derek."

"Derek!" she shrieks. "Derek's here? Why is he here?"

"Calm down," he says, touching her shoulder. "He mustn't have had time to call you yet."

"Where is he? What happened?"

"He was one of the first responders on the scene. He's just in for routine observation. Mild smoke inhalation."

"W-what? What room?"

"Level 3, room 11."

She starts for the elevator. "Lib, do you mind waiting down here?"

I'm about to say, *"No"* when Will drapes his arm over my shoulders, pulls me to his side, and says, "She'll be fine. I'll take good care of her."

159

I push him away as the elevator doors open and she disappears inside. "Labia?" I gripe, sucking on my tooth. "Really?"

He bursts into laughter. "You wanted a performance, so I gave you one."

Huffing, I step up to his chest and throw my arms over his shoulders, breathing him in. "Are you okay? What happened? How's Bryce and Derek? You must've been so worried."

He rests his forehead against mine, and I'm acutely aware that someone we know might see us. I just don't care right now. He seems fragile, and I want to know he's okay.

"Gareth blew up the apartment."

I rear back. "Who's Gareth?"

"Bryce's cousin."

"His cousin! But why? Why would he do that? And how...?"

He shakes his head. "Don't know. Apparently, he wanted to kill Alexis."

"Oh, my God!"

"He's a creepy fuck. Always has been."

A shiver runs the length of my spine. "Was anyone else hurt? The news report said someone died."

"Yeah. Gareth did."

Resting my head on his chest, I squeeze him tight, glad he wasn't there when this unfolded. "How awful for Bryce."

"Dude's a mess. I've never seen him like this." Will presses his lips to my head and inhales. "I've missed you."

I smile. "It's only been four days."

"Four days too long."

Not wanting to—because he's warm and comforting and smells like fresh trees and clean dirt—I pry myself off him and step back before someone sees us.

"Don't do that." He tugs me to him again. "There's no one here."

Pushing against his chest, I argue, "Carly could come back at any second."

"Let her."

"Will." I sigh.

"What?"

"Now's not the time to announce we're together."

"Then when is? It's been months."

"I don't know. Soon."

"How soon?"

"Just… soon."

Turning on my heel, I storm off, not knowing where I'm going. The only public places a hospital has is a gift shop and café, and I need neither so steer myself outside, warm summer air spiraling around me and sweeping my hair off my shoulders as I head down the steps.

"Elizabeth, where are you going?"

"To wait in my car."

He follows, and when I click my key fob to unlock the doors, he gets in and takes a seat. I'm reluctant, but I do the same, and we sit in silence for a moment before he drums a beat on my dashboard.

I cover my face with my hands and grumble. "You're so frustrating."

"Pot calling kettle black."

I give him an *"Oh really?"* look, but he ignores it. "Why do you desperately want everyone to know we're a couple? What is it to anyone but us?"

"It's everything, sweetheart."

"No, it's not."

"It is. It makes us accountable."

He's right. I know he is. And I feel stupid for fighting it. But I don't have a choice, at least for now.

Turning to face him, I drop my hands to my lap.

He doesn't look my way, instead keeps drumming his fingers on the dash. "Why do you desperately want to keep us a secret?"

"I don't," I choke out.

"Doesn't seem that way, Lib. Seems like you're ashamed, or scared, or… I don't fuckin' know."

The corners of my mouth rise a little at hearing him call me Lib. So casual. So comfortable. He's always said Elizabeth or sweetheart, or Labia.

Reaching out, I hold his hands still. "We can't make us official until you know the real me."

His eyes finally meet mine. "The real you? What are you talking about?"

"There's so much you don't know about me. Stuff you may not like, and stuff I don't want you to know because it might scare you away."

"What do you mean 'scare me away'? Nothing about you will scare me away."

"You don't know that, and that's why I don't want to change what we've got going on right now."

He lifts his hand to the nape of his neck and narrows his eyes at me. "Let me get this straight. You don't want to move forward, and you don't want to go back."

"Yes. No." I huff. "Kinda."

"That's the stupidest thing I've ever heard." Will throws his body against the seat and scrubs his face with his hands.

"No, it's not stupid. It's logical."

"Fuck logical, Elizabeth."

"Will, please—"

"Tell me what you're hiding."

"I... I can't," I plead. "Not yet. Please just give me more time."

Drawing in a deep breath through his nostrils, he then puffs it out, opens the passenger side door, and gets out.

"Where are you going?"

"Back to work."

"Will!"

"Call me when you want to show me the 'real' you. I'll be waiting and ready."

He closes the door and walks away, one hand in his pocket, the other gripping his hair. My shoulders slump, and tears pool in my eyes. And for the first time in a very long time, I hate the cards I've been dealt.

Damn it!

CHAPTER SIXTEEN

I don't see him for a couple of weeks, and it's like a part of me died. I miss him, like a kick-to-the-stomach miss him. Painful, lonely, almost debilitating. I miss his eyes and his lips, and the way his beard tickles my neck when we cuddle in front of the TV. I miss Molly and Casper, Princess Fiona, Shrek, and the fish. I even miss Romeo and Juliet, although I miss them the least. I miss the way he consumes all the space in a room but never lets you feel crowded, and how he tastes when we kiss goodnight. But most of all, I miss the sound of his voice and how his hand feels holding mine.

He's my Prince Charming, and I want my fairy tale back.

"So how many fucklets are going to be at this birthday party?" Carly asks as Derek pulls his truck into Albert Park.

It's Lucy's son, Alexander's, first birthday party, and Bryce has thrown a big shindig for his nephew. Massive marquee, jumping castles, ball pits, and slides. Anyone who is anyone is going to be there, except for Will.

When Carly begged me to attend with her, she mentioned Will had a family thing on, thinking him being there might deter me in saying yes. Unbeknown to her, it wouldn't have because I *want* to see him. I *need* to see him.

His absence has made me realise I'm ready to show him the *real* me, consequences be dammed. He's either going to embrace it, which terrifies me, or run for the hills, which will shatter my heart. Either way, he deserves to know what truly being with me entails.

"You can't call children fucklets," I say as I unlatch my seatbelt.

"I can. And they are." She does the same, and we all get out of the car.

The sun instantly scalds my freckled, sun-hating skin, so I hurry along, grateful the marquee is enclosed and air-conditioned. I'm wearing navy linen shorts, a white cami, and sandals, and my hair has grown so much I can now fit all of it into a decent ponytail.

As we step inside the marquee, a man dressed as a train conductor hands us a lollypop. I hold my hand up and decline, as does Derek, but Carly snatches all three. I roll my eyes and shake my head at her. She's either going to be the best or worst mother one day, and I honestly can't wait.

Glancing around the makeshift play centre and the never-ending stream of parents and kids, my heart squeezes a little. The giggling, the squealing, the innocence—it's all music to my ears.

"I stuck," a little girl cries out as she tries to pedal her trike between two gym mats.

"Hang on a second, sweetie." I rush over, squat down, and set her free, smiling when she says, "Fank you" before pedalling off.

"I would've left her there," Carly mumbles.

She helps me up but then laughs because she's joking. At least I think she's joking.

"You would not—"

"Yo."

I startle at the sound of Will's voice, heat crawling over my skin like a colony of fire ants as he steps up beside us, beer in hand, a lazy grin on his face. He's wearing a black polo shirt—collar up—grey shorts, and sunglasses on his head. He looks neat but delectably rugged all at once, and I have to bite my lip to prevent myself from biting him.

"And if it isn't my favourite redheaded walking vagina."

Mischief crinkles his eyes as he lifts my hand and kisses the back of it.

I don't know what to do or say because I've missed his lips and what he does with them.

Desperate to caress his cheek, I swallow, my fingers stiff. But when he winks and lets my hand go, his eyes tell me our ruse is still in full swing, that's he's giving me the time I asked for, even though I don't want it anymore.

Blinking, I switch on my inner actress and scrunch my nose before wiping the back of my hand down the front of his top. One last performance, then it's out with the truth.

"Carly, a word. Now!"

She practically shrivels on the spot, and so she should. She lied, on purpose. And now I have to pretend to be mad.

I pivot and head for an empty table in one of the corners of the marquee, Carly following behind. And when we're out of everyone's earshot, I blast her with my icy damnation.

"You little liar! You said he wasn't coming. This is a new low, even for you."

"Don't get your labia in a knot." She sticks her tongue out and clamps it between her teeth.

I point to my face. "I'm not laughing. Is my face laughing?"

"No, but then again, it doesn't laugh often. You need to laugh more, starting with now. Laugh, this really is quite funny," she goads.

I agree; it is funny, but not for the reasons she thinks.

"Oh, I'll be laughing," I say, narrowing my eyes at her. "Mark my words. I'll be laughing like a hyena when I get my revenge."

She takes a seat and stares at Derek as he talks with Lucy, Will, and some other people, Alexander desperately trying to lunge out of a woman's arms and into Derek's.

"I don't like hyenas," she says solemnly. "They're ugly-looking, kind of like the by-product of a dog and clown."

I sink into the seat next to her. "What's wrong?"

"Am I forgiven already?"

"No. Your time will come. In the meantime, tell me why you look so deflated and no longer want to be here."

She nods toward Lucy. "I don't trust her."

"Why? I thought the two of you got along well."

"We do. She's lovely. I just don't trust her."

"There's got to be a reason why, Carls."

"Not really." She shrugs. "I just feel as if I'm missing something. Call it a sixth sense."

"What could you be missing?"

"I think Lucy and Derek dated before she turned lezzie. They have a history. That much is obvious."

"So? History is the operative word here. In the past. Yesteryear."

Carly looks down at her fingers and fiddles with her aunt's ring, twisting it back and forth. "I get that. I just don't think it's entirely in the past."

I rest my chin on my hand. "What makes you say that?"

"God, I don't know," she snaps.

"Hey! I'm just trying to help." I push up from the table. "I'm going to get a drink. Do you want one?"

She recoils and gives me a sorry face. "No."

"Fairy bread?"

"No, thank you."

Smiling, I know what she'll like because she's a sucker for all things mini. "I saw some mini-pizzas and hot dogs. How 'bout those?"

Her pout morphs into a grin. "You had me at mini."

"Thought as much. I'll be back in a minute."

I make my way toward the buffet at the opposite corner of the marquee and am about to get our drinks when a hand slides onto my hip.

"Don't hate me, sweetheart," Will murmurs into my ear.

The hairs on the back of my neck dance, and I momentarily close my eyes. "I don't," I say, breathing out.

"I'm sorry. I'm sorry for walking away from you that day. I'm sorry for not ringing, and I'm sorry for calling you a redheaded walking vagina."

Laughter bursts from my chest. "Yes, well, you're not forgiven for *that*."

"But I'm forgiven for everything else?"

"Yes, of course." I turn into him. "It's me who needs to ask you for forgiveness."

Will rears back a little, brows pinched.

"No, I do. I'm sorry for holding us back. I'm sorry for not being completely honest with you, and I'm sorry for not trusting you with the real me."

He cups my cheek. "Lib—"

"Don't touch me!" Carly shouts.

We snap our heads to where she's standing a few metres away.

"Don't ever touch me again." She wrenches her arm from Derek and storms past us on her way out of the marquee.

"Carly!" I call after her just as Derek stops next to us.

"Fuck!" he snaps.

Will grabs his arm. "Mate, there's kids around. Watch your language."

He runs his hands over his shaved head. "I've fucked up."

I point my finger at him. "What did you do?"

"I… Shit!"

Torn between leaving to go after Carly and staying to tell Will everything I need to tell him, I choose my best friend when he says, "Go. We'll talk later."

I nod and leave, soon finding Carly outside.

"What happened?" I rest my hand on her back, her shoulders bobbing as she sobs.

"I… I just want to leave."

"Okay. I'll get Will to drive us home."

She wipes her eyes. "Will?"

"Yeah. He won't mind." I wipe a tear from her cheek, my heart breaking at her distress. "Are you sure you don't want to stay and sort it out?"

She shakes her head adamantly. "No."

"Okay. I'll be back in a minute."

I head into the marquee again. Derek is standing with Bryce and

Lucy, his head in his hands. I don't know what he's done, but what-ever it is, it looks bad. *Shit!*

Not wanting to leave Carly alone for long, I approach Will who's with the guy he was talking to earlier. "Hi. Sorry to interrupt—"

"Elizabeth, have you met Matt?"

I shake my head. "No."

"He plays bass in the band."

"Oh, that's right. Nice to meet you."

Matt tips his head, flicks his eyebrows, and grins while looking me up and down.

I narrow my eyes at him but focus back on Will. "I know this is a big ask, but would you mind taking Carly and me home? We came here with Derek, and she doesn't want to see him right now."

"Anything for my favourite Labia—"

I grab his arm. "Knock it off."

"But you wanted—"

"That doesn't matter right now."

His eyes widen, and he passes Matt his beer. "Later, mate."

I sigh, relieved. "Thank you."

"No sweat, sweetheart." He places his hand on the small of my back. "Let's go."

"Libby, hold up."

I pause and turn to Derek, who's stepping over toddlers to get to me.

"Is she okay?"

"What do you think?" I snap. "I don't know what you've done, but I... I've never seen her this upset."

"Just tell her I'm sorry and that I love her, and I should've told her."

"Told her what?"

"Just tell her that. Please."

His eyes beg me, and a small, sympathetic shred of my being feels sorry for the guy. He's obviously kept something from her, for whatever reason, and now it's backfired. I guess I can relate to his predicament. Sort of.

"I'll tell her. But you need to tell her yourself. You understand? *You* need to make this right."

"I will, when she lets me."

"A word of advice, Derek… she won't, so don't wait too long."

Will slaps him on the back. "I'll get her home safe."

"Thanks. Wait!" He points to both of us. "Are you two a thing?"

Will scoffs. "Nah, mate. She hates me."

I smile. "Let's just say he's growing on me."

As we leave the marquee, he leans in, his breath hot on my neck, and murmurs, "I can grow for you anytime you want, sweetheart."

I nudge him with my elbow. "I know."

* * *

CARLY SOBBED the entire way home and went straight to her room when we entered the house. Will kept Sasha occupied while I consoled her, and when she finally told me what happened, my heart broke for her. I also knew I had to tell Will my secret. And I had to tell him now.

"Is she okay?" Will asks as I enter the living room.

I shake my head. "No."

"What happened?"

"I think you should ask Derek. It's probably best you hear it from him."

"That bad, ay?"

"Depends how you look at it. I guess I see both sides." I fiddle with the hem of my cami.

"You wanna talk?"

"I do."

He pats the spot on the sofa next to him. "Come here, sweetheart. I hate it when you're so far away."

My chest squeezes with love and apprehension, and my hands tremble. "I can't have kids," I blurt before taking a seat. "I mean, there's more to it than that, but the bottom line is, I had cancer in my fallopian tube when I was fourteen, so both tubes were removed. I'm sterile, and I'm okay with that. I have a classroom full of kids. They're my kids, and I love each and every one of them. That's why I became a teacher, to help raise kids I didn't bring into the world. It's the next best thing. I—"

"Whoa!" He blinks. "Slow down." Will reaches for my hands and pulls me onto his lap. "You had cancer?"

"Yes. I suffer from Cowden Syndrome. You probably haven't heard of it because it's rare. It's inherited. Runs on Dad's side of the family. Basically, I get multiple noncancerous growths on various parts of my body, but I have an increased risk of developing certain types of cancers. Breast, thyroid, endometrial, which is what I already had. I see a specialist every month and have scans multiple times a year."

"Shit, Lib." His misty eyes chase mine. "I'm sorry."

"Don't be. I'm not. It is what it is, but it does mean I'll never have kids, and if you stay with me, you won't either. And I... I don't want to be responsible for that. You're great with kids. Really great, and you deserve to have them. This is my brick wall in life, and I don't want to be the reason for it becoming yours as well."

He rubs the pad of his thumb across my cheek, and I close my eyes and lean into his touch.

"Can't you do IVF?"

"I can," I say, opening my eyes, "but I don't want to."

He doesn't convince me I'm wrong like so many before him have, and I love him even more for it. I lived with this disease for most of my life, so it's not like I haven't thought deeply about my decision.

"I don't want to pass this disease on," I say, continuing to explain. "And if I have kids, there's an exponential chance I will pass it on. I want it to stop with me." I take his hand in mine. "I've made peace with my decision, I truly have, but you don't have to. This is my life, but it doesn't have to be yours. And I'm okay with that. I mean, I'll be heartbroken, of course, but I understand."

Will gently tucks a tendril of my hair behind my ear. "I don't want kids either."

I rear back. "What? Of course you do. Why wouldn't you?"

"Because I don't. My kids are my animals. They're enough. Always have been."

Swiping his hand away, I stand. "You're just saying that. Don't brush this off like it's nothing."

He stands too. "I'm not."

"I think you are."

"Don't tell me what I think and feel, Elizabeth."

"I'm not."

"Yeah, you are."

"Damn it, Will! I just want you to let this all sink in, properly. Really understand what it means. I'm locked into this lifestyle; you're not."

"I know what it means."

"You don't. You need to think about this for longer than five fucking minutes," I seethe.

The doorbell rings, and we both look toward the front door.

I sigh, my shoulders slumping. "I need to get that."

"I'm not going anywhere, sweetheart."

Huffing, I make my way to the door, look into the peephole, and find Lucy on the doorstep. "Shit!"

"Who is it?" Will whispers, his beard tickling my ear.

"Jesus!" I nearly jump out of my skin at his close proximity. "It's Lucy." Scowling at him, I open the door and say, "Hi" hoping she doesn't want to speak to Carly.

"Hi." She gives Will a quizzical glance then focuses back on me. "Is Carly here?"

Crap! "Yes, she is."

"Can I come in?"

It's probably not a good idea, but I step back and gesture for her to enter. "Surrre. I don't think she'll speak to you though."

Lucy glides past me like an ethereal being, and I swear for a second that she *is* Belle from *Beauty and the Beast.*

"So, she told you." Lucy hangs her hands, one over the other, in front of her waist.

"She did."

171

A half-smile creeps onto her face, and she points to Will then to me. "Are the two of you…?"

"Maybe," I snap.

Her smile widens. "That's wonderful!"

Will winks at Lucy and lifts his chin, smug-like.

I turn to him. "Go home."

His smugness vanishes. "What? Why?"

"Take the time to think about what I've told you. *Really* take the time. You can't do that here, now, with all this shit going on."

"You're kicking me out?"

"Yes, but"—I stretch up on my tippytoes and lightly peck his lips—"I'm hoping you'll come back. And if you don't, I understand, and I won't hold it against you."

Will threads his hand across the back of my head and pulls me to him, teasing my lips apart with his tongue, his kiss firm and direct.

"I'll see you tomorrow, sweetheart."

CHAPTER SEVENTEEN

*C*arly and Derek sorted their shit out in the weeks that followed, thank God, and it was now time for Will and me to do the same.

He sent me numerous texts, telling me he thought about what I said and that his mind remained unchanged. It was what I wanted to hear, of course, but as painful as it was, I deliberately kept him at bay, forcing distance between us in the hope it would give him time to factor in every aspect that needed factoring. So I'd continuously replied to his texts, saying *Take more time.* I didn't want him pursuing a future with me if he wasn't one hundred per cent sure I was worth the sacrifice. Because that's exactly what being with me is—a sacrifice, a severing of ties to parenthood. And a decision like that deserves more than a sweeping thought.

Yawning, I stretch as I shuffle into the kitchen and switch on the kettle, phone in hand, Will's latest messages on the screen.

Will: Elizabeth, stop avoiding me.

Will: I don't need more time

A flicker of pain tickles my chest, and I rest my palm over my heart, unsure whether or not he really has thought about what being with me means. I know I can't avoid him any longer, and I don't want to. Every moment spent with him sparks new hope in ways I didn't know existed.

In a perfect world, I'd be enough for him and he'd be enough for me. We'd fill each other's voids and soothe the constant white noise. We'd smile for the other, bleed for the other, breathe for the other. We'd love enough. We'd be enough.

But the world isn't perfect. It's the water's edge, enticing but rippled, murky and unclear, and the only way to find out what's underneath is to dip in your toe and hope for the best.

I'm ready to dip now; I just hope he is, too, like he says he is, but for the right reasons.

Leaning against the kitchen cupboards, I draw in a deep breath, about to reply, when another text comes through.

Will: Knock knock.

I giggle.

Me: Who's there?

Will: Open your front door and see

My head springs up, and I shuffle in my slippers along the hallway, my skin prickling with excitement when a towering shadow swims across the frosted glass panel beside the front door.

This is it, make or break.

Puffing out a breath, I shake my hands, shedding the tension from my body, and unlatch the lock, swinging open the door to find him standing on the doorstep wearing a white polo shirt, collar—as always—up. His sunglasses are perched on his head, and one hand is in the back pocket of his jeans, the other braced on the doorframe, his inked bicep taut and deliciously obtrusive.

"Hi," I say, exhaling with a whoosh.

He looks me up and down, a lazy grin forming on his face. "Mornin', sweetheart."

I glance down, unsure what he's stirred about, only to find that my sleep shirt is stained.

Scrunching up the spot, my laugh is a little foolish. "I... er... I spilled my Milo last night."

He steps closer. "Cute."

I step back. "It's not cute. It's piggy."

He steps closer again, a predatory glint in his eyes. "Cute piggy."

"Wait!" I hold up my hand. "We need to talk first."

Will wraps his fingers around mine and brings my wrist to his lips, his eyes alight with mischief and lust as he presses a kiss to my skin.

My knees wobble.

My eyelids close.

"There's nothing to talk about," he whispers.

My eyes snap open again, and I snatch my hand back and place it on my hip. "Oh, yes, there is! I need you to take this seriously."

"I am."

"No, you're not." I point at him. "You have sex eyes. Nothing is serious with you when you have sex eyes."

Will chuckles and waggles his damn sex eyes.

Growling, I turn on my heel and head back to the kitchen. "Coffee?"

I don't wait for his answer; he's having one whether he likes it or not.

Grabbing the coffee and sugar canisters, I lift an eyebrow when he stops in the doorway and speaks.

"I am taking this seriously, Elizabeth."

"Just because you used my full name does not mean you're taking this seriously." I open the cupboard, pull out a coffee mug, and slam it on the benchtop. "I won't have kids, Will. *Ever.*"

"I know."

"And I might get cancer again."

He pushes off the doorframe, moves to where I'm standing, and takes my hands in his, his voice calm. "I know."

"My life isn't simple. It's an ugly time bomb that might explode or simply tick forever. I don't have a choice in this, but you do."

"I know."

Tears prick my eyes. "Stop saying that."

"What else do you want me to say?"

"I... I don't know... that it scares you as much as it scares me." A tear spills from my eye onto my cheek.

Will reaches up and wipes it away. "But it doesn't."

"Well, it should."

"Why? Because all men and women should want kids and live the perfect, cosy life?"

"Yes!"

"Believe it or not, not everyone wants that." He trails his fingertips along my hairline then tucks a tendril behind my ear. "It's boring."

I scoff. "That's stupid."

"It's not stupid. I don't want boring, I never have. I want fun, excitement, the unknown. I want a challenge, not what everyone else wants or has. I want the good times and the hard times. I want *you*."

"But why?" I sob. "Why do you want me?"

"Because you're hot as fuck."

I shove him. "I'm serious!"

He grabs for me again. "I know! I'm sorry. I know."

We stare each other down before he says, voice calm, "Because you're serious when I'm not. Because you're short and I'm tall. Because I make you smile when you don't want to smile. Because you're fierce and see the world for what it is. Because you're smart, funny, beautiful, kind, and fucking annoying. Because you're you, sweetheart. That's why I want you. That's why I choose *you*."

"But you shouldn't have to choose." I close my eyes, inhaling deeply before slowly breathing out. "I'll be the reason you're not a father, and one day, you'll resent me for it. You'll regret this choice you were forced to make, and I can't…. I just don't think I can live with that."

"You're not forcing me to make this choice. It was made long before you came along."

I close my eyes, praying he's telling me the truth. "So this is why you never settled down, because you told every woman you dated you didn't want children?"

"Yes, and no."

"No?"

He smirks. "None of them were you."

I can't help the smile that lights my eyes. "Are you sure?"

"There's no question here."

"We'll never have the fairy tale we deserve."

Will shakes his head and smiles. "You don't get it, do you? We can make our own fairy tale, together."

"But—"

"No buts. You get me, and I get you. We fit. Sometimes it's a squash—" He looks himself over then gives me a sheepish grin. "—but we fit. Like a pipe to an elbow joint."

I blink. "A what?"

Sliding his fingers under my arms, he hoists me onto the benchtop and settles between my legs, his hands on my thighs. "Not all pieces that connect are the same." He tips my chin up. "You're one piece, and I'm the other." Leaning forward, he softly pecks my lips. "We're not the same, but we connect."

I'm about to tell him he's the sweetest man I've ever known when he lifts his hand and makes a circle with his thumb and pointer finger and then pokes his other pointer finger inside it, pulling out and repeating the motion several times.

"See?" He grins, all teeth and tenacity. "Connection."

I push at his chest and laugh. "I'll give you connection."

Will growls and reaches around my back, squeezing my arse before sliding my body across the benchtop into his. I gasp, my core a flutter of desire as I lock my ankles behind his back.

Searching his stormy sex eyes, I want to ask one more time if he's sure I'm worth the sacrifice, but it's as if he knows what I'm thinking, his pinched expression saying I should shut the hell up and focus on the fact that his cock is now pressing my clit.

Pushing the thought out of my mind, I surrender and rock into him, reaching down to cup my hand over his erection and giving him a light squeeze. He growls again, threads his hand into my hair, and pulls me to his mouth, his kiss hungry as he rocks his cock into the palm of my hand, hard and unashamed.

Will's tongue sweeps mine a little faster, a little messier, and all I want is to feel his silky warm skin against mine.

Lifting his t-shirt over his head, I let him take over and remove it while I unbutton the top of my sleep shirt. He tosses his tee on the floor then coaxes the lapels of mine apart, his fingers skating across my breasts. My nipples peak, and I dig my heels into his arse and grab at the buckle of his jeans, frustrated as I fumble with the zip.

"Off," I demand, pushing the denim over his arse and down his legs.

Will kisses my neck and nibbles my earlobe, his lips featherlight as he trails them down my body, over my collarbone, and between my breasts, a growl emanating from his throat when his teeth snag the centre of my bra.

"Off," he mumbles, sliding my shirt from my shoulders as I reach back and unhook the clasp.

I remove it and lean back on my hands, legs spread, chest bare.

"Fuck me, you're beautiful," he says, cupping my breasts.

Will rubs the pads of his thumbs over my nipples before leaning down and sucking one into his mouth. My nerve endings fizzle to life, heat surging my body so fast I almost combust.

Gasping, my head falls back, and I arch into him as he swaps breasts then runs his hands along my thighs, pushing up the hem of my shirt.

"Touch me," I beg, not recognising my voice or the words coming out of my mouth. I've never begged anyone for anything.

He presses his finger to my clit.

My pulse spikes.

My underwear sticks to my skin.

He groans, so I rock against his finger and bite my lip, my heavy-lidded eyes holding his.

Will doesn't hesitate and tears my panties down my legs, spreads my knees apart, and leans forward, his tongue a continuous, delicious lash.

A moan so arduous and filthy sweeps past my lips, my back bowing as I grip the edge of the benchtop. Will props my feet on his shoulders then slides two fingers inside me, his lips and beard glistening as he smiles like a greedy devil. I want to smile, too, but I can't, the pressure and sensation with each slide, twitch, and flick are almost too much to bear.

"Will," I pant.

He plunges his fingers deeper, brows drawn, muscles tense, his fingertips stroking the perfect spot. Heat explodes all over my body, and I cry out, writhing uncontrollably.

"That's it, sweetheart." He pumps me over and over, slower and slower until he slides his fingers out, yanks his underwear down, and presses the tip of his cock against my clit.

"Oh God!" I scream as he drives into me, rears back, and drives in again, his hands gripping my hips as his body slams mine like a drumbeat—quick, fast, relentless, his rhythm perfect.

Will roars, dirty and guttural, and I almost come again just from the sheer sexiness of it. Everything about him is wild and animalistic—the ink etched across his skin, the sweat-dampened hair on his chest, the heavy and hooded look in his eyes. He's no clean-cut, prim and proper Prince Charming, and I sure as hell don't want him to be. Not now, not ever.

His eyes meet mine, sparkling as he smiles, our breathing laboured. And just like that, dark and dirty turns to light.

"Come here," he says and offers his hand to pull me up.

Wrapping my arms around his broad shoulders, I kiss him hard, holding him tight, never wanting to let go. He chose me. He *wants* me, just as I am—a little damaged but not broken. And for the first time in my life, I can see a happily ever after.

I relax, snuggle into the crook of his neck, and murmur, "I love you." I don't care if he doesn't say it back. I said it for me, and for now, that's enough.

"Er... can we come in now?" Carly calls out from the hallway.

My body stiffens, and I jerk back, eyes wide, the shade *"mortification"* my new complexion.

"Shit!" I shove Will away and pull my shirt over my shoulders. "Uh... just a minute," I sing out.

He lifts his jeans and chuckles as he fastens his zip and button.

"Stop laughing," I hiss. "Where's my underwear?"

"Don't know. I tossed them."

I try to murder him with my eyeballs.

"I think I see them on the table," Carly says. "Which is disgusting, by the way. I eat there."

Oh, my God! "No, you don't," I snap. "You eat in the lounge room." I point to my underwear and mouth, *"Quick!"* to Will. *"Go get them."*

He strides over to the table and glances down the hallway. "Hey, Jaws."

"Hey!"

He picks up my underwear and twirls it around his finger before tipping his chin and adding, "Mate."

Mate? My face burns hotter than a jalapeno.

"Derek?" I mouth, cringing.

Will nods once, and I simply want to strangle him. How can he be so cool, calm, and collected? So relaxed and proud?

He's a nutcase.

Snatching my underwear from his twirling fingertip, I quickly step into them, pull them up, and smooth down my shirt and hair.

"Uh… you can come in now," I croak.

Carly skips into the room, her smile obnoxious and sleazy. "That sounded so hot." She sits her arse on the breakfast barstool as if I'm about to dish up a feast with a side of sexual gossip.

I gape at her.

"I knew it! I knew something was going on." She picks up an apple from the fruit bowl, tosses it into the air, and catches it before spinning her chair to face Derek. "What did I say, huh?"

He presses his lips together, shrugs, and opens his hands, ready to take a catch.

Carly takes a bite then tosses it his way.

Are you kidding me? They're playing catch right after listening to my pound-town session. Who does that?

I can't look at them. I can't look at Will. I can't even be in this room right now.

"Be right back," I mumble and hightail it out of there.

After heading straight for my bathroom, I close the door, grab a handful of toilet paper, and clean myself up.

"Lib," Carly says as she knocks on my door. "You okay?"

I take in my reflection in the mirror, cheeks as red as my hair, and burst into laughter. "Yes."

The door creaks open, and I bury my head in my hands and peek at her through my spread fingers. "Oh, my God!"

"You can say that again." She bites her lip. "So Will...? What? How? When?"

"It's a long story."

"Best you tell me before I punch you in the tit."

I wash my hands and attempt to fix my hair.

"You look like a slutty Troll Doll."

"Stop it." I laugh. "I do not."

"Do." Carly leans against the doorframe, crosses her arms over her chest, and points at my girly bits. "What I want to know is how the fuck does he fit in there?"

I look down then back up again. "I have no idea." Drying my hands on the towel, I add, "But he does. Perfectly."

"I heard," she drawls.

We both head into my bedroom and sit down on the bed.

"I'm sorry I didn't tell you," I say. "But you had a lot going on with Derek, and I didn't want to add to that."

"Libby, I'm your best friend. When there's a new cock in your life, you need to tell me."

"I know." I grab my seashell cushion and hug it to my chest. "We just had a few things to sort out first."

"Things?" She touches my hand. "Does he know?"

"About my illness? Yes."

"Good." Carly lets out a breath. "Will's a great guy, Lib."

"I know." I scrunch my face and spit out, "We've kinda been dating for a few months."

"A *few months?*" She stands and narrows her eyes at me. "I can't believe you."

I stand, too, and quickly kiss her cheek. "Yeah, sorry."

Carly playfully shoves me, so I shove her back.

We head into the kitchen, and I've the overwhelming need to wipe down the benchtop, so I grab a cloth and rush to scrub the surface.

"You fucked on the bench?" Carly says, eyebrows high.

Will grins.

She nudges his shoulder. "Nice!"

I roll my eyes and rinse the cloth at the sink.

"So does this mean you're coming with us tonight?" she asks.

I half turn and glance over my shoulder. "Tonight?"

"Yeah, to Bryce and Lexi's for the guys' jam session."

Will drums his fingers on the benchtop. "Yep, she's coming."

"I am?"

They all smile at me. "You are!"

CHAPTER EIGHTEEN

"*H*i, guys, come in," Alexis says as she opens the door to the City Towers villa.

She gives Carly a hug and kiss on the cheek, followed by Will, then me. At first, I feel a little weird; Alexis and I aren't close. But she has a warm, welcoming aura about her, and after a quick squeeze and excited giggle, I feel less like a tag-along when she moves on to Derek.

"Come here, you. So much has happened since the penthouse blew up, and I haven't properly thanked you for all you did that day." She wraps her arms around him and hugs him tight.

"Okay, okay. That's enough. Anyone would think he's a damn hero," Bryce says, smiling as he strides barefoot into the foyer, wearing jeans and a shirt, sleeves rolled up, beer in hand.

Alexis playfully rolls her eyes, lets go of Derek, and moves to Bryce, her long blonde hair cascading down her back as she drapes her hands over his broad shoulders. "Everyone knows you're my one and only hero."

Carly puts her finger to her mouth and gags.

Bryce smirks.

Oh wow!

"There it is," Will murmurs behind his hand. "That's the look that makes all women drop their panties." He reaches into the back of my jeans and basically gives me a wedgie.

"What are you do—"

"Making sure they stay up."

"Oh, my God!" I swipe his hand away and inconspicuously try to un-wedgie myself.

Carly scrunches her face and says, "You got worms?"

"No! I'm just…." I huff. "Never mind."

Will rests his arm on my shoulder and pulls me into his side. "Bryce, you remember Lib?"

"I do." He reaches out, takes my hand, and lifts it to his lips. "Welcome, Ms Hanson."

My eyes grow wide, but Alexis just smiles.

"Okay, okay." Will playfully shoves him back. "Anyone would think you're a damn billionaire."

Bryce chuckles. "Come in, guys. It's not the same as the penthouse, but it'll have to do."

We step into the living area, and I'm in awe. *It'll have to do? Is he nuts? This place is incredible.* Creamy white walls, mahogany door trims and countertops, gold fixtures and fittings, leather sofas. Even the floor-to-ceiling, gold-embroidered sheer curtains are opulent.

"There's a bathroom and toilet on this level, as well as one upstairs. Feel free to use either," Alexis says. She waddles behind a bar counter and pops open a bottle of wine. "Drinks are here. Help yourselves."

Bryce slides in behind her and takes four beers out of the fridge. "We'll be in the studio, my love. Come in when you're ready."

He kisses her neck and gently caresses her full belly, and I can't help but look away.

"You'll get used to it," Carly says. "They can't keep their hands off one another. They're like rich, horny rabbits."

Alexis laughs. "We are not!"

Bryce kisses her one more time. "We are!"

She shakes her head. "We'll be in soon." Alexis opens another bottle of wine. "Libby, what would you like, white, red, or this non-alcoholic pink shit I have to drink?"

"Oh." I cringe. "Just a glass of red, thanks."

"Carls?"

"White for me."

She goes about pouring the drinks as the men follow Bryce into another room, and Carly and I take a seat on the sofa behind Charlotte—Alexis's seven-year-old daughter—who's sitting in front of a giant TV on the plushest rug I've ever seen.

"What ya watchin', squirt?" Carly asks.

Both Charlotte and I answer, "*The Little Mermaid.*"

Her twinkling blue eyes land on mine. "You like *The Little Mermaid?*"

I slide off the sofa and onto the floor next to her. "I do! It's my favourite movie ever."

She smiles and hands me her Ariel doll. "Here, you can play with this one. You have the same hair."

I take it from her and hold it next to my face.

She giggles. "I'll play with Ursula."

Charlotte pulls a yuck face, and I copy.

"What's wrong with Ursula?" Carly asks. "She looks like a baaad bitch."

"Aunty Carls, you just swore."

Carly raises her hands. "Sorry."

"For that"—Charlotte tosses Ursula to Carly—"you can play with her."

Carly tosses it back. "I don't play with dolls."

"You sure 'bout that?" Alexis drawls.

Carly glares at her friend of thirty-plus years. Alexis just winks.

Chuckling at the both of them, I leave them to their devices and focus back on the movie. "Ooh, ooh!" I nudge Charlotte. "I love this bit!"

"Me too!" She picks up a fork that's lying among her toys.

"A dinglehopper!" we both say at the same time Scuttle—the eccentric seagull—says it in the movie.

Charlotte threads the fork into her hair and starts combing it. I laugh, and she hands it to me before running off and returning moments later with another fork.

"Now you have a dinglehopper, and I have one."

"Why thank you, Charlotte."

"My friends call me Charli. You're my friend now, so you can call me Charli too."

"My friends call me Libby."

She hugs me. "I like you, Libby."

"Naww, I like you too, Charli."

We sit there, enthralled, combing our hair with dinglehoppers until Ariel—and Charlotte—start singing "Part of Your World."

"This is one of my favourite songs," she says, eyes alight.

"Mine too!"

She frowns. "Then why aren't you singing?"

"Oh." I shake my head. "I can't sing."

"Sure you can. You just open your mouth and say the words in your best voice."

Gah! My heart! What a sweetie.

I scrunch my face. "My best voice isn't very good."

She pouts, and it tugs perfectly on my guilt strings.

"Okay. I'll sing it with you, but you have to promise not to laugh."

"I'd never do that." Charlotte holds up her little finger. "Pinkie swear."

We lock pinkies then sing the rest of the song, joining in with Ariel as she sings about wanting to be a part of the human world, and it strikes me that even in an innocent kids' Disney movie, we tend to want what we don't or can't have. We create an ideal of the perfect life and strive to achieve it, all the while forgetting true perfection is what we make of it. It's human nature, I guess. Well... in Ariel's case, it's mermaid nature.

Giggling when the song ends and Sebastian the crab crashes into the scene, I almost jump a mile when Will whispers into my ear, "Why do you have a fork in your hair?"

"Jeeesusss." I cover my heart with my hand and turn to find him sitting on the sofa behind me. "You scared the crap out of me."

His eyes are dreamy, his smile even dreamier.

"What?" I have to move away; he's too damn sexy.

Grasping the handle of the fork, I comb my hair and add, "It's not a fork."

"Looks like a fork to me."

"It's a dinglehopper, Will," Charlotte says.

"A what?"

"A dingle— Never mind." I slide it out of my hair then glance around, noticing Alexis and Carly are no longer in the room. "Where is everyone?"

"In the studio."

"Oh. Sorry, I didn't realise. I was just watching—"

"*The Little Mermaid?*"

My cheeks flush with embarrassment. "Yeah."

He licks his lips, gives me his sex-eyes, then takes a swig of his beer. "Cute."

"Don't," I say, pointing at him as I stand up. "I know what you're doing."

Will chuckles then scruffs Charlotte's hair. "Thanks for looking after Libby while I was gone."

"Anytime. I like her. We're friends."

Biting back my laughter, I hand her the fork. "Thank you for lending me your dinglehopper."

She stands up and gives me a hug. "Keep it. Mum won't mind."

"Really?" I'm not about to take their cutlery home, so I go along with her beautiful gesture so that I don't offend or upset her. "I've always wanted one of my own. Thank you so much."

"You're welcome." She fiddles with her fingers and twists her body from side to side, seemingly proud of herself. And so she should be—she's such a delightful child.

"Bye, Charli."

I wave as Will takes my hand in his and leads me into the studio, a room filled with instruments and lined with soundproof, carpeted panels, much like Will's music room only bigger. There's even a pool table, barstools, and sofas.

"Wow! This is impressive," I say.

"Believe it or not, Bryce had one double the size before the fire," he murmurs. "Shame it burnt down."

"This is certainly nothing to sneeze at. The villa is stunning."

"Oh, we know," Alexis says. "The design and building team at City Towers are exceptional. They've pulled out all stops to make this villa seem like home while the penthouse is being rebuilt."

"So did the entire penthouse burn down?"

"No." Alexis hands me my glass of wine. "Structurally, the place is sound, thank God! But, internally, it's completely destroyed. The walls, carpets, furniture, pretty much everything sustained smoke, fire, and water damage."

"I'm so sorry."

She sucks in a breath and glances at Bryce. "It is what it is. Now we rebuild and move on. We have each other, and that's all that matters."

His eyes are full of love as he smiles at her sadly before looking away.

"I'm just glad you're all okay," I say.

"We're getting there." She sips her non-alcoholic pink shit then points to us both. "So, you and Will, huh?"

"Yeah." I slide my hand into the back pocket of his jeans and glance up at him. "He's everything I never knew I wanted."

"Naww, I'm so happy for you both. You make an adorable couple."

"She loves me." Will beams, eyeing me over the rim of his beer bottle as he tips his head back for another swig.

My eyebrows nearly hit the roof, and I choke. "Wha—"

"That's what you said after we fucked in the kitchen."

I choke again, and Alexis covers her mouth with her hand, muffling her laugh.

"I—"

"Yeah, you did, Lib," Carly adds. She leans over the pool table and takes a shot, sinking two balls.

Will raises his beer. "Jaws!"

Hoping to change the subject, I ask, "Why do you call her that?"

"Because she's a shark. You know, pool shark. Whooped Derek's arse the night we met her."

"She did not." Derek removes his leather jacket then takes the pool cue from Carly. "I let you win, baby."

Will coughs into his hand. "Bullshit."

"You think you can beat her, smartarse?"

"No! She's motherfucking Jaws."

Carly chomps her teeth together, and I laugh. The nickname suits her.

"So what are you gonna play for us tonight?" Alexis asks as she makes her way over to where Bryce is propped on a barstool.

He lifts her with ease onto his lap. "What do you want us to play?"

"Fleetwood."

Will groans.

Bryce smirks. *Damn!*

"If Alexis wants Fleetwood, then Fleetwood it is."

"Fine. But it's 'The Chain' or nothing."

Alexis happy-claps.

"How 'bout you, sweetheart?" Will asks. "What do you want us to play?"

"Oh." I shake my head. "I don't mind."

"Pick a song, preferably one with a wicked beat."

I shrug. "You choose. I don't really know that many."

"Come on... 'Sunday Bloody Sunday,' 'Seven Nation Army,' 'Map of the Problematique,' 'My Generation'—"

"Ooh, yes! I like that one."

He kisses my head. "Done."

"And 'In the Air Tonight'."

"No can do. I don't have a gorilla suit." Will swigs the last of his beer, his eyes mischievous.

I rest the rim of my wine glass on my bottom lip and playfully glare at him. "How convenient for you."

Alexis slides off Bryce's lap and says, "Be right back," before scurrying out of the room. Perhaps she needs to pee. I'm not sure how far along in her pregnancy she is, but by the looks of her belly, I'd say she's in the pee-every-other-minute trimester.

"She got worms too?" Carly prompts.

Derek laughs. "So what about you, baby, what do you want us to play?"

She slams the cue tip into the white ball, sending it hurtling towards the black, the black landing in the corner pocket. "How 'bout the *Jaws* theme song!"

Will and I burst into laughter.

Even Bryce throws his head back, amused. "That'll be game over, mate," he says, flicking through what looks like sheets of music.

Derek raises his hands and rests them on his shaved head. "Fuck me."

Carly puts down the cue, saunters over to him, and slides her hands around his waist. "With pleasure." She lifts the hem of his t-shirt and runs her hands up his back.

I can't help but smile at them because Carly deserves what she's found with Derek. They may have had a rocky start, but rocks form the base of most solid foundations. Without them, we'd just have sand, and most things sink into sand.

I'm confident these two won't sink.

"You look happy, sweetheart," Will murmurs.

I divert my gaze to him and blink. "I am."

"Because you love me?"

"Oh, my God!" I wriggle out of his grip. "Can we just move past that already?"

He chuckles. "Not gonna happen."

Before I can put up some lame form of defence, Alexis waddles back into the room. "Will, can I borrow you for a second?"

He points to his chest then fires Bryce a shit-eating grin. "Sure."

Bryce narrows his gaze then shrugs and goes back to flicking through the sheet music.

"Lib," Carly says. "Rack 'em up. You're breaking."

"But I'm worse than Derek."

"Hey!" He picks up a guitar and tunes it. "For the last time, I let her win."

"He's so cute," she says condescendingly.

I trudge to the pool table, place my wine glass on a ledge, and chalk my cue. "You've been warned. I really do suck at pool."

"That's because you suck at math."

"I do not suck at math. I'll have you know I'm better than most of our faculty, especially Oliver."

"Speaking of Mr Bunt," she says, wobbling her head like she always does when she says his name, "have you told him about Will yet?"

"It's none of his business."

"I know that. I just want to be there when you do it."

Rolling my eyes, I bend over and try to line the cue between my knuckles. "Why? What's the big deal?"

"What's the big deal?" She rests her hands on the edge of the table. "Are you serious?"

"Yes. Why wouldn't I be?" I push the cue and hit nothing but air. "Argh! See? I suck. You may as well play with yourself."

She raises a seductive eyebrow. "I do."

Derek nods.

"You know what I mean," I say.

"Libby, Libby, Libby." Carly moves to my side, rearranges the position of the cue in my hand, then steps back. "Move your arm back nice and slow, then bring it forward just as slowly. When you're as good as me, that's when you can slam the shit out of it."

I do as I'm told and hit the white ball, but it doesn't hit anything else.

"You're supposed to aim for the coloured balls, yeah?"

I give her a deadpan look.

"Math, remember? It's all about angles."

"Since when are you any good at math?" I ask.

"Since it was the only subject at school I ever enjoyed."

"Really?"

"Helped that the teacher was a fucking god!"

Derek raises his eyebrow at her.

She blows him a kiss. "Anyway, back to Mr Cunt." Carly holds up her hand. "Sorry, I mean Bunt. Mr Bunt."

"What about him?"

"He likes you, Lib. Little wanker has had a little stiffy for you for quite some time."

"You're wrong. The guy's a jerk. A decent teacher, yes, but a selfish jerk nonetheless. The only little stiffy he has is for himself."

She cackles. "Jerk or not, he likes you."

"Who likes you?" Will questions, his voice muffled.

Carly and I turn toward the door to find Will in a full-length gorilla suit, Alexis behind him with a grin so wide I'm not sure where it starts and ends.

"Dude," Derek says.

Bryce clutches his waist and lets out a belly laugh. "I fucking love you, honey."

Alexis waddles past and winks at me. "Libby wanted the gorilla suit, so I rang the entertainment department and, voila, they had one."

I bite my lip and finally burst into laughter when Will gallops like a gorilla toward me, making *oo-oo* and *aah-aah* noises before engulfing and lifting me into his furry arms.

"This is a once-off, Elizabeth, because I love you too." He mashes his hairy, plastic face against mine then puts me down, sits behind the drums, and pounds his chest a few times.

I cover my mouth with my hand and shake my head, astounded.

"How the hell am I supposed to pick up the sticks?" he says, fumbling for a second before managing to somehow hold them and tap the snare.

Giddiness tingles my fingertips, toes, and spine when Bryce strums the electric guitar and Derek starts singing about feeling something in the air tonight.

"Oh, my God!" I say, taking a seat on the sofa, clapping and giggling like the girls in my class.

Alexis and Carly take a seat beside me, Carly wolf-whistling and Alexis sounding a "Whooo!"

Despite the hilarity of an ape playing the drums, the guys are exceptionally talented, Derek's voice as smooth as oil, and Bryce's fingers faultless. But as good as they are, I'm not paying much attention to them, instead completely stunned as what Will just said to me finally sinks in.

"He loves me too," I blurt quietly, but loud enough for Alexis and Carly to hear.

"We know," they say simultaneously.

I blink. "Oh. Good."

Carly squeezes my leg. "It's more than good, sweets. It's fucking excellent!"

Bursting into laughter yet again, I focus back on Will, loving his jovial personality as he pretends to sniff his armpits and do stupid gorilla-type things like scratch his head between taps.

"Ready?" Alexis prompts.

Bracing myself for the infamous drum solo, we ready our hands and air drum the beat along with him, Will slamming the drums in quick succession, his entire body bouncing with the beat.

I squeal and stomp my feat, laughing uncontrollably. It's the best thing I've ever seen.

The song winds down, and I don't know what comes over me, but I pretty much charge him, wrapping my arms around his neck and knocking him from his stool, both of us crashing to the ground with me on top of him.

"I take it you like the suit," he says, voice muffled by his mask.

"Yes, you dork."

"It's fuckin' itchy." He throws the mask off. "And I can't fuckin' breathe."

Placing my hands on either side of his face, I lean forward and kiss him, soft but firm before pulling back.

Will pounds his chest again then grabs my hips. "Come on, let's go make some gorilla babies."

CHAPTER NINETEEN

*M*y eyes grow wide the same time his do.

"Shit, sweetheart." He sits up, me astride him, and holds me tight. "I'm sorry. I didn't mean to say—"

"It's okay." I trail my fingertips down the side of his face, following his hairline, the sorrow and remorse in his eyes more painful than his words. "It's an easy thing to say, right?"

He buries his head in my chest. "Yes, but it's still shitful."

"Hey! Trust me, it won't be the last time you say it either. Believe it or not, my mum and sister still slip up."

"What did he say wrong?" Alexis whispers loud enough for me to hear.

I look over at her. "I can't have children."

"Oh!" She touches her belly. "I'm… I'm so sorry."

"Thank you, but apologies aren't necessary." I stand and brush myself off. "I've known for a long time."

Holding out my hands to help Will up, which in hindsight is ridiculous given his size compared to mine, I grin when he takes them anyway and unfurls like… well… like a giant gorilla.

"I need to get this thing off and see to my woman."

I scoff. "I'm not your *woman*."

"You are." He reaches behind his neck, turning in a circle, frustrated when he can't reach the zip.

"Come here, let me help you."

"Nah, leave him in it. It's an improvement."

Will picks up the mask and launches it at Derek. "Chuck that on, then we'll have improvement."

I laugh. "Is it always like this with you guys?"

"Yes," Alexis and Carly say, both unperturbed.

I'm glad; I kinda like it. I've never had a group of friends with partners before, and the playful—mind you, somewhat insulting at times—interaction is rather lovely.

Will steps out of the suit and threads his arms over mine from behind, hugging me tight. "I'm sorry," he whispers.

Turning in his arms to face him, I skate my fingertips over his inked arm and whisper back, "I know."

He leans down and pecks my lips. Soft. Quick. Sensual. The tenderness almost buckles my knees and takes my breath away.

"Right," I pant, "I'm glad we sorted that out." Patting his chest, I push back a little and turn to Alexis. "Thank you for finding the suit."

She waggles her eyebrows at Will. "Anytime."

"No, not 'anytime.' *One* time."

I shrug. "I don't know... I think it should become part of your act."

Will's answer is a flat "No!"

"Actually," Derek says, looking at the mask in his hand. "I think you might be on to something."

Bryce smirks.

"Sweetheart, what are you doing to me?"

I laugh. "I'm kidding. You don't need it. You're all really great without the gimmick. I loved it."

"It's a great song," Bryce says.

"Agreed." Will nibbles my earlobe. "One of the best drum fills of all time."

I squirm at the ticklish feathering of his lips. "What's a drum fill?"

"It's a short passage, a riff, which is used to 'fill' the transition between parts of a song. Like a guitar solo."

"Oh!"

"I'll show you." Will lets me go, sits behind the drums again, and nods toward Bryce, saying "'Wipeout'" before drumming a beat. Bryce joins in with the guitar, and I instantly recognise the infamous beach song.

After a few more seconds, Will holds the snare still and says, "Another good fill is in 'Africa' by Toto." He plays that, too, and again, I recognise it, which is interesting given I've never paid much attention to drumbeats before. I've never had reason to. Now, though, I'm enjoying relating to something he is so passionate about.

"And 'Be Somebody' by Kings of Leon," he adds. "Fucking great beats."

Alexis practically moans. "I lovvve Kings."

"We know," Derek says.

She moans again and locks eyes with Bryce. "That night when I saw them live at the Tel V Awards...."

"Honey." He clicks his neck from side to side, voice low, almost predatory.

She sucks in a breath and shakes her head as if to compose herself.

"So they were *that* good?" I ask, eyes wide.

She doesn't look at me, instead keeping her eyes fixed on Bryce. "They were. But he"—she gestures toward him—"was *much* better." She plays with her bottom lip. "Best night of my life."

"And mine," he says.

The room grows silent as they both take each other in. I've heard it said many times that two people can create electricity, and I've always thought that saying to be stupid. But oh my God, sparks are flying between these two. I'm almost tempted to duck in fear of being electrocuted.

"I think they're going to fuck," Carly says.

"I think we are too." Alexis teases Bryce with a smile, and he growls.

"Right." Will taps his sticks together. "How 'bout a bit of Grohl and Nirvana? 'Smells Like Teen Spirit.' Haven't played that one in a while."

Derek and Bryce both strum their guitars after Will counts them in, and they play the Nirvana song. Now I've never been one of those girls to go gaga over rock stars; I've always found them sweaty and gross. But Will, behind a drum set? Someone hold my beer, wine, whatever the hell I'm drinking.

Biting my thumbnail, warmth spreads across my body, settling at my core as I take in the way his muscles tense with every hit, tap, and smash, his pecs firm while the rest of his body bounces to his beat.

Sweat forms on his brow, concentration etching his face as he loses himself in the song, and there's absolutely nothing gross about it. Quite the opposite—erotic and incredibly sexy.

"They're incredibly sexy when they play, aren't they?" Alexis says, nudging me, eyes on Bryce.

Shit! Did I say that bit out loud?

I exhale. "So it's not just me then?"

"No!" Carly and Alexis both say. They give each other a knowing look then glance at me and smile, and I'm beginning to understand what that look means.

"I'm screwed."

Carly laughs. "Why?"

"Because if he keeps this up, this sexy, sweaty, fuckable rock god stuff, that's all we'll be doing… screwing."

Alexis stands and gathers our empty wine glasses. "Welcome to my life."

"And mine." Carly stands and helps her. "You know, we should have our own band name, like how the wives and girlfriends of footballers are called WAGs."

"How 'bout the Burnt Burgers?" Alexis suggests.

What an awful name.

"Yes!" Carly laughs. "Perfect!"

"How is that perfect?" I ask.

She clutches her waist. "Trust me, it is."

"So would my fellow Burnt Burgers like another glass of wine?" Alexis jiggles while holding up the empty flutes.

"Is that even a question?" Carly replies.

I shrug. "Sure, why not."

We continue to drink and fawn over the guys as they play Alexis her Fleetwood, some Kings, followed by Muse, and finishing with "My Generation". I've never had so much silly fun, dancing around, singing along, drinking, and trying to play pool, to the point of not wanting to leave. *Ever!*

"M-m-mummm myyyyy generation," I sing, twirling around.

"Someone's having fun." Will slides his hand across the small of my back and tugs me to him.

I stop twirling and look around the room for the fun person. "Who?"

"Annnd a bit too much to drink." He chuckles and takes my wine glass from my hand.

"Hey!" I pout. "I have nnnot."

"Sweetheart"—he tips the glass upside down—"it's empty. And the song is finished."

Snapping my head from left to right, I realise he's correct just as the room starts spinning. "Wheee!" I giggle. "Who moved the ground?" I look down at our feet, trying to find the culprit.

Carly laughs. "I've never seen her this drunk. It's excellent!"

"Lies!" I point at her but somehow poke Will. "I've never ssseen youuu this drunk."

"I'm over here." She waves her three hands.

"I think it's time to get you in bed," Will says.

I shimmy down his tree-trunk body. "Yesss. Let's do the bed."

"As kinky as that sounds, sweetheart, I'll pass."

"You pass? Y-You can't pass. I pass." I try to shimmy back up, but my body won't work. "Wh… why am I nnnot working?" I fall back onto my bum and roll around, laughing. "I'm not working." I snort.

"Oh goodness! Please tell me you're staying in one of the suites," Alexis says.

"We are." Will scoops me up as if I'm a little flower.

"I'm nnnot a flower," I assure him.

He chuckles. "Glad to know."

"I'm Libby."

"Yes, you are."

My head falls back, and I wonder where my body has gone. I hope it comes back. I like my body, for the most part. I mean it's a little broken, but it's mine.

"You need a hand getting her to your room?" Bryce asks.

"Nup. I got it." He swings me around.

"I'm flying."

"Have fun," Alexis says.

We fly around the hotel until I float onto a cloud.

"I li—ike this cloud. This cloud is myyy friend."

He chuckles. "I can tell."

Will undoes my sneakers and jeans then tugs them off.

"You f-found my body."

He kisses my leg. "I never lost it."

"Do m-myyy feet smell?"

"Yes."

I cry. "They're bad feet."

"They're not. Feet are supposed to smell."

"You smell."

The cloud moves and my blouse opens itself and flies away.

"Do I just?"

"Yesss, you smell like a yummy tree."

He sniffs. "A yummy tree?"

"Yes, nom nom nom." I pretend I'm the Cookie Monster. "Me love cookie. Nom nom nom. I want to eat you."

Will bursts into laughter. "The feeling is mutual, sweetheart."

I try to bite him, but he's not there.

"You need to open your eyes to eat."

"They are open."

He touches my face. "You're cute as fuck when you're drunk."

"You're cute as fuck."

"And you're worth every sacrifice in the world."

"You are." I take a deep breath and exhale, my cloud swallowing me. "You're my Prince Charm—"

* * *

I WAKE THE NEXT DAY, my body hot, limbs heavy, my head pounding like ritual drums. At first, I think I'm in some hellish heaven, the room ethereal white, my eyes burning like a bitch.

"Am I dead?" I grumble.

Will mumbles, "I hope not."

"Where am I?"

"In bed."

"Who's bed?"

"Bryce's."

"*What?*" I shoot up, blinking as my heart attacks my chest. "How—"

Will chuckles, his giant arms pulling me back to the mattress. "Relax. We're in one of his suites."

Groaning, I cover my face with my hands and bury my head into the crook of his neck. "What happened?"

"You enjoyed yourself."

"How much?"

"A lot."

"Oh, my God! I can't remember anything after 'My Generation'."

"Yep, that sounds about right."

"How did I get here?"

"You flew."

"What?" I can't help but laugh, even though I have a strong feeling last night is not a laughing matter. "How embarrassing. I'm so sorry. Alexis and Bryce must think I'm…. I don't even know what they must think."

He rolls me onto my back, his finger teasing circles around my breasts. "They think you're great." He leans down and sucks my nipple into his mouth before releasing it with a pop. "Just like I do." His masterful hands massage my chest as he trails his lips down my stomach.

I close my eyes and squirm under the tickle of his beard. "I think you're great too."

"I know."

Threading my fingers through his hair, I grip him tight when he nudges my clit. "And how do you know that?"

"Because you love me."

I smile. "You love me too."

"I do."

He dips his tongue, and I squirm, my head turning to the side, my eyes catching sight of the alarm clock.

"Holy shit!" I clamp his head with my thighs. "It's past one."

"So?"

"So I have school tomorrow. It's the first day of term two. I've got so much to do and prepare."

"That reminds me, Carly said she needs me to drop by the office and fill in some paperwork for the job I did before Christmas, so do you want me to pick you up at the end of the day?"

"Oh. Sure."

He tries to pry my legs apart, his voice stern. "Elizabeth."

"But…." I groan, the digital display taunting me.

"Relax. You've got plenty of time."

"But I don't. I—" I yelp when his teeth graze my knee.

"Open. Your. Legs."

Surrendering, I let my legs fall limp, and he flicks his tongue over my clit.

"Oh Gawd!"

"Thought so."

"Shut up and eat." I peek an eye open to see his reaction; I've never said anything like that before.

Will cocks an eyebrow, slides his hands under my arse, and says, "Me love cookies," before diving between my legs and growling like Cookie Monster.

I squeal and squirm, laughing. "What are you doing?"

"Repaying the favour."

"What?"

"Never mind."

Holding me firm, he laps a little slower. I grip his head and rock against his face, delighting in the bridge of his nose and the bristles on his chin. Soft, hard, rough, smooth.

K.M. GOLLAND

He moans. "That's it, sweetheart. Fuck my tongue."

Will tilts my pelvis, angling me higher while he grabs a pillow and wedges it underneath my arse.

"What are you doi—?"

"Preparing my breakfast."

I laugh. "You can't say that."

"Yes, I can."

"No, you can't. I'm not a meal."

He stops, and I wait for him to say my name like he usually does, but he doesn't. He just sucks his fingers slowly, then slides them inside me, pumping slow before speeding up, dipping to flick, suck, and nip my clit.

Heat surges to my head, stars bursting behind my closed eyes, and I cry out and arch my back, my core clenching as an orgasm rockets through me. Will holds me down as my core contracts, his lips firm over my clit.

He growls, eyes wide, before burying his face in my arousal.

He's so wild and ravenous and easily the single most sexy thing I've ever seen.

Getting to his knees, nose and beard glistening, he licks his lips then slowly strokes his cock, his hand firm but delicate. My throat goes dry, and I draw in a much-needed breath, panting as he confidently palms his shaft, a bead of precum pumping to the tip of his crown.

He looks so... so beautiful. Beautifully rough and rugged. Beautifully raw and sensual. Beautifully virile. He's so damn beautiful that tears sting my eyes.

I blink them back. "I don't want this to end."

He grins. "Neither do I."

"No. Us. I don't want us to end."

His brows pinch. "Neither do I."

"But what if it does? My life is a ticking time bomb, remember? And bombs explode."

He stops milking himself and leans forward, hands firm on the mattress on either side of my head. "If it explodes, I'll be there to pick up the pieces."

"And if it doesn't explode? If it just ticks and ticks and tortures us?"

"Then we'll set our own tick." Will seals my mouth with a kiss so soft and passionate that I no longer care about the what-ifs and maybes. I no longer care for the perfect path I always thought I would take. Perfect paths are overrated. They don't allow for what's hidden on the side. And life is, after all, all about discovery.

Lifting me to the tip of his cock, he says, "Tick," before pushing inside me then rocking back and pushing again. "Tick." And again and again. "Tick, tick."

I smile and brace for the ride.

"You forget I'm a drummer, sweetheart. I create my own beat."

Boy, oh boy, does he ever.

* * *

THE FOLLOWING day is both exciting and hectic. The kids all tell me about their Easter holidays and what they did during their two weeks off—some camping, some chilling at home, most gorging themselves on chocolate.

Evan is quiet, which isn't unusual, but it certainly unsettles my stomach, given the fun topics we discuss and activities we do, but more so when he refuses to remove his jumper as the day grows warmer. I can tell he's uncomfortably hot, his cheeks red, his hair sticky with sweat.

My gut tells me something isn't right, so when the final bell rings, I head outside the classroom to speak to his mother, but she isn't waiting where she normally does.

"Where's Mum today?" I ask him.

He shrugs. "She's late."

"Okay. Well, wait here with me until she arrives. I need to speak with her."

The schoolyard grows quiet as children run from the grounds, and parents drive away. It always reminds me of the aftermath of a tornado.

I take a seat on the bench beside him, facing the carpark. "Did she tell you she might be late?"

"No." He sits on his hands and swings his legs.

"Hm... maybe I should give her a call."

He doesn't answer me, and my concern amplifies tenfold.

Looking up, I see Will enter the office building, so I wave and hold up my hand as if to say I'll be five minutes. Truth be told, I don't know how long I'll be.

"There she is!" Evan blurts and darts off.

"Evan, wait!" I jog after him when he stops by a Holden Commodore parked across two parking spaces.

Evan's mum is sitting in the passenger seat, her boyfriend—I assume—behind the wheel.

She opens the door and only half gets out. "Evan, get in the car."

"Ms Hunter," I say, puffing as I stop by the driver's side. "Can I have a quick word?"

She looks at her boyfriend then shakes her head. "Um... now's not a good time."

"I just really need a momen—"

"You fucking deaf?" the boyfriend snaps through his open window. I jerk back. "I beg your pardon?"

He tips a can of Beam and Coke to his mouth, skolls it, then crushes the can and tosses it at my feet. "Nosey bitch."

My chest seizes, and I look at Evan through the back window, terror filling his wide-open eyes. I need him to get out of that car, *now*. I don't know how I'm going to do it, but I do know that. The longer he stays there, the longer he's in danger.

Straightening my shoulder, I say, "I'm sorry, but I must insist."

"Fuck off!"

He fumbles to turn on the ignition, so I do the first thing I can think to do and reach into the car, yanking out the keys.

"You're drunk," I say, holding them to my chest. "You shouldn't be driving."

"Fucking *bitch!*" His eyes flame and bead like the devil's as he opens the door and stumbles out.

"Stewart, no!"

"Shut up, Eliza. You fuckin' shut your whore mouth."

He slams the car door and lunges for me, but thanks to Will's boxing classes, I dart out of his way, once, twice, but the third time, I'm not so lucky.

Pain slams the side of my face, fire burning my scalp as his hand catches my hair and pulls. I scream and stumble like a rag doll, fear rippling through my body. His fist collides with my jaw, and I see bright lights and waves of black. I try to blink them away, try to focus enough to stay conscious and fight back. Because if I don't, I believe deep within the bowels of my being that he could very well kill me.

A metallic taste coats my tongue, and I choke a little before composing myself and throwing an uppercut, which is good enough to break his hold and have him falling backwards.

Agony blankets my hand, and the pain is so severe that I know I've broken it, but the adrenaline pumping through my veins keeps me alert enough to brace for another charge when he's suddenly tackled to the ground in a tumble of limbs.

Blinking back the cloud of darkness, I fall to my knees and cradle my wrist as Will grapples with the guy until he's subdued in a headlock, his face turning red, his eyes slowly closing, Will's arm tight and unrelenting.

"Will!" I cry out.

He doesn't look up, just holds firm, his face a mask of unbridled fury.

I scream, "Will!"

Finally, his eyes meet mine, and he lets the guy go, scrambles to his feet, and drops to his knees in front of me.

"Lib." He cups my face, his touch featherlight. "Jesus! What'd he do to you?"

"I'm okay," I choke out, "but I think my hand is broken."

He cradles my arm and wipes my cheek. "You're bleeding. Where are you bleeding?"

"My mouth." I spit some blood. "I dropped my guard."

"Sweetheart," he says, pressing his lips to my head. "You did good."

I manage a small laugh. "I learned from the best."

Will helps me to my feet just as Carly runs toward us, phone in hand.

"The police are on their way." She takes one look at me and says, "Shit!" before bringing her phone to her ear again and asking for an ambulance.

The guy grumbles and tries to stand, his arms and legs like noodles.

"Stay the fuck down or I'll kill you," Will seethes.

I touch his chest and gesture toward Evan, fearing he's seen, and possibly experienced, enough violence already.

Ms Hunter gets out of the car, walks over to her boyfriend, and kicks him in the gut. "You crazy arsehole! I hate you!" She kicks him again. "I hate you! I hate you!"

All I can hear and see is Evan crying, and it breaks my heart. No child should ever be subjected to this. "Will." I gesture toward Evan.

Will pulls Ms Hunter away from her boyfriend then opens the car door, kneels down, and tells Evan it's okay and that he's safe.

Evan pushes past him and rushes to my side. "Ms Hanson," he cries.

His little arms wrap around me, and no matter the pain tearing through every inch of my body, I know he's safe.

It's all that matters.

My sweet boy is safe.

CHAPTER TWENTY

"We're going in that?" I point to the old, rickety rowboat, which isn't much bigger than Will.

"Yes. Get in." He taps my arse with the oar.

Jumping forward, I rub the spot and narrow my eyes. "You're so bossy."

Will puts down the oar, steps up to me, and lifts my wrist to his lips. There's a small scar from the surgery, but after several months of recovery and rehabilitation, my broken bones have healed, and my hand is pretty much functioning as normal.

I pressed charges against Stewart Stonewall, as did Ms Hunter, and he's currently being held in the Melbourne Remand Centre, no bail, with his committal hearing set for this coming December. I'm nervous for the outcome, but for the most part, I'm trying not to think about it. It's out of my hands now, and I need to focus on the aspects of my life that I do control.

I found out not too long after the incident that Stewart had dislocated Evan's shoulder during the school holidays when he threw him against the wall. He also held a knife to his throat and broke several of Ms Hunter's ribs. The night before that awful day at school, Stewart used Evan as a boxing bag, and he was bruised pretty much from top to toe, which is why he refused to remove his jumper when I asked.

My heart still bleeds for him, and I'll forever feel guilty for not doing something sooner, despite Ms Hunter telling me Stewart hadn't laid a hand on Evan prior to the school holidays. He always targeted her, and she'd been a willing sacrifice if it meant her son was safe.

The thing is, with Stewart in their lives, Evan had never been safe. But he is now, and he's thriving, and all is once again good in the world.

"How's it feeling today?" Will asks as he detaches his lips from my wrist.

I bend it back and forth and smile. "Good as new."

"Excellent!" He hands me the oar. "You can help me row."

"What? Ripped off."

He laughs just as a family of magpies sing in a nearby tree, the sun's shimmering reflection on the lake bright and beautiful. I inhale and push my sunglasses up the bridge of my nose. Everything is perfect... despite Will wanting to risk my life to go row boating.

"Fine." I sigh. "I'll get into this death trap, but only because I love you."

We've been living together in his magical cottage for a couple of months now. It's a dream come true. Every day, I wake up, as if I'm in my own fairy tale. But I do miss Sasha terribly. Carly, not so much.

Okay, maybe a little.

He kisses my scar again, winks, then scoops me into his arms, the sunlight illuminating the golden streaks in his beard. I giggle. He kinda sparkles like Edward Cullen in *Twilight*.

Placing me on my feet next to the boat, Will holds my hand as I carefully step in and take a seat.

"Please don't tip us," I say, gripping the sides.

The boat wobbles when he steps aboard, but we stay upright. We survive.

Will pushes off from the shore, and we float toward the centre of the lake, the water as smooth as glass.

I lean over the edge and skate my fingertips across the surface. "This is quite a lovely idea."

We've just come from my routine ultrasounds, and Will thought this would be a nice way to distract me from my thoughts, even though I told him there were no "thoughts" in the first place. But that's a lie, and he knows it.

"So have you rowed before?" I ask, hoping his answer is yes.

"No."

"Oh. Well… you're doing a great job. Keep it up."

I don't know why I'm so nervous. Maybe it's because he's in one of his quiet man-of-few-words moods. He gets like this sometimes and says it's because I say enough for us both.

I've yet to figure out if that's a good thing or not.

Rowing along the shoreline, I lean back and rest on my hands, admiring the view. The sleeves of his white shirt are rolled up, tight against his biceps, and I'm most thankful as his arms flex delightfully when he rows, the muscles in his neck taut.

I want to lick them.

"Elizabeth," he warns.

"Yes, William?" I smirk, but I've no doubt it's nowhere near as good as Bryce's.

"Stop fucking me with your eyes."

"Me?" I touch my chest. "I'd do no such thing."

He stops rowing, and we drift, the boat all of sudden rocking more than I'm comfortable with.

"What are you doing?"

He goes to stand, steadying himself with his arms, before reaching for the waistband of his shorts. "I'm repaying the favour."

"What?"

"You fuck me, I fuck you."

"Will!" I try to tug him back down to sit. "Okay! Stop it! Sit down. Please! I'll stop eye-fucking you. I promise."

He deliberately rocks the boat before sitting, and I scream.

"Why did I agree to this?"

"Because I'm *very* convincing."

He is. Too convincing. I need to get on top of that.

Clasping the oars, he continues to row when the sound of bongo drums and a violin fill the air, the tune overly familiar.

I tilt my ear toward the sound. "Can you hear that?"

He nods, a smile lifting the corner of his lip.

I twist, trying to pinpoint the origin. "It sounds like 'Kiss the Girl' from *The Little Mermaid*."

We row around a corner past a weeping willow, the tune growing louder, and I gasp when I spot Derek, Bryce, Alexis, Carly, Charlotte, and Lucy standing on the bank of the lake, all of them dressed as various water creatures.

Eyes wide, my hand shoots up to cover my mouth. "What on Earth?"

Alexis is a flamingo with her newborn, Brayden, in one arm, a microphone in her other hand. Charlotte is a turtle, also with a microphone in hand. Derek is a crab, again with a microphone. Lucy's a fish, positioned behind a keyboard. Bryce is a guitar-wielding frog. And Carly is an obnoxious seagull with two Golden Retriever pups on leads.

I burst into laughter. "Did you do this?"

He shrugs. "I don't know what you're talking about."

My heart swells; it's the fakest most pathetic shrug I've ever seen in my life.

Laughing again, I choke and blink back tears as Derek sings about kissing the girl, Alexis and Charlotte on back-up vocals, Carly twisting in circles as the puppies play at her feet.

"Oh, my God!" I point at her. "She got more puppies! She's insane!" I slap my palm to my head. "She really must miss me."

Will belly laughs. "Yeah, she must."

Charlotte waves as she dances, so I wave back then cover my face with my hands, peeking through my spread fingers. "I can't believe you got a billionaire to dress up as a frog."

Will puts down the oars, pulls out his phone, and snaps a photo.

"I didn't. Alexis did." He slides the phone back into his pocket. "That will be used as blackmail one day."

"Oooh." I laugh. "You're game."

We float in a circle as Derek sings about not being scared and to just kiss the girl, and I blush, waiting for my kiss when Carly squawks, "Ya ya ya yaaaaa," just like Scuttle did in the movie.

The ear-piercing noise echoes across the lake, and I fear she just unintentionally called an entire colony of the things. That, or she's about to find a mate.

"A seagull suits her," Will says.

Throwing my head back in laughter, I almost roll out of the boat.

"Whoa, sweetheart." He steadies me and leans forward, the music dying down as our crazy friends all whisper into the microphone, "Kiss the girl."

His eyes meet mine, and he reaches into his pocket. I draw in a breath, my heart pounding so hard I'm scared it'll beat right through my chest.

Biting my lip, I blink when he pulls out a piece of chewing gum, unwraps it, and pops it into his mouth. *Is he kidding me?*

"Gum?" he offers, holding out the packet.

I almost frown but stop myself. "No, thanks." I force a smile but don't have to try too hard, because—let's face it—what he's organised is incredibly sweet.

The gang whisper again, "Kiss the girl."

He cups my jaw and kisses me softly before pulling back. "You ready?"

My eyes grow wide, my heart hammering once again. "For what?"

The damn jerk deliberately tips the boat, and we splash into the water, coldness swirling all over my body as I flail to the surface, coughing.

"Will!" I tread water, only to find it's shallow enough to stand. "What did you do that for?"

He flicks water from his head and lunges for me, securing me in his arms as he twirls us in a circle. "I had to make it authentic."

Remembering Eric and Ariel did, in fact, end up in the water, I laugh and whack his chest. "You sure did that!"

Pushing away from him, keen to get to the shore, he secures me once again, holds me tight, and says, "I love you, Elizabeth Hanson. And I told you I'd give you your fairy tale." He gestures to our crazy friends and the surrounding lake. "This is me doing that."

"Oh, Will." I slide my hands up the back of his neck and pull him to my lips.

He's cold but warm, his skin wet and slippery as our hungered mouths ravish one another's.

"I can't believe you watched *The Little Mermaid*," I mumble between kisses.

"Believe it."

"How? Where?"

"At Bryce and Lexi's. Bryce even tried to make me watch *Lady and the Tramp* as well. Weirdo."

I grab his face and kiss him again, in awe of everything that he is and does. "I love you too, Will."

"Get a room!" Alexis calls out.

Carly whistles.

Laughing, I flip them the bird.

"Watch out for the eels!" Charlotte shouts.

Will pulls back. "Eels?" He looks between us into the murky water. "What is she talking about?"

Biting back my smile, I keep my voice neutral. "Yeah. Didn't you know there are eels in here."

"Fuck that shit!" He hoists me over his shoulder, and I squeal as he carries me out of the water and places me on solid ground again.

"I'm kidding." I laugh. "There are no eels."

He glares at the lake as if it's pulled a swifty on him.

The gang waddle along the grassy shore toward us, and I crack up laughing again; Derek and Bryce look priceless.

"You guys are crazy," I say. "That was excellent!"

Charlotte runs up to me and gives me a hug. "Did you like my singing, Libby?"

I release her arms and bend toward her, holding her hands between us. "I did! You sounded just like Ariel."

The little joy blushes and turns her hips back and forth, and it's the cutest thing.

"Charli-bear, come here," Alexis says and winks to her daughter.

Will takes the puppies from Carly and hands me their leads. "Meet our babies."

"What?" my mouth falls open, and I drop to my knees. "What are you talking about?" Both puppies wiggle around me, licking and pawing my face. I pick one up, and then the other. "Hi there." They squirm like giant fluffy worms, and I have to put them down again for fear they'll squirm right out of my hold.

Will squats and picks one up, letting it lick his entire face. "We can have babies, sweetheart. They just might have four legs, or scales, or feathers."

Pure joy washes over my body, warmth fizzling at my cheeks as my heart all but bursts. This man, this giant, sweet, incredible man. I love him so damn much I can barely breathe. "They're just... I'm just..." Tears stream down my face. I'm so overwhelmed I can't even speak. "Are they... brother and sister?"

He shakes his head and smiles. "No. Separate litters."

"What are you going to name them?" Charlotte asks.

"I... I don't know."

She looks up at Alexis. "Mum, I want a puppy."

Alexis's eyes nearly grow wider than her face. "Nooo."

"But—"

"No buts, ratbag."

Bryce lifts Charlotte onto his shoulders, and I can't help but laugh at what is simply a turtle on top of a frog.

I giggle. "You all look ridiculous."

"We know," Bryce says.

Continuing to laugh, I apologise for their misfortune. "I'm so sorry."

He holds Charlotte firm with one arm then slaps Will on the back. "Well worth it, mate."

Will tickles Charlotte's leg, and she almost knees Bryce in the face. "Beats that time we performed 'November Rain,' huh?" He waggles his eyebrows at Bryce.

Bryce chuckles.

"*Nothing* beats 'November Rain,'" Alexis says.

"Yeah. At least we didn't have to wear godawful costumes when we performed that for Lexi." Derek snaps his claw-like hands and frowns.

Carly bursts into laughter and points to Derek. "I've just realised... I've got crabs."

We all facepalm.

* * *

AFTER A CHANGE of clothes and a picnic lunch by the lake, we headed home and settled the pups, both of them sleeping on the floor beside our bed.

"So what do you want to call them?" Will asks, spooning me as we watch them snooze.

I wiggle back and snuggle against him. "I'm going to name the girl Snow White, and the boy Prince."

He tightens his grip and nuzzles my ear. "I love the names, sweetheart. They're perfect."

Revelling in his warm body embracing mine, we fall asleep in each other's arms until I'm woken by a puppy's whimper sometime in the early hours of the morning.

"Hey, babies," I whisper. "It's okay."

I carefully lift Will's python arm off my chest, and he grumbles and snorts but doesn't wake up.

Reaching out to turn on the bedside lamp, I pat my fingers on the nightstand in search of the switch until I skate across it and press it down, a soft light illuminating the room and catching the glint of a diamond ring on my finger.

Blinking all the blinks, I shake my head, scrub my eyes, then hold out my hand before bringing it close to my face. "What. The. Fuck. Is. That?"

I scrub my eyes again, convinced I must be dreaming.

I'm not.

"Holy shit!" I whisper.

"Will you marry me?"

Practically jumping out of my skin, I turn in Will's direction. He's lying on his side, head propped up by his hand, his eyes mischievous but timid as they search mine.

I snap my head to look at the ring again, then back at him, my mouth agape. "When did you—?"

His smug smile grows. "Well... will you?"

"Y-Yes! Yes, of course I'll marry you."

Lunging into his arms, I sob as he catches me then rolls us until I'm on my back and he's hovering over me, his eyes gleaming as they roam my face, his thumb playing with my bottom lip.

He looks hot as sin and teddy-bear cute all at once, and I can't believe this is my life. That I'm happy and now engaged to the man of my dreams, dreams I never knew were possible.

"Yes, William," I say, blinking back tears. "I'll marry you."

"I'm gonna spend every waking moment making you the happiest princess alive."

I nod and blink again. "And what about the non-waking moments?"

"Those too. Every damn moment of every damn day, sweet-heart. From here on in, it's just you and me... and Snow White, Prince, Molly, Casper..."

Laughing, I skate my fingers down the sides of his face and grip his chin. "Kiss the girl, fiancé."

Eyes glimmering, he slowly lowers his lips to mine, sealing our engagement with the softest of kisses. A wave of warmth and insurmountable joy crashes over me, and I giggle and hug him tight, peeking over his shoulder at the stunning diamond on my finger.

"It's a princess cut," I say.

He scoffs as if there was no other choice. "Of course."

The puppies bark, and I drape my hand over the side of the bed, my fingers soon gobbled up in slobber and sharp teeth. I have everything I've ever wanted: the perfect guy, the perfect job, a home, and kids. Animal-kids.

Often, our fairy tale can seem out of reach, but the magic of fairy tales is what we make of them because we're all princesses, with or without a prince.

I'm just lucky I finally found mine.

EPILOGUE

"*I*s it too much?" I ask Carly, Fiona, and Alexis as I twirl my Cinderella-inspired wedding gown, silk, tule, and shimmering chiffon swishing as I spin one way and then the next.

Fi playfully rolls her eyes. "Yes."

"No!" Alexis places her hands on my shoulders and turns me to face the mirror. "It's not. It's almost perfect."

"Almost?"

"You're missing one thing."

"Oh! Of course! My tiara!" I hoist up my dress and skip to the bedside table in the bridal suite of City Manor, a 19th century homestead that Bryce bought a little over a year ago.

Nestled among pristine rose gardens and perfectly manicured hedges, City Manor sits on a generous allotment on the city's fringe. When Bryce showed us his new acquisition with the intent to bring a country escape to the city, I couldn't believe my luck. It was absolutely perfect. Mystical, magical... a fairy tale castle in a fairy tale setting.

Collecting the delicate crystal tiara in my hand, I bite my lip. "I completely forgot to give this to the hairdresser to put in my hair. I'm such an idiot."

"Here." Carly takes it from me. "I'll do it."

"Are you sure?"

She points to her head. "This doesn't just happen. It takes skill and know-how."

"But you didn't do your hair, Carls. The hairdresser did."

She scoffs. "Not today, I didn't. But every other day, I do."

I look to Alexis and Fi for support, and they quickly turn around and busy themselves.

Carly huffs. "Just stand still. I've got you. Haven't I *always* got you?"

Tears prick my eyes, and I'm not sure if it's because of the tiara now digging into my scalp or because of my best friend's words.

"Yes," I whisper. "You have always got me. And I know I don't tell you this enough, but I'm so thankful you do."

She studies the top of my head before glancing down at my face, her smoky eyes glassy. "Don't you dare cry, Labia. You're ugly when you cry. You can't be ugly today."

I choke on my teary laugh and splutter, "Bitch."

Carly plumps my red curls to sit on my shoulders then steps back, holding me at arm's length. "There. Almost perfect."

"Almost? Why do you both keep saying 'almost'?"

She glances at Alexis, who steps up to me with a white box.

"We thought you should wear these," Alexis says.

Curious, I take the box, lower myself onto the corner of the bed, and open it to find one Jimmy Choo replica glass slipper.

"Oh, my God!" I shriek. "Are these Cinderella's—"

"Yes!" Alexis nods like a maniac, her teeth almost brighter than the crystals on the expensive and overly extravagant high heel.

"But..." I suspend the shoe, rotating it in my hand.

Hundreds of tiny crystals embellish the entire satin surface, accentuated by a large crystal flower motif on the toe. I'm almost afraid to touch it for fear it'll smash in my hand.

"H-How?" I stutter. "Hang on, wait!" I lift the tissue paper in the box. "Where's the other one?"

Alexis takes the stiletto from me, lowers to her knee, and slips it onto my foot. "Where do you think it is?"

I wrack my brain for the smallest of seconds before recognition dawns. "Will!" I laugh. "Of course he has it."

Carly smiles then collects three bouquets and hands one to Fi and one to Alexis. They all turn to me, each of them stunning in powder-blue, body-hugging gowns.

"Are you ready?" Carly asks

"No. How am I going to walk down the aisle in one shoe?"

"If Cinderella can do it, so can you."

"You're right," I say, standing up. I point my glass-slipper-covered toe. "Okay, let's do this."

Gathering up my dress, I hobble toward the door when it opens and Dad pops his head in, Mum not so reserved as she barges past him.

"Come on, Elizabeth. Everyone's waiting." She gives Fi an awkward glance. "Izzy has emptied her basket of rose petals already, and poor Charlotte keeps picking them up and putting them back in for her."

Alexis laughs. "Is my daughter fussing over minor imperfections?"

Both Mum and Dad say, "Yes."

She laughs again. "That's my girl."

Fi, Mum, Alexis, and Carly file out of the room, and as I'm about to follow them, Dad lets go of the door and gently places his hands on my shoulders.

"My princess—" He clears his throat. "—you look beautiful."

I slide my arms around his waist. "Thanks, Dad. I feel beautiful."

"Whether you feel it or not, you always are and always have been."

Tears once again prick my eyes, and I inwardly curse them. "Stop it. You're making me cry."

He reaches into the inner pocket of his suit jacket, pulls out a handkerchief, and then gently dabs the tip of it to the corners of my eyes.

"Thank you. Thank you for always having faith in me to find what *I* was looking for in my own time."

"I've always had faith in you, darling. Your life is your own. It always has been, and it always will be." He pockets the hankie again. "Now, let's get you married to your prince."

Holding out his arm, I loop mine around his and walk beside him.

He stops. "Why are you limping?"

I laugh. "You'll see."

* * *

WITH DAD'S ASSISTANCE, I hobble down the mahogany spiral staircase and out into the garden, hundreds of white, plump roses in bloom, their sweet perfume filling the air. The sun beams high in the sky, a gentle breeze providing the perfect temperature.

An ivory carpet separates two sections of wooden chairs, each with a powder-blue bow tied to the back, and a rose-covered archway frames the garden where Izzy, Charlotte, and Brayden cast handfuls of rose petals into the air as they slowly make their way toward Will, Bryce, Derek, and Matt.

One by one, my bridesmaids follow as "Inevitable", the Live Trepidation marriage song—played at both Alexis and Bryce's, and Carly and Derek's weddings—sounds through the speakers.

My eyes lock on Will, and I draw in a deep breath, holding it for as long as I can. He stands at the end of the aisle, ruggedly handsome in his tuxedo, my missing glass slipper presented in the palms of his hands.

Choking back tears, I thank my lucky stars he pushed himself into my life. I don't know how, but he knew me better than I knew myself and persisted when most wouldn't. He knew we were a pair, and he knew he could give me my happily ever after. This day. This enchanted moment and beyond.

"Ready?" Dad asks.

I nod. "Yes."

Hobbling down the aisle, I giggle with each awkward step, my cheeks burning and no doubt redder than my hair. I want to kill my husband-to-be but kiss him endlessly at the same time. Not only has he thought to present me with my very own glass slipper, but he also got me an authentic dinglehopper for my birthday, which is also currently wedged into the back of my hair.

He thinks of everything I don't and says everything I won't.

My missing part, my entire heart.

I stop before him, and he lowers to one knee, lifts the hem of my dress, and secures the glass slipper to my foot. Our guests clap, and I let out a delighted sob, feeling very much the princess he promised I'd be.

"Perfect fit," he says and stands, his misty eyes alight with pride as he holds out his hand.

Dad lays mine on top of it and says, "Yes, you are both the perfect fit." He kisses my cheek then claps Will on the back. "Look after her."

"I will, sir. Every moment of every day."

Will brings my hand to his lips and kisses my knuckles, and I know he'll do exactly what he just said he'll do. I know because we're connected, mind, body, and soul, and a connection like that isn't easily broken.

It's forever.

Eternal.

A fairy tale.

Because fairy tales are real. We just have to believe in them.

EXTENDED EPILOGUE

"*W*ill!" I yell. "Wake up. I think it's time."

I hear him groan from our bedroom, and given it's nearly midnight, I don't blame him.

"I'm coming," he grumbles.

"It's okay, Snow. Mummy's here. You're doing so good, girl." I kneel by the whelping box and pat her head.

Will stumbles into our living room, stretching his gigantic frame as he yawns. "She punch 'em out yet?"

I glare at him. "I'll punch *you* out in a minute."

He chuckles and combs his hand along Prince's back. "I'm kidding, sweetheart. What's happening?"

"I think her waters just broke because she's been licking a wet patch on the sheet underneath her. She's been panting pretty hard, too, and shaking." I flick my hands, a little panicked. "Okay, so I've got towels, sterile scissors, rubber gloves, antiseptic, dental floss—"

"Dental floss?" Will gives me his unexplained phenomenon expression.

"Yes. To tie the umbilical cords if we need to." I huff. "I've told you this already."

He scrubs his hand down the back of his neck and yawns again.

"So, I've got the floss, a heating pad, the heat lamp is on, the vet is on call… what else?" I look around the room, and that dreaded feeling you get when you know you're forgetting something settles in my stomach. "Ice cream!"

"What the hell do you need ice cream for? You hungry?"

"No, it's not for me, it's for her. It's to keep her blood sugar levels up. Plus, she's about to 'punch' out many babies. Bitch deserves ice cream. Don't even argue with me on this."

He holds up his hands. "I'm not arguing, sweetheart. Whatever you say goes. You got this."

Prince tries to climb onto his lap, and he lets him. The two of them are best mates, inseparable, especially after Molly passed away last year. Prince has filled a void only a loyal dog can.

"Who's gonna be a dad soon?" Will coos, scruffing Prince's ears. "You are." Prince licks his face. "Yes, you are, big boy. Are you ready?"

Prince barks.

"Will! Keep him calm. Snow doesn't need you two goofing off right now. She needs serenity. Tranquillity. Shit! I forgot to put on my playlist."

He stops scruffing Prince's ears. "You're what?"

"My birthing playlist for Snow."

Will cracks up laughing and crawls onto the floor next to me. "What's on it… 'Who Let the Dogs Out'?"

I whack his arm. "Very funny."

He hugs me to him. "Just breathe. She knows what to do by instinct; she'll do most of the work."

Sighing, I slump against him. "I know. I'm just nervous." I run my hand ever so softly down the back of Snow's head. It might sound silly, but I'll never experience giving birth, and this will be the closest I'll ever come. I don't want to let her down. "Not long now, girl."

She shuffles and licks herself again, and this time her tail lifts, and a balloon-like membrane sac appears.

I gasp. "Look, it's the first puppy."

Excitement rolls over me, and I quickly put on my gloves. "Grab a towel and the scissors, quick!"

Will does as I tell him, and we both wait with bated breath as Snow pushes out her first puppy and starts licking the sac to break it open.

"Should we help her?" I ask.

"Just give her a second."

She bites the sac, and I almost shriek, fearing she's going to bite the puppy. But she doesn't. She just keeps licking and licking until we hear a tiny cry.

Both Will and I exhale.

"Oh, my God!" I say, tears spilling from my eyes. "We're grand-parents."

Snow chews into the umbilical cord, and it's both gross and amazing. Once she's chewed through, releasing her pup, I quickly scoop the tiny thing up and rub it down with a towel, gently rolling it over in my hand.

"It's a boy!"

Prince hangs his head over the box as if to approve of his son. He licks Snow's head, and she licks him back, and my heart near explodes.

"All right, you two, that's enough." Will guides Prince back a little, and I place the puppy down near Snow's teats.

She licks herself again, and another sac appears.

"Whoa! There's another one already," I say, bouncing on my knees. "This is so exciting."

Will squeezes my shoulder as Snow pushes out her second puppy before licking, chewing, and freeing it from the sac. Once again, I clean it up and check for the sex.

"It's another boy!"

I pat her head and encourage her. "You're such a good mumma, girl. Yes, you are." I offer her some water, and she takes a small sip, nowhere near enough to keep her hydrated. "Quick! Grab one of the small organic ice cream tubs from the freezer," I say to Will.

He jumps to his feet and is back in seconds, two tubs in his hands. He passes one to me then rips off the lid of the one he's still holding before offering it to Prince.

I frown. "What are you doing?"

"Don't you think he deserves one too?"

"No! Not really. I don't see him lying here, 'punching out' *seven* puppies. I mean, why don't you both just kick back and smoke a friggin' cigar?"

He looks at Prince, who's happily licking the ice cream out of the tub. "That's not a bad idea, hey, mate."

I bite back my smile; there's no way I can be mad—I love both of my babies equally.

Tearing off the lid, I offer my tub to Snow, relieved when she starts licking enthusiastically.

"Good girl!" I pat her head. "You need your energy, Mumma."

Roughly four hours later, Snow gives birth to her sixth puppy.

"Surely this one is a girl?" Will says, waiting as I turn it over.

"Nope. Another boy."

"That's *six* boys. How many did the vet say she could see on the scan?"

I scrunch my nose. "Seven."

"Come on, girl." Will pats her head while helping me keep the puppies suckling on her teats. "One more. You can do this."

She licks his nose, and he cringes. "Did she just put birth juices on my face?"

I laugh. "Yes."

"That's fucking gross."

"It's not." I giggle. "It's lovely. It's natural. It's—"

"Fucking gross."

Wiping his face with his sleeve, he then moves Prince closer. "Lick him. That's what he's here for."

Snow licks herself again, and moments later, the seventh puppy plops out onto the sheet. Like the others, Snow breaks the membrane and licks her pup. But unlike the others, this one doesn't cry.

My chest tightens. "Somethings wrong. It's… it's not crying."

I pick it up and gently rub it the same way I did the other six, but it feels different. Too still. Too quiet.

Tears pool in my eyes and trickle down my cheeks. I wasn't

prepared to lose any. I mean, I knew we could, but I never believed we would.

"It's okay, baby girl," I say to Snow. "You've done so good. I'm so proud of you."

Will takes the puppy from me, determination flaring his eyes. "Not on my watch."

Holding my breath, I watch in awe and horror as he sticks his little finger inside the puppy's mouth then gently pushes on its tummy. It doesn't respond, so he makes a cone with his hand, covers the puppy's nose, and blows a puff of air while still pushing on its tummy.

My heart skips a beat, and I freeze, my chest constricted, my hands shaking.

A loud cry pierces the air, the loudest yet, and I finally let out the breath I've been holding.

"Oh, my God!" I cover my mouth with my hands. "It's alive."

Will places the puppy next to Snow then kneels back, sits on his heels, and wipes his brow with the back of his hand. I could kiss him. Forever and ever.

"Holy shit!" he says. "I really do need a cigar now."

Tears streaming down my face, I throw my arms around him and ply his head and face with kisses. "You're my hero, William Butler."

"Anything for my girls," he mumbles into the crook of my neck.

"Speaking of girls, should we check?"

He nods.

"You do it. This one is your miracle."

Gently lifting the final puppy, he turns it over, and I wait while he inspects.

"It's a—"

"A what?" I blurt.

"A…"

"Will! For shit's sake, tell me."

"It's a girl, sweetheart."

I clap like a seal. "Six boys and one girl. Oh, my God! I'm gonna call her Happy."

His eyebrows pinch, curiously. "Happy?"

"Yes. And I'm gonna call the others Doppy, Doc, Grumpy, Sleepy, Sneezy, and Bashful." I remove my gloves and wipe my hands on a towel. "Snow White and her Seven Dwarfs."

Taking a seat in Will's lap, I snuggle against his chest as his python arms hold me tight.

"Thank you," I say, sleep beckoning as exhaustion takes over.

He nuzzles my cheek. "For what?"

"For giving me my fairy tale."

THE END

Turn over for a sneak peek at *Commitment* (Temptation #6)
Tash and Dean's story

COMMITMENT PROLOGUE

*T*hirteen years. That's how long Dean and I have been married. Thirteen years of ups, downs, forwards, backwards, whirlywhirls and somersaults. Whatever the obstacle we'd faced during that time, we'd nailed it. And not just nailed it; we'd MacGyvered the arse out of it.

Our matrimonial knot was tied in front of friends and family in a large Catholic church before God on a scorchin' hot December afternoon. Skin was tacky. Napes were damp. And underneath my dress, I had a makeshift steam oven between my legs that, had I baked a cake in, would've put Betty Crocker to shame. But despite the awful heatwave we'd experienced that day, I'd still rocked my white halter-neck, taffeta wedding dress like nobody's business. Yep, Natasha Jones—that's me—had been the most beautiful human-meringue to have ever lived.

The perfect bride at the perfect wedding to the perfect man.

Smiling as I drove my car into the driveway of our house, I thought back to that day and to just how far Dean and I've come. Like most couples, we'd started out by working our arses off to save for a deposit on a home, soon after becoming proud owners of a gigantic mortgage. We'd parented a cat and then a dog—our safe and happy furry test subjects successfully proving we could try parenting a real baby human. Enter said baby human number one: William, who was born two years after we married, followed by baby human number two: Thomas, three years later.

My boys.

I loved them.

But they near destroyed my vagina.

How the tunnel of Tash still operated after pushing out those beasts was beyond me, and yet it somehow did. In fact, it was scheduled to operate later tonight. *That's right... bring on anniversary sexytimes.* Bring on a candlelit dinner, a full body massage, a hot steamy bubble bath, schnappies and a fuckalicious fuckfest with my man. Bring on the rarity that is a child-free evening. Bliss.

Grinning devilishly, I got out of my car and skipped to my front door, waving at my neighbour before pausing and pulling out my phone to check my hair and makeup on the selfie cam. I'd performed a rearview mirror beauty touch-up at the traffic lights and had even sprayed some deodorant on my armpits for added effect. And just because it was our anniversary, I'd de-fuzzed myself the night before.

All of myself.

Yes... Tashy's clam was no longer bearded.

Since giving birth, my window of horniness had shrunk from a floor-to-ceiling panel to a porthole on a tugboat... a *toy* tugboat. I'd gone from yee-haw to yee-naw, and quite frankly, I normally couldn't be bothered. Sex was boring. A chore. And I hated chores. It also involved getting naked—something else I hated.

Don't get me wrong, my husband was hot, and I loved him. In the years we'd been together, he'd barely changed physically whereas I had. My boobs had become droobs. My arse resembled a tail. I had flabdominals and bat-wing arms, and the bags under my eyes could hold a week's worth of shopping. Everything I possessed was loose and tired, but that was motherhood.

Despite loving and being attracted to Dean, and despite my teeny tugboat porthole of horniness, I just wasn't all that interested in meaningless do-it-for-the-hell-of-it sex anymore. There was nothing remotely exciting about it. Nothing spontaneous. And at the end of a long exhausting day, the last thing I wanted was a whole five minutes of belly flab flabbing while having to act out an orgasm worthy of an Academy Award.

Except for tonight!

Tonight was different.

I'd planned on digging out my sexy nightie, one that hid the bits I wanted kept hidden. I'd also picked up some wine and donuts, and we had "Love Actually" on DVD. It was perfect. Romantic. And did I mention there were *no kids?*

Pulling a duckface at my phone and running my tongue across the top row of my teeth, I nodded in approval before turning the key to my front door, stepping inside our entrance hall and nearly having a fucking heart attack.

"Surprise!"

"Shiiit! What the ff… fig tree is going on?" I screamed, clutching my chest and staring wide-eyed at my sons, both William and Thomas in battle stance and pointing sword-shaped balloons at me. *Yes, balloons, as in air-filled latex objects from hell.*

"Prepare to die, mother," William declared, stepping forward.

The balloon neared.

I backed up.

"Yes, prepare to die a horrible death, evil wench."

"Thomas!" I scowled at my youngest spawn. "Don't call me that." *What the hell is going on? Where are my candles, rose petals and smooth sounds of Lionel Ritchie filtering from the stereo? Where is Dean?*

Thomas put his hand to his mouth and whispered, "Just go with it, Mum. I'm acting."

"But… but…" I shook my head in bewilderment. "But why?"

He stepped forward again, this time pointing the sword-balloon directly at my chest. "Do not speak, or I shall slit your throat."

The balloon made a hellish screeching noise as it molested my skin, causing my heart rate to elevate and an ear-piercing squeal to leave my mouth. I hated balloons. *Despised* them.

I was a proud Globophobic.

"Get that thing away from me!" I yelled, swatting it and then making a dash for my bedroom.

As I ran past the kitchen, two insane children hot on my tail, Dean sprung out from behind a wall, causing my bladder to lose some of its contents. *Jesus Christ, for the love of Depend!*

I wasn't sure whether to clutch my chest or vagina as I focused on my husband who was dressed in a white shirt and grey tights, his outstretched arm wielding one of the boys' non-balloon toy swords.

"Halt, you heathens," he announced dramatically, chest puffed, his arm guiding me to stand behind him. "How dare thee cause m'lady such distress?"

The boys stopped suddenly and stared dumbfounded at their father, taking in his attire and unusual choice of words.

"What's a heeven?" Thomas whispered to William.

"I don't know. I think it's Robin Hood speak for bad guy."

Thomas scrunched his nose and nodded. "Oh. Dad's weird."

"You are no match for us, girly man," William declared, aiming his balloon at Dean.

Girly man? I couldn't help it and giggled. The whole scenario was crazy.

Dean widened his stance and held his arms out, defensively. "Hey! There's nothing girly 'bout what I'm packing."

My gaze dropped to 'what he was packing', which was beautifully accentuated in tight cotton Lycra. Pronounced. Snug. Confronting. I clamped my teeth around my lip, wanting that package. I wanted it in between my legs, rubbed across my face... I just plain wanted it.

Staring at his bulge, it occurred to me that it would remain out of reach because children murder sexytimes. *This always happens.*

My heart sank. The one night I was up for it, I wasn't going to get it.

There was never any time for Tash and Dean, Dean and Tash. It was always us *and* the boys, or work, or... life. No sexytimes. No tunnel of Tash exploration.

That was *marriage*.

Raising my eyes to meet my husband's endearing sweet face, I put on a smile for what he'd orchestrated. Sure, it wasn't what I'd had in mind, wasn't what I'd hoped for. But this was Dean. He was my goofy man, my entertaining, caring, safe and secure man.

He was my *normal*.

ACKNOWLEDGMENTS

I'd like to first and foremost thank those vocal readers who ~~begged~~ politely asked me to write Will and Libby's story because they weren't yet finished with the *Temptation Series* characters. I was of two minds whether to write this book, but thanks to the overwhelming encouragement over the years, I finally sat down and let this story unfold. And I'm so glad I did. Will and Libby are one of my favourite couples. So, thank you from the bottom of my heart. I hope you enjoyed them as much I did.

To my copy editor, Kayla Robichaux—I loved working with you on this book. A perfect fit. And, funnily enough—and as we quickly discovered—your brother is kinda Will, lol. Also, I ~~promise~~ will try to stop shouting in caps moving forward, *winks.

To my content editor, Sali Benbow-Powers—We didn't "Sandra" on this book, thank goodness, but it was still a fun journey all the same. Also, I ~~promise~~ will try to never write a stinky-feet scene again, *winks.

To my mum—You're always so keen to read my work, and I love you very much for that. Your enthusiasm towards my writing has, at times, been the only reason I kept writing through some of the toughest moments in my life. You pull me out of dark clouds and ~~gently push~~ shove me where I need to go. I love you endlessly x

ALSO BY K.M. GOLLAND

TEMPTATION SERIES

Temptation

Satisfaction

Fulfillment

Attainment

TEMPTATION SERIES STANDALONES

Attraction

Connection

Commitment

WILD NIGHTS

Revue

Reveal

Resist

PLIGHT

DISCOVERING STELLA

UNSPOKEN WORDS

ABOUT THE AUTHOR

Born and raised in Melbourne, K.M. Golland is a best-selling author with HarperCollins, and a two-time Romance Book of the Year award nominee.
A lover of rabbits, doughnuts, bridges, and cars, she's also quite happy to support a *very* healthy high heel obsession.

Connect with K.M. Golland
Website
Email

Sign up to my mailing list for the latest news, book releases, and sales.